THE TEN SHIRT

How the United States National Soccer Team (Might Have) Won The 1982 World Cup

Michael Maddox

PUBLISHING COMPANY
www.figure18publishing.com

THE TEN SHIRT
How the United States National
Soccer Team (Might Have) Won
The 1982 World Cup

Published by Figure 18 Publishing (www.figure18publishing.com)

ISBN 978-0-578-02034-1

Printed in USA

Rosters and other extras are available at www.thetenshirt.com

For

Theresa, Beth, and Jimmy

My Tens

INTRODUCTION

A few years ago, a friend loaned me a book he thought I might enjoy. That book, *OFFSIDE: Soccer and American Exceptionalism* sat on my nightstand for awhile, then my desk, before it was finally relegated to the shelf in my office. It wasn't designed to be a page-turner but, with in-depth analyses and loads of sports history, it was fascinating as a reference tool.

One of the themes of the work is that the "American sports space" (their term) was determined in the early part of the twentieth century, giving us the situation we have now – the big three-and-one-half. After television became the driving force in sports, the scene in the United States was set in stone. That's where I thought, *What if things had been different?*

If soccer had developed one major league instead of several competing leagues, it may have been in a position to reap the benefits when television was introduced to the mix. *Maybe not*, but the thought was intriguing and I decided to run with it.

The Ten Shirt is a fun look back at a history where soccer didn't miss out on a place in the American sports picture and where the United States learned to excel at a game that wasn't born here.

Thanks to Andrei Markovits and Steven Hellerman for their fantastic book, and to David for thinking I might like it (it's still on my shelf!). Also to Fernando Fiore and John Robinson for their wonderful books on World Cup history. Thanks Kerry, for helping me with the editing and for providing moral support.

1

Chapter 1

LESLIE KING

"Sub, sir," the kid asked politely from the touch-line at midfield, shortly after the second half began.

The linesman nodded in acknowledgement and turned his attention back to the task at hand. The Celtic strikers ventured offside frequently, and Zachary Lane wasn't about to be caught out of position. He had been able to relax during the first half since the Mariners' lone forward had seldom touched the ball, although he was keenly aware of the verbal abuse his counterparts had endured, (and it *was* actually worse when the other team spoke English). These "friendly" matches were never much fun, but the twenty bucks (for 90 minutes work) was nearly two weeks worth of gas for the struggling college student. Luckily, for him, the guests from Glasgow had scored just before the halftime whistle, relieving some of the pressure.

Lane had officiated at the Beach Center at least a dozen times during these summer scrimmages. Clubs from Europe would routinely visit *America's Largest Resort City* in the summer to take in the sights at the oceanfront, and take on the hometown team. The Mariners enjoyed moderate success in the Eastern Conference of the United Soccer League, which was a step below the first division North American Soccer League. These summer exhibition matches were lucrative fundraisers for the second-division club, and provided excellent tryout opportunities for hopeful signees. Today, 17-year-old Virginia Beach native Leslie King was one of them. Sort of.

"What the...?" Reserve goalkeeper Mark Stevens was the first to notice.

"That's the new kid. King, I think." Assistant coach Sonny Smith offered an answer, not really sure himself what was going on. His job was mainly administrative, and he was only on the bench today because his doctor had insisted he get out of his office and start exercising. Smith thought watching others run was a start.

Leslie King was well known in the club soccer community as an immense talent with a penchant for causing trouble. Depending on who you asked, he was either the *second coming of Archie Stark*, or *the spawn of Satan himself.* More often than not, the opinion was based on whose side you were supporting – his, or the one he just defeated single-handedly. Able to take over a match seemingly whenever he wanted, King was the kind of player who toyed with opponents (and coaches) in ways unique to his own style and personality.

He was late for his trial with the Mariners, and was inserting himself into the game without permission from the coaching staff. In fact, he had not even approached the bench while jogging from the parking lot. King had changed clothes in his red Mustang and, with his Pioneer car stereo blaring Led Zeppelin's *Dazed and Confused* from a new pair of Jensen 6 x 9's, laced up his PUMAs. Apparently, the players on the bench cared much more about this break in protocol than Leslie did.

Since he stood at the touchline with his back to them, they couldn't see it but he cracked a smile when he overheard their complaints. They sounded a little like Mary Sue had when he left her house twenty minutes earlier. She hadn't approved of his behavior either.

"Come on!" referee Mike Riley shouted to King after yet another Celtic shot was wide of the frame, setting up another Mariner goal kick. Virginia Beach's bunker defense had allowed the green-and-white to dominate possession in the second half. Head Coach Shawn McIlvenny believed in his 4-5-1 system, and was thinking to himself that it was a good thing they had dropped back more numbers to protect against this elevated attack. Then he noticed his latest, and what would be his best ever, coaching decision.

"Lancaster! Come out!" King yelled to the Mariners' lone striker as he prepared to jog onto the soft Bermuda-grass pitch. He tucked in his navy blue jersey and adjusted his thick, white headband.

Reggie Lancaster was beginning the last year of a three-year contract with the Mariners and was, as a player, a shell of his former self. His leadership and professionalism, as well as his ability to persuade several outstanding players to follow him to the beach, had helped transform the squad from near-bankruptcy to a real contender for the league championship this season. His ability to get behind defenses, however, had disappeared with the cartilage in his left knee.

"Mack! What is this?" the thirty-three-year-old asked his coach.

"Not sure, but have a seat and check it out with me," his friend replied.

Reggie Lancaster had once possessed the kind of raw speed that was nearly superhuman. He seemed to be able to reach maximum velocity in just two steps and his scoring touch was legendary. He won the ASL's "Golden Boot" three consecutive years, and had broken the league scoring record of 27 goals with four games left in the 65-66 season, finishing with 30. The Tornado striker also led the league in offside calls each of those seasons, but had started to make improvements in this area by studying the tendencies of the linesmen and classifying them as *ball-watchers* or *back-watchers*. Injuries sidelined him most of the 1966-1967 season, and he was released by Dallas when his contract expired.

Leslie King was making his professional soccer debut three months after turning seventeen, and a week after completing his junior year of high school. Two years ago, his father had agreed to a trial only after Leslie graduated from high school and the enterprising son had taken extra classes, and some summer school, and graduated from Kempsville High a year early. His 145 I.Q. had helped him achieve a solid 2.0 grade point average while exerting minimal effort. Leslie saw high school as a nuisance, and was determined to get out as soon as he could. *Finally*, he thought, *his time had arrived.*

As Reggie jogged toward the bench, he noticed King was wearing his identical jersey, complete with sponsor patches, a white number nine, and LANCASTER on back. Before he could say anything, the teenager offered a mock apology.

6

"Sorry, mine was in the wash," he said, with a wry smile.

"Where'd you get that?" Lancaster asked.

"Are you kidding? Half the kids in town have one of these."

The former US National Team striker had joined the Mariners in the summer of 1967, and sales of his jersey had always been strong and steady, even as his production on the field waned. Largely due to his involvement in the community, Reggie Lancaster was more popular than ever and was frequently rumored to be the *next* coach of the Mariners.

Coach McIlvenny had called the King household two weeks earlier himself to invite Leslie to this scrimmage, and was anxious to see if the kid had what it took to play at this level. At six feet, three inches, and nearly two hundred pounds, this *kid* would actually be one of the biggest players on the field today, matched only by Celtic's center back, Darren O'Shay, and both keepers. He had seen Leslie play several times over the past three years. At club matches with his Beach FC team, he always stood out even though he "played up" with older players. Mack was especially impressed at the way the kid was able to control a match from his forward position. He was known mostly for what he could do *with* the ball, but what really wowed the coach was his work rate *without* it. He would come back deep into the midfield to get the ball; track back on defense and make the hard tackle; pressure the other team's backs relentlessly - and foul them harder than they did him.

Pete King had answered the phone when Mack called, since Leslie was over at the high school playing pickup games with the pub team he had joined at fifteen. He would be home soon. The best player on the "Spanky's" squad still wasn't old enough to join the gang at the bar afterwards, but he knew they were talking about him over their beers, which was very cool. The ribbing from the guys was intense – until they walked onto the pitch, where Leslie was the man in charge. (He had finally started shaving, so that was one less target for his teammates to aim for.) The two men agreed that Leslie was ready to attend a trial, and that a future in pro soccer was certainly a possibility. The date was set, and the call ended. That was the easy part.

While Captain King ran his ship with an iron hand, his household was ruled by Leslie's mother. After graduating from Villanova in 1948 with her Master's Degree in English, Karen Pressley started her teaching career in the Philadelphia public school system. Two years later she met Peter King, a junior lieutenant in the United States Navy, at a friend's wedding in Baltimore and they were married, after a six-month courtship, on Christmas Day, 1950. Karen King was not thrilled about leaving teaching, but embraced her new life as a Navy wife, and eventually a mother, when Leslie Michael King was born on March 5th, 1952. *She* would have to be convinced that this was the best decision for their only child.

"He's a smart-aleck kid, Mack. What are you up to?" asked Reggie, after grabbing some water and joining the others on the bench.

"Have you seen him play?" the coach answered the question with one of his own. "Hmmm?"

8

Reggie grunted, "OK, let's see what he's got."

The first ten minutes of the second half looked like more of the first, with the Celtic midfielders controlling the ball while searching for the proper time and place for the perfect cross. The Mariners' low-pressure, defend-with-numbers plan was doing what it always did, which was justify itself by allowing the opponent to keep possession in Virginia Beach's half of the field. Lancaster had spent most of the first half, and all his six minutes of the second half, watching his team defend, while standing at the midfield stripe. He had his routine down: The occasional long clearance was chased and then, when possession was regained by the Glasgow defender or keeper, he'd retreat to midfield to start all over again. The substitute striker was not so sophisticated.

"He moves pretty good, for a big guy," McIlvenny noticed.

"I'd like to see him get a touch soon, you know, before he gets tired," Reggie replied, adding a nudge to Mack's ribs.

His first four minutes were spent just warming up, moving in and out of the defense while preparing for a pass in case his team won back the ball, but King was starting to get antsy. Celtic's holding midfielder, Ireland Under-21 Seamus Donnelly, had controlled this match from the start and the Mariners' minimal pressure only made his job easier. The amount of space given this guy, in Leslie's opinion, was bordering on criminal, and someone had to do something. At the fifty-five minute mark, someone did.

Donnelly had a penchant for drifting back into the space just in front of his defenders since the pressure there was nominal (opposing midfielders tended to stay back, and their forwards tried to stay high, leaving a gap defensively) and he could orchestrate the attack with his trademark long passes. King had noticed that each time Seamus received a pass from his right side he would let it run across his body and collect it with the inside of his preferred left foot. He had also noticed that the lack of pressure on the midfielder was making him complacent, and he was simply stopping the ball under his feet to survey the landscape.

"What's going on here, Mack? You're not gonna let this punk kid just show up and do what he wants, are you?" Mark Stevens whispered in McIlvenny's ear. It took a lot of nerve for the backup keeper to walk the length of the bench to question his coach, since he was still fighting for the starting spot, but this display of petulance had rubbed the 26-year-old the wrong way.

"Mark, if this kid is what I think he is you'll be glad he's on our team. If not, he'll be gone in about half an hour," the head coach replied, checking his wristwatch. "Humor me, please?" he asked.

"You should know some of the guys are really ticked off," Stevens added as he turned away.

"Thanks," Mack answered gruffly. "Hewitt! Get warm! You too, Brooks!" he called down to the end of the bench, summoning his reserve forwards who were always griping about playing time. "Be ready if King screws up."

They, of course, heard *when* instead of *if*, and smiled at each other.

Leslie King saw it in his mind about a minute before it actually happened: *Ball is played wide to right mid, Pat O'Malley, who sees no crossing target, and turns it back to the inside. He puts it on his passing foot and propels it on the ground toward Donnelly, who patiently waits for the ball to arrive. Planting his right foot, the Celtic playmaker broadens his stance and softly collects the leather sphere with the inside of his left foot, preparing for the next searching pass.* All occurring while the Mariners' young striker stood ten yards behind him.

He had the timing down and, when the opportunity presented itself, he was ready. As soon as O'Malley's pass was on its way, King made a quick run downfield for a few yards, then turned and sprinted directly for Donnelly. Coming from behind, he was totally unnoticed and he chewed up the fifteen yards in just under the two seconds it took for the ball to arrive at its destination.

Leslie's slide began nearly two yards behind Donnelly, as he dropped his left hip onto the smooth Bermuda turf. As his left knee bent to absorb the shock, his right leg straightened, reaching out to a spot between the legs of, and about eighteen inches in front of, the Celtic man. The toe of King's boot grabbed the ball just as it came off Donnelly's foot, and he planted the studs of his left boot into the soft grass. His forward progress stopped as he began to rise up from the ground with the ball on his foot and a man on his hip.

Seamus Donnelly was lifted two feet off the ground by King's momentum and sent face-first into the turf. His scream made players on both sides wince, but there was no time to dwell on the carnage. Unfortunately for the visitors, King had risen at midfield and instantly bolted toward the goal as their teammate cried in agony on the pitch, holding his crotch and wondering what had just happened.

"Play on!" the referee yelled, heading off the inevitable complaints as he was racing to catch up with the counter-attack.

"That was pretty cool, man," Joey Brooks said to his warm up partner.

"Yeah, but he's not in there to play defense," Don Hewitt responded.

Leslie King had always had deceptive speed - the kind of player who didn't look fast, but always seemed to get to the ball first. This was different, though, since the goal was still forty yards away and the two Glasgow central defenders were hot on his tail. He had gotten the jump on them after stealing the ball from Donnelly – they were simply stunned – by making a twenty yard pass to himself right between them and running as hard as he could to catch up.

He knew he would have no help on this break-away since all his teammates were bunkered in, most within thirty yards of the Virginia Beach goal. He was also confident he could handle the situation, having experienced every possible one-v-everyone scenario known to man, either on the pitch or in his imagination. This was one of his favorites.

King ran at top speed until he was about thirty yards from goal. Since the defender on his right was closer, he would be the first victim. Leslie simply cut in front of him and slowed slightly, making him decide: Slow down or foul. The center back thought he had help, so the decision was to concede. Then, as the second defender passed him and tried to get his feet turned around, the kid chopped the ball to his left and, in a blink, he was behind the last Celtic player.

In the one-v-two breakaway it never mattered which defender was closer to King, since he could finish with deadly precision with either foot. And the finishing was what made Leslie King special. Due more to his killer instinct than his technical skills, he could always be counted on to put the ball in the net. He simply did not get rattled, no matter the stakes, and it was as if the game slowed down for him in the penalty box.

As the second Celtic back tried to regain his balance, he saw Leslie's navy blue jersey flash over his right shoulder. King pulled back his left foot in preparation for a blast between the keeper and the near post. The opposing goalkeeper launched all six and a half feet of himself toward the post, cutting off King's best possible shot angle.

Leslie could have put the ball in the space just above the diving keeper, since he knew it was virtually impossible to change directions once in the air, but this was a special occasion. Instead, he pivoted on the ball with his studs, turned to the right, and gently placed the ball on the ground just inside the far post. Mariners 1, Celtic 1.

Reggie Lancaster always did his *airplane*. Joey Brooks liked to perform multiple back-flips. Don Hewitt hadn't scored for the club yet, but said he would slide on his knees right in front of the opponent's bench. Or stand on top of the sponsor boards and taunt the visiting fans. Or maybe grab a corner flag like a microphone, and do his best hip-shaking Elvis impersonation.

Leslie King simply grabbed the ball from the back of the net and ran to midfield, where he placed it on the center spot and waited for the Celtic kickoff.

"Wow," was all Brooks could spit out.

Hewitt nodded in agreement, and they both jogged back to the bench. Neither wanted to miss the rest of this show - or thought they were going in any time soon.

Sonny Smith slowly rose from the bench and waddled over to Coach McIlvenny's side. He was normally the calmer half of this duo who had been coaching together for almost nine years, including four at the University of Virginia prior to the Mariners.

"I have my checkbook in my pocket. Give me a number, and it will be done," Smith said. "My *personal* checkbook," he added for effect.

"Calm down, Sonny," Mack replied, with a laugh. "I think there may be more where that came from."

Shawn McIlvenny needed a break. The club had new owners, again, and he had been told his contract would be terminated after this season unless he could

14

produce a serious run at the USL championship. Nothing less would do and, at fifty-four, he didn't need this kind of pressure.

Not much was said on the pitch after King's goal. Mostly cries from the Celtic players to "Pick it up, boys!" or "Let's get it back!" The Mariners' players were simply trading glances with each other, their coach, and the tall blond-haired kid in the dark blue "LANCASTER" jersey. The roughly seven-thousand fans at this businessman's special filled the humid June afternoon with deafening cheers for the home team and their new striker.

Standing at midfield, soaking it all in, Leslie was remembering an Albert Schweitzer quote his mother had read to him years before:

Success is not the key to happiness. Happiness is the key to success. If you love what you are doing, you will be successful.

"Well, I *do* love this," he said softly, to himself.

King's new teammates were invigorated, and the visitors seemed to wilt a bit in the heat, which led to a complete reversal of the first half. Two more goals would be scored by the Mariners, both set up by Leslie's hard work, and the match ended 3-1 for the home team.

Now it was time for business.

"Captain King! Glad you could make it," Coach McIlvenny welcomed Leslie's father to his Beach Center office with a handshake. "Your son made quite an impression out there, as I'm sure you noticed."

"No, actually I just arrived," Pete King said. "How did it go?"

Sonny stepped right in, "Your boy played very well and we would like to talk to him about a contract." He was trying to stay professional, but his enthusiasm was showing through. "Scored a heck of a goal and assisted on two more...in only forty minutes!"

"Captain Pete King, this is my assistant, Sonny Smith. Sonny handles the administrative issues, so I can concentrate on the coaching side of things," Mack said as he took back control of the conversation. "Let's sit down, please."

As the players filtered out of the locker room, most stopped just outside the gate that led to the parking lot to sign a few autographs or mingle with friends. Leslie made a right turn into the lobby and headed down the hall to Coach McIlvenny's office, just past the small trophy case. King noticed that the most recent date on anything was from the 1950's, and he swore to himself that he would help get his team back on track. Leslie King was a Virginia Beach boy, and the Mariners had always been his team.

The meeting lasted less than twenty minutes. Leslie had a one-year contract offer for $225 per month, league minimum, contingent upon his passing a physical with the team doctor - and receiving the blessing of his mother. Pete knew Karen would agree once

16

she saw the look on her son's face, but he tried to convince the coaches it would be a hard sell.

After the terms were agreed upon, Coach Smith took Leslie to his office to make the arrangements for his physical exam. Mack and Pete walked to the lobby together.

"You know what's funny about this?" Captain King asked.

"No, what?"

"Since he was a kid, Les has been saying he was going to be the first American soccer player to sign a million-dollar contract. Wrote a story predicting it when he was in the third grade, if you can believe that. He always had this vivid imagination. Big difference, though, between his story and reality."

"I dunno, how old was he in the story?"

"Twenty-one, I think. Why?"

"Four years. Could happen, who knows?" the coach thought aloud.

"Sure. I guess we'll just have to wait and see," he laughed at the absurdity. His wife was the only person who believed absolutely in her son's potential, and she alone would see him achieve his goal.

Sadly, Pete King would never even see his son play professionally.

Chapter 2

BILLY FORD

"One last thing, and this one is non-negotiable," the incoming Chairman and CEO said to his predecessor, John Riccardo, and the other board members in the Chrysler Room of the Waldorf Towers in New York.

"Sure Lee, what is it?" For such a high profile transfer of power the process had been easier than expected, but some small issues were inevitable.

Iacocca pointed his index finger toward the ceiling and proclaimed, "Billy Ford must go!"

"What? Who's Billy Ford?" Riccardo was not much of a sports fan, but his ignorance of Detroit Chrysler FC's greatest-ever acquisition was truly remarkable.

The midfielder had joined the squad last season after a spectacular showing at the World Cup in Argentina. Even though the United States had been eliminated in the first round, Ford made the All-Tournament Team, and the Philadelphia native was suddenly being courted by some of the biggest clubs in the world. Rumors had him going to Manchester United, Real Madrid, New York (both the Cosmos and the Americans were interested), and the Los Angeles Aztecs. Detroit made the most lucrative offer, and Billy d in late July. His $1.8 million transfer fee was a w American record.

"You're kidding, right?" asked Tom Whitlow, President of Pentastar Marketing, Chrysler Corporation's second-most profitable subsidiary, next to Chrysler Defense. Tom's group had oversight of the soccer team, as well as the stadium operations, and he could not believe that anyone in the Detroit area had not heard of *his* Mr. Ford. Besides, *he* was responsible for making sure they had. "The guy's in half our commercials, and is currently our leading scorer!" Billy had four goals in his last five games.

Iacocca reiterated, "I don't care how good he is, Tom, I will not have *Chrysler* on the front of his jersey and *FORD* on his back! C'mon, guys, can't you see how this looks?" He just knew his former boss, Henry Ford, would delight in the irony.

Whitlow said he'd take care of it (he had an idea), and the meeting was adjourned. Several members of the board lost sleep that night over the thought of their star player in an opponent's lineup. Three days later, on September 15, 1979, a press conference was called to make the announcement.

Seventeen thousand royal blue-and-white striped "BILLY" jerseys would be sold in the next two weeks.

Billy Ford grew up in the Bartram Village projects of West Philadelphia, two blocks from Bartram Park on the Schuylkill River. Drug dealers, prostitutes, and gangs of young hoodlums frequently stood between

20

him and the dirt fields where he and his pals would play soccer after school.

Augustine Ford knew of the potential dangers on the street. She had lost her husband when Billy was only two months old, and worried about their son every day. Despite her fears, she would never try to keep him from his after-school games or the five-a-side tournaments on the weekends. She knew it could be his ticket out.

The former Augie Banks was well-liked in the neighborhood. The gentlemen appreciated that she still retained the physique she had had as high school track star. Nicknamed *the fastest little filly in Philly*, she was best known for her back-to-back State Championships in the 100 yard dash. And Mrs. Ford could still run.

After high school, she and her 20-year-old boyfriend, Tommy, set their sights on qualifying for the 1956 Olympics in Melbourne. Thomas Ford was one of the country's top hurdlers and she was a shoo-in for a spot on the 4x100 relay team - until they found out Augie was pregnant. They were married two weeks later by a minister friend of the Banks family in a small, family-only ceremony. They exchanged wedding rings instead of Christmas presents.

While her husband trained, Augie worked two jobs to support the newlyweds. She would never know that Tommy had been approached by one of his old friends from the South Philly neighborhood where he grew up. "Fat Joe" Munroe made a strong case: Lots of cash, low probability of trouble, multiple opportunities. And he knew Ford was desperate, since his little lady could not possibly keep up her pace much longer.

21

William Thomas (Billy) Ford was born on May 5, 1955, at the Children's Hospital of Philadelphia, delivered by Dr. Jonathan Speed, who was working the overnight shift only because someone had called in sick. Despite her obvious pain, Augie laughed out loud when he introduced himself. Tommy covered his mouth with his left hand and shook the man's hand with his right. The poor doctor did not get the joke.

The job that took Billy's father was not unlike the three others they had performed. Simple holdups at remote convenience stores, with the clerk always in on the deal. Munroe's boys would offer a percentage of the till to overnight workers and make it look like the store employee was roughed up, just enough to avoid suspicion. When Tommy arrived at the Quick-E-Mart on 34th, the owner was unexpectedly behind the counter, filling in for a new hire with a case of cold feet. After pulling his mask down to hide his face the robber grabbed his unloaded gun from the glove box and went inside, planning on spending a few minutes with some college kid and leaving with the loot. Instead he was met with a shotgun blast to the chest. He died at the scene.

The first part of the deal made between the twelve-year-old and his mother made perfect sense. He wanted to join a club team and finally get to play on a real pitch with a real jersey. Number five, of course. Mom wanted him to focus on school so he had to maintain at least a B average at all times, and stay out of trouble. No problem.

It was the other detail of their arrangement that frustrated the boy, at times, to tears. Augustine Banks Ford, former national sprint champion and almost-Olympic-medalist (16-year-old Wilma Rudolph got hers instead) insisted that Billy beat her in a foot race before he could play club soccer. Big problem.

For his first fourteen years, Billy's body parts never seemed to be in synch. Pudgy, pigeon-toed, and blessed with feet two sizes too big, running at all, let alone running *fast*, was not something he seemed destined for. If he had grown up next to a real, full-sized soccer pitch he might not have fallen in love with the game, but the small dirt field at Bartram didn't require much running ability to stand out. It was all about the skills - and Billy Ford had 'em.

Fortunately, eighth grade was special for Billy. He grew six inches and gained almost thirty pounds, was finally noticed by Natalie Johnson, and he became the fastest boy in Bartram Village. Puberty brought so many changes: Hair in weird places, sudden leaping ability (he could not only touch the rim, but grab it!), feelings about girls, chest muscles and, best of all, speed. It was all wonderful. Being fast was the best.

The tryout notice was printed on yellow paper with the Fury's maroon logo at the top. Posted at the top left corner of the Community News bulletin board outside the school's main office, Billy knew it was placed there specifically for him. And it could only mean one thing: It was time to challenge Mom.

The Philadelphia Fury announces tryouts for youth players age 14 and up.

This Saturday, 10:00 am, at Franklin Field

On the campus of the University of Pennsylvania.

All participants under 18 must have a parent or guardian present.

Good luck!

The field at Bartram Park was Billy's home turf, so he chose the venue. As agreed, Augie then got to pick the race. Her famous quick start normally would have made the choice easy. 40 yards, maybe 50, and after the first ten it would be over. He would never have a chance to even think about catching up. Perhaps the mother in her persuaded Mrs. Ford to choose the 100 yard dash to decide Billy's fate. She had noticed the changes in her son and thought it was time to give him a fair shot at something he wanted very badly. Augie was not ready for the outcome.

She met him at the park after school, 4:30 sharp, just as Billy finished setting up the course. 60 yards down, slight dogleg to the right at the orange cone, 40 more to the finish line. Bartram just had no way to lay out a straight hundred-yard course. Augie noticed how calm her son seemed and wondered what was up.

"He should be nervous," she mumbled to herself, while stretching her quads.

"We'll go on *your* start," the man-boy stated, matter-of-factly, as he walked over to greet his adversary with a hug. He was a little taller than her now.

"Will we?" his mother responded with a laugh, not sure if he was joking.

"Sure, ladies first," he couldn't resist a little wink.

The Augustine Ford of thirty-two was still the competitor she had been at eighteen. When she stepped into the imaginary starting blocks with her old Brooks running shoes, she ceased to be "Mom". *He is going to regret that*, she swore to herself.

Dust flew when Augie's powerful legs blasted her from the four-point stance. She chewed up the first ten yards in world-class time and it felt good. A little pang of guilt hit her about the 35-yard mark, when she thought Billy was going to have to wait a little longer to play club soccer, but it lasted only an instant.

Tommy Ford had been described as a *runner's runner* by his coach at Temple University. His near-perfect form was filmed and used by high school track coaches around the country as a training aid. Every aspect of his technique was considered flawless, except the odd way he held his left hand. He kept it clenched in a fist, while his right one was always in the preferred knife shape. No one knew why, or attempted to fix it.

When Billy flew past his mother roughly forty yards into the race, she was surprised. When she noticed his near-perfect form, she was impressed. But when she saw that fist on his left hand, she broke down and cried.

"Sore loser!" Billy called out from the finish line. From fifty yards away he could not see the tears on her face or hear the sobbing. He could only see that his opponent was bent over with her hands on her knees, breathing deeply, barely half-way into the course.

Augie straightened up and jogged to her son, who was waiting for her with a jug of cool water. He was confused when he saw her face up close.

"You alright?" he asked, thinking she had cramped up or pulled a muscle. "We can have a rematch if you want, when you feel better," he offered.

"I feel great," she said as she wiped the tears from her eyes. Augie hesitated a few seconds, soaking it all in. "Blew me away out there, didn't you?"

Billy smiled, "Yeah, but I didn't think you'd cry if you lost. Why did you stop?"

"I saw someone who reminded me of your father," Augie confessed. "And I had buried him pretty deep in here," she added, pointing to her heart.

"So you were sad?" Billy asked, still a little confused.

"No," his mother replied, "I was happy. I *am* happy. Very happy."

Billy reluctantly accepted her story, since it came with a wide smile.

"Say, you sure seemed confident before the race. How did you know you could beat me?" The competitor wasn't completely gone.

"Research. Your best hundred-yard dash time was eleven-five, when you were eighteen. I've been running under eleven for two months now, and Mr. Hudson said there was no way you could be faster now than you were then," Billy explained, not knowing that he was invoking the name of one of his mother's old flames.

"George Hudson said *that*!" She pretended to be upset, but was glad George had taken an interest in her son. He was a good man. Then she realized what else Billy had said. "*Under* eleven seconds! Are you kidding?"

"Sure of it," her son replied. "He's been timing me at the high school track, and I beat most of the varsity guys. My best so far is ten-seven, but I think I can beat ten-five by the time school is out."

"My son, the track star," Augie mused. "Who would have..," she was interrupted.

"*Soccer* star, Mom. Your son, the soccer star," Billy corrected her.

"Are you ready for Saturday?" she asked.

"Been planning for this my whole life," Billy Ford answered, in his most serious voice. They both laughed, and headed home. Celebratory pizza was for dinner tonight.

Franklin Field was brimming with activity by 9:30, and the line for tryouts was twenty-deep by the time the Fords arrived. Billy had wanted to leave earlier, but the Saturday bus schedule wasn't as convenient as it was on weekdays. Augie did not want to wait at the stadium for an hour before the signups started, so they agreed to take the 8:45 and hope for the best. Unlike on race day, Billy was showing some nerves so his mother told him the story of Dr. Speed. He, of course, thought she was making it up just to distract him. She promised to show him the birth certificate when they got home.

Once the players were divided by age, the coaching staff put the prospects through a series of warm-up exercises, then sent them directly into five-a-side matches to small goals. It took five minutes for Bob Ehlinger to notice Billy Ford. As General Manager of the franchise, he was most interested in the older players but found himself mesmerized by the left-footer dribbling around the other fourteen-year-olds.

"That kid is something special," he said to staff coach, Trevor Hall. "If he can run, make sure we sign him."

Billy Ford stood out on the small fields, but he was spectacular on the large ones. His speed and strength combined with a soft touch and silky moves to make a player too much for his peers to handle. He was moved up to play with the sixteens, where he continued to impress. In fact, he was better suited to play with the older boys since they were more likely to read his runs, and offer more support when he had the ball.

At the end of the morning session, the majority of the youngsters were given a yellow Fury t-shirt, told how special they were for trying out, and asked to leave.

The remaining boys and their families were invited to have lunch with the first team players in the field house at the west end of the stadium.

After welcoming the group, Fury Head Coach Jack Masters provided a brief history of the "maroon and yellow" for any who weren't already aware:

"When the North American Soccer League formed 1½ years ago, from the merger of the United Soccer Association and the National Professional Soccer League, the owners of Philly's two main clubs also agreed to merge and join the first division. The Atoms and the Ukrainians joined forces and began play last fall as the Fury."

Applause erupted from the young fans-turned-prospects, most of whom already had licensed t-shirts, jerseys, posters, or pennants with the Fury logo. The club was a leader in merchandise sales, and these kids (and their friends) were the prime marketing targets. The front office staff had even begun watching Eagles and Phillies games simply to count all the yellow shirts in the stands.

Coach Masters continued, "As most of you know, the club immediately began construction of the Fury Youth Academy at FDR Park. I am pleased to announce that the Academy's six fields are complete, and the indoor facility and clubhouse will be done in time for the winter season. This state-of-the-art complex will serve as the training ground for all our squads, from the first team down to the fourteens, and will be used for all amateur matches. The first team will still play here at Penn - at least until the stadium is done sometime next year. The new stadium will be across Broad Street from FDR."

Most of the players had reservations about leaving Franklin Field due to its significant home field advantage, but realized that a move to a larger capacity stadium was economically necessary. Veterans Stadium would be the new 65,000-seat home of the Fury and the NFL's Eagles. The Phillies had lobbied hard to be included, but realistically could not compete with the two biggest players on the Philadelphia sports scene. Baseball would continue to be played at Connie Mack Stadium.

"The youth teams will play all home matches at the Academy, and will be in a regional league consisting of teams from New York to Washington, DC. For you parents, this a big step. While your boys will still live at home and attend school, they will spend a significant amount of time with the club. Boys, if you decide to sign an amateur contract with the Fury, the club will own the rights to you, as a player, for about four years, until you turn eighteen. We will invest a great deal of money and time in your development with the hope that you will someday be here as a professional. We will provide you the tools, but you must work very hard."

Bob Ehlinger was banking on the Academy. The USSFA ruling of 1966 had been ignored by most of the bigger clubs, mainly due to the recent major changes in the league structure. There was just too much going on to worry about youth contract regulations. But Ehlinger realized the potential of the academy system right away. The "Youth Academy Regulations and Guidelines" was presented by the Federation at its Annual General Meeting on Saturday, February 26, 1966 in Chicago. Among the minutiae in the forty-three pages was the following gem:

a. Players of any age may contract to play professionally as long as minimum salary, transfer windows, and any other requirements are met pursuant to league rules at the time of the contract.

b. Amateur contracts are only allowed for players at least eighteen years old, and are intended for reserve or developmental players. A player who plays in any competition for a professional team must be paid for his play pursuant to league rules in place at the time. Amateur contracts may not exceed one calendar year in length.

(1) Exception. A player under the age of eighteen may be signed to an amateur contract under the following conditions:

(a) Player must be at least fourteen years old.

(b) Player must have parent or guardian consent in writing.

(c) A fully accredited academy is in place (See 104.1.d-f).

(d) Contract must be terminated at player's eighteenth birthday.

c. Clubs may charge a transfer fee for any player currently under contract, whether professional or amateur, regardless of age. Fees are negotiable and are determined by the clubs involved.

The goal of the Fury Academy was to develop players for a professional career. If some were sold to other clubs while under contract, the transfer fees could offset the cost of developing the ones who were kept. A delicate balance, but one that Bob thought he could maintain. He would become the authority in transfers and academy management.

31

The boys chowed down on cheese steaks and pizza while listening to Coach Masters. After lunch, all were marched to the training room for physicals and to take care of paperwork. Augie signed Billy's contract without hesitation, to his great satisfaction.

"Five-eight, one-hundred forty-five pounds," she read off the physical evaluation form. "Let's see, with two inches of afro and about ten pounds of pizza."

Billy responded, "No, the nurse smushed my hair down. I do feel like I ate ten pounds of pizza, though. I hope we don't play for awhile. I'd be as slow as you."

A well-deserved punch in the arm was followed by a hug and an embarrassing kiss on the cheek, which made it worthwhile.

Chapter 3

BARRETT GREY

"Welcome home, son," Tom Grey practically gushed. He was not an emotional man, but the old Marine actually felt a tear welling up when he saw Barrett, now twenty-one, step from the doorway of his Gulfstream II.

"Hi, Dad," he replied with a big bear hug and a few tears of his own. Thomas Barrett Grey III smiled at his mother, who had purposely remained in the background.

More than anyone else, Margaret Grey was responsible for brokering the deal that would bring her son home from Mexico City to the Dallas Tornado. Barrett's agent had contacted several American clubs looking for a way to get his prime client back in the States, but he had been personally directed not to contact Dallas. Grey led his team with eighteen goals last year, and had become a hot commodity in this season's transfer market. After a poor showing in the 78-79 season, the Tornado needed a reliable goal-scorer but Coach Miller had been told, in no uncertain terms, that a certain Club America forward was not to be pursued.

Margaret Grey thought the feud between her husband and their only son had gone on long enough, and her fear for Barrett's life finally forced her to step in and take action. The crime rate in the Mexican capital was always a concern, but an American billionaire's son provided a stellar target for kidnappers who had turned increasingly brazen. She never involved herself in Tom's business, but this had become personal.

"I want you to sign Tommy," she had blurted out during their anniversary dinner date. The couple met for dinner at Kirby's Steakhouse on April twenty-sixth every year. Tom had proposed to Margaret here, while he was still working as a field engineer for Lone Star Steel. She was a secretary for the company and he liked the way the little gal could stand up to the boys in the office. She was pretty easy on the eyes, too.

Tom was stunned. "Maggie, you know how I feel about this," he said after gathering his thoughts, and swallowing a bite of his medium-rare filet. He also knew she wouldn't let up.

"Do not misunderstand me. I want Tommy here, playing for your team, and you are going to take care of it." She left little room for negotiation.

Tom had purchased the Tornado in 1971, after his company was bought by Mobil Oil. Grey Petroleum had made him a wealthy man when he went public five years before, but the buyout put his net worth at just under a billion dollars. He tried to stay out of the daily operations of his teams (he was also majority-owner of the Dallas Cowboys) but occasionally would let his opinion be known.

"Damn it, he doesn't even call himself Tommy anymore. What makes you think he wants to move back here?" It bothered him that his son had started using his middle name when he left home for Mexico four years earlier.

"I've talked to his wife, Rosa. She is a wonderful girl, Tom, and I want to have them here when they start their family," Margaret answered, "and she wants to be here, too." She looked him square in the eye and said, "So it's settled then."

The richest man in Texas never had a chance.

"Don't I get a say in this?" He asked, but already knew the answer.

"No." Margaret smiled and Tom remembered their first dinner here, twenty-six years ago. When they argued, which wasn't often, she always won. And Tom told himself each time how lucky he was.

"Hon, you know how Al is," he reminded her of Coach Miller's stubbornness. "He won't like me meddling in personnel decisions," he added as a last resort.

"Of course, dear, he's the only man I know who's as bull-headed as you. But, he needs a striker and I need Tommy here, and you own the team. So, you see how easy this is?" She added another smile.

"Have you...," Tom cut himself off. "Of course you have. Al's already on board isn't he?" He just realized he was the last to know.

"Yes, dear," Margaret answered demurely. "But you get to make the announcement," she added, to cheer him up.

35

Tommy, as he was known then, started playing soccer with the neighborhood boys when he was seven. Their games always seemed to end up in the Grey's back yard, partly due to its twelve sprawling acres of prime University Park real estate, and partly because of Margaret's knack for making the best Kool-Aid popsicles in town. (She added a little extra sugar and used real Popsicle sticks, not old spoons like some other moms used.)

It was the best kind of environment for developing young players: No coaching, no parents, no rules, no positions, and no referees. Any coaching that was done was usually attempted by the older guys, and promptly ignored by the younger ones. The real coaching was all done by example, and no one realized it. The guys who played on club teams really enjoyed the freedom of these pickup games. Because of the inherent competitive nature of young boys, the rules were simple: Beat the other player, score goals. And if you can humiliate him in the process, even better! The games were sometimes brutal, but the ones who could handle the pressure invariably got better.

Up until the early 1950's, most American youngsters had few options to play organized soccer. Pro teams were reluctant to sign an unproven player, so the vast majority of the twenty-four ASL franchises looked overseas for talent. Only a few soccer hotbeds existed in the United States, in cities like New York, Los Angeles, and St. Louis.

It took the United States' victory over mighty England at the 1950 World Cup in Brazil to change the course. Although media coverage was initially sparse (the St. Louis Post-Dispatch was the only American newspaper with a reporter at the match in Belo Horizonte) the story spread rapidly, and the team was eventually greeted as conquering heroes, even though they had only won that one match. That fall new fans came out in droves to support the league and, within three years, soccer would surpass baseball as our national pastime.

Professional soccer had been popular for over twenty years, with most ASL teams drawing enough to keep their owners well in the black, but it was starting to see some competition for fans from the National Football League, which had recently expanded to thirteen teams, including their first on the West Coast. Many immigrants who had played and followed soccer in their home countries were starting to support their local football teams in order to appear more "American". Football, and also baseball, welcomed the new fans, but could never persuade them to teach these new games to their children. Due to this fresh *soccer nationalism*, their kids could now assimilate into their American communities easier *because* of soccer, not in spite of it.

The 1950's saw unrivalled prosperity, the beginning of the Cold War, and the first American youth soccer boom. All the demographics were covered: Second-generation immigrants, inner-city minorities, rural farmers' kids, suburban blue- and white-collar families. The world's game had found a home in the United States, but the big crowds of the 1950-51 season were less important, in the long run, than the interest in the sport by the children.

Increases in attendance at almost all the ASL games allowed the owners to spend more for players, mostly foreign, which added to the excitement of the league. Youth soccer leagues started to spring up in all areas of the country, and participation grew by leaps and bounds through the decade. But the real turning point occurred when the United States Soccer Football Association, in association with the National Soccer Coaches Association of America, created the United States Youth Soccer Association.

Formed in 1958, the USYSA formalized the rules for the nation's many youth leagues, set coaching standards, and formed the first regional and national competitions for amateur players under nineteen years old. President Eisenhower championed the new organization and spoke at the inaugural AGM, regaling the crowd with stories of his exploits on the soccer pitch at West Point, even though his playing days were cut short when he suffered a serious knee injury following a hard tackle. *Against Navy*, he claimed.

By the time Tommy Grey was in his teens it was common to see American players starring in the North American Soccer League or in the European leagues who could match the money, primarily England, Spain, or Italy. Additional homegrown players increased the popularity of the league, which in turn provided more opportunities as the number of first-division teams grew to thirty by 1970. This, of course, led to increased recruitment of American youth players by both the domestic and foreign leagues. The formation of the American Premier League in 1972 would again raise the level of soccer in the United States to a new high.

While the 1960's saw tremendous gains for soccer in all areas, the 70's were much more focused. At the end of the 1970-71 season, a consensus was reached among a majority of NASL club owners to create a new league with a much higher profile. The expansion of the other pro sports in the United States was causing increased competition for fans, but the introduction of television coverage added another layer of possibilities. Led by New York Cosmos owner Ahmet Ertegun, the league leaders reached an agreement that would elevate soccer to a previously unimaginable level. Ertegun was a visionary who saw a partnership with television as the logical way to grow soccer in the United States.

The American Premier League kicked off on August 14, 1972, when the New York Cosmos met St. Louis at Busch Memorial Stadium. ABC broadcast the match on its *Monday Night Soccer* show, and the rest of the twenty-team league played the following Saturday. The network pledged $2 million per year for the first two seasons and, in addition to *MNS* which had debuted in 1970, would produce *Wide World of Soccer* each week to show highlights of league games. A revenue-sharing plan would make sure all the teams, not just those in large markets, benefited from the increased exposure.

Dallas entered the APL as the last champions of the now-defunct North American Soccer League. Tom Grey had purchased the struggling team a year earlier from Lamar Hunt and had seen an immediate return on his investment. Since the lack of a scoring punch had kept the Tornado out of the playoffs the last four seasons, Grey's first act was to sign Jairzinho from Olympique de Marseille. The Brazilian had joined the French squad after a spectacular showing at the 1970 World Cup in Mexico, helping his country lift the Jules Rimet trophy for the third time, but was unhappy with his new team. Mirko Stojanovic provided leadership in the goal and, with the addition of Jairzinho, the Tornado had the goals that had been missing since

Reggie Lancaster left for Virginia four years earlier. Despite a slow start, the team finished with a 10-8-6 record which was good enough for second place in the Southern Division, and a playoff berth. Dallas cruised through the playoffs and won their first NASL championship.

Tommy Grey was allowed to train with his dad's team for the first time when he was fifteen. He was used to frequenting the training grounds, had kicked balls around the Cotton Bowl during pre-game warm-ups, and had hung out with the players at his home, but the locker room was still a scary place for the scrawny teenager. Coach Newman had suggested it to Tom and, though a little nervous, he had given the go-ahead. He knew Ron would look out for Tommy, but couldn't be sure how the players would take it. Over the next two years, they grew to expect the younger Grey not only to be at training, but to contribute as if he was on the team. Before long they all forgot he was still a teenager. Barrett's growth as a player had been accelerated by his exposure to the professionals and his passion for the game had grown with it.

After-practice sessions were the best, especially during the preseason before school started. He was able to stay for hours and work on the things he enjoyed most, like scoring goals, and fix some of his weaknesses. Kyle Rote, Jr. was especially fond of helping Tommy with his *studies*. Rote was under intense scrutiny after his high-profile rookie season in 1973, where he had led the league in scoring with 10 goals and 10 assists. He knew he would have to work harder than ever to keep up with his Rookie-of-the-Year stats. Kyle was an expert on physical fitness, and practiced what he preached. His success on TV's *Superstars* competition showed the world what kind of athlete he was when he won in 1974, 1976, and 1977.

Tommy Grey was very athletic, but he was still a kid and could barely keep up with his older training partner. Skill drills, emphasizing touch and striking ability, allowed Tommy to compete with, and at times get the best of, his mentor. The two would practice hitting the crossbar from twenty-five yards, and then run wind sprints inside the penalty box for half an hour. Pushing each other to improve, the duo became good friends and looked forward to playing together on the Tornado. It was Kyle, though, who would unknowingly convince Tommy to leave it all behind to pursue his dream in Mexico.

The Grey's housekeeper, Beatriz Mendoza, had practically raised little Tommy and he thought of her as a second mother. He always spoke Spanish with Beatriz, even though her English was impeccable, and they shared a passion for soccer. She had grown up in Chimalhuacan, just east of Mexico City, and had been a fan of Club America since she could remember. Beatriz told Tommy often of the exhilaration she and her family felt each time their beloved Club America defeated archrival Chivas of Guadalajara. Her greatest source of pride was that her cousin Eduardo had been hired as a scout for the yellow-and-blue. It was as close as any member of her family had ever gotten to actually *playing* in the cavernous Azteca Stadium.

In the summer of 1975 seventeen-year-old Tommy Grey was on top of the world. His youth club team, the Texans, had won their regional title for the second year in a row and he had scored a hat-trick in the final against Atlanta. He had grown up and was finally able to compete with Kyle in some of his physical challenges. The 1970 Pontiac GTO Sport Coupe he drove was a serious chick-magnet and, since his little sister had finally gotten her license, he didn't have to drive her around anymore. All was good in the world.

"Hey Kyle," Tommy greeted his mentor and friend to the field.

"Ready to get your butt kicked again today?" Rote responded with a smile.

"What do you mean *again*? It must be old age, gramps. Your memory is fading fast," he said to the twenty-five-year-old.

Their training sessions almost always started this way, and the trash-talk would last until they left for the day.

"Talked to Newman last night," Kyle ignored the jab about his age and got serious for a moment. "He said he's been talking to your dad about signing you."

"Must be nice, having an old man who owns a pro team," he added, not really meaning anything by it.

Tommy stopped in his tracks. "What does that mean? I'm not good enough to play here otherwise?" he asked abruptly.

"No, that's not what I meant. It's just that, maybe, it makes it a little easier, that's all," Kyle answered and realized then that he should have kept his mouth shut.

Tommy arrived home fifteen minutes later and was greeted by Beatriz when he entered the house. She had heard his car and suspected something was wrong. He should have been gone for at least two hours.

"Can you call Eduardo for me?" he asked before saying hello, "I want a trial with America." The scout had dined at the Grey home several times while in Dallas visiting his cousin. He always left an open invitation, if Tommy ever wanted to move south.

The housekeeper was not completely shocked. "Tommy, are you sure?" she asked, "What about playing here, for the Tornado? With Kyle?"

"B, I need to know that I can do it on my own," he answered, in Spanish of course. He sat down on a barstool and looked her in the eye. "That cannot happen here in Dallas, or probably anywhere in this country. Everyone knows me as *Tom Grey's son*, and I just realized what that does for me – and I don't want it."

Beatriz agreed to call her cousin right away, but warned Tommy that she couldn't guarantee anything. "I'll see what Eduardo can do," she said, "but no promises."

"That's exactly what I want," he replied with a smile and a hug, "Gracias, B."

It is often said in Mexico that Club America was founded in 1916, but reborn in 1959, when the club was purchased by Emilio Azcarraga Milmo. The owner of *Televisa*, he was a visionary businessman who understood the importance of marketing football as a form of entertainment. Shortly after his acquisition, Azcarraga sought to set himself up as the traditional bad guy, instrumental to every Mexican soap opera. He would be the antagonist that his fans could rail against for the common good, while both sides prayed for success when the squad played their arch-rivals from Guadalajara. Azcarraga immediately offended fans by buying expensive foreign players, which was a terrible insult to his loyal followers. Within five years, though, the team was back on top of the Mexican league, and the Club America brand was known worldwide. Despite this new openness to foreign players, the requested trial for an American was unprecedented.

Tommy arrived in Mexico City ten days after his request from Beatriz was granted. She had pleaded with her cousin Eduardo, and he agreed to let the Grey boy try out with a number of locals who were being assembled for the annual "Open Trial". Club America staged these events more for show than to actually find talent, as a way to remind the fans that they were still a club of the people. Several dozen players from around the capital would lace up their boots and give it all they had, most knowing they had no chance - but the thrill was worth a few bruises and sore muscles.

"Grey," he replied to the coach's first question.

"Si.....Barrett," he replied to the second. Surely, no one here would know his middle name.

"Numero cuarenta siete," Barrett was told and handed a royal blue practice vest with "47" stenciled on its front in gold. Not his usual "eleven", but it would have to do. He was directed to a crowd in front of the main practice field. Once the others were checked in, play started on each of the four manicured pitches with the coaching staff feigning interest and talking over ice water and cigarettes.

After the initial thirty-minute session, players were given a break and reshuffled so that the better ones were on the main field, directly in front of the head coach and his assistants. A few of the local players were legitimate contenders for a spot on the reserve squad, so the added pressure would, hopefully, force one to the top of the heap. Raising the stakes even higher, legendary striker Enrique Borja had joined the coaching staff in the stands. Borja was a hero to most of the men in the stadium, having led the Mexican League in scoring three straight years from 1970-1973, and for helping to defeat Toluca for the league championship in '71. Luckily for Barrett Grey, he had a keen eye for talent.

During the initial session Grey played sweeper, directing from the back and conserving his energy. His vision and field-awareness were far beyond his years, and his new teammates figured out quickly that the white boy could help them look good. Of course, most of the locals saw themselves as the next great America goal-scorer, so they were glad Barrett offered to play in the back. His training regimen with Kyle had forced him to become a complete player, as competent at sweeper as he was at forward. He also knew that playing in the back was a great way to show off his leadership skills, not to mention the opportunity to get forward when the opposition least expected it.

45

After the break, Barrett resumed his role in front of the keeper, and kept his new team organized and on the attack throughout the next thirty-minute period. During the break, Grey asked one of his strikers if he would like to switch positions, to give the guy a rest. He agreed, and Barrett started the final thirty minute period in his usual, and most comfortable, role. It only took eight minutes for *El Leyenda* to call him off the field.

Enrique Borja was never the most skilled or athletic player, but had a knack for scoring goals like no Club America striker before or since. He was a student of the game, and believed his hard work on and off the field made all the difference. Hours spent practicing his finishing, polishing his moves, studying defenders and goalkeepers, all helped him produce seventy goals in only three seasons. The legendary forward was not easily impressed, but he liked what he saw on the field this sunny afternoon.

"Who is that? Is he the American?" Borja asked Raul Cardenas when Grey switched to forward. The Head Coach hadn't really been paying attention.

"One of the defenders, I guess. Looks like he thinks he's a striker, now," Cardenas replied with a laugh. He wasn't aware of any *gringos* at the tryout.

"No, that one is a soccer player. Watch how he moves off the ball. He is good enough to play in the back for our reserves right now, and I'd like to see if he can score," Borja said, mostly to himself. "Jorge, how old is number forty-seven?" he asked his assistant. Play began with the referee's whistle.

"Mmmm, let's see, seventeen. Wow, he's only seventeen," Jorge responded as he read from his notebook. "Barrett Grey...Dallas, Texas, USA...six feet two...one hundred seventy pounds," he said, "that's all I have."

Three minutes into the period Grey found himself one-on-one with the opposing side's left back, wide out on his right flank. He headed straight for the poor defender, faked left, went right and sent in a driven cross that should have been finished. His teammate, some guy called "Pablo", was too tired to jump high enough to head the ball down, and the shot sailed harmlessly over the crossbar. The delivery, however, raised a few eyebrows in the coaches' box.

Four minutes later Barrett was pushed up to the other team's eighteen, with their center back draped all over him. His jersey had not left the defender's hand in over two minutes, since he had placed himself at the lone center forward position. Luis Corrada, a well-liked local player, was at left mid and had been playing long balls to the forwards all day – with no payoff. This time, his forty-five yard pass was received on Barrett Grey's chest. Grey noticed that the back had been trying to force him to his left, so much that he was almost daring him to use his weaker foot. *OK,* Barrett thought, *here you go.*

A slight head fake just before the ball made contact with his chest made the defender think he was going to place the ball on his right foot. This forced the big back to dig in and hold his ground. Grey cushioned the ball with his left pectoral muscle and dropped it two yards in front of him, slightly to his right. Farther away than he wanted, but not impossible. The added distance actually helped him in one regard, since there was less time to think about the options. He simply reacted to the ball as it bounced off the grass like he had done in practice hundreds of times before.

The American striker took three quick steps forward before pivoting on his right foot, almost 180°, and unleashed a booming shot that beat the keeper to the upper left corner of his goal. As his teammates congratulated him on a spectacular strike, Grey looked past them at the defender who had been marking him, or at least had been trying to. "You should see what I can do with my *right* foot," he said to the dejected man, in perfect Spanish. Barrett then noticed the middle-aged man on the sidelines, trying to get his attention.

About time, he said to himself, as he jogged toward the bench.

Chapter 4

JIMMY MAXWELL

"Too small," Coach Messina answered, knowing full well that he would be questioned again. "Five-foot-nothin', and what, about a hundred pounds – soaking wet?"

"But Tom, you can see this kid's a player, can't you?" Gary Rickman was adamant. The Maxwell boy was small, but he had displayed a level of skill the St. Louis coaches had never seen in a youth player. Actually five-four and one-hundred twenty pounds, dry, he was still among the *least* imposing sixteen-year-olds at this tryout.

"Sure Gary, we'll sign him," Messina replied, "and tomorrow Petey will dip him in marinara sauce and have him for lunch." He was referring to Stoyan Petrov, the hard man of St. Louis Busch Soccer Club. "This discussion is over," the head coach added.

Rickman conceded, but tucked Jimmy Maxwell's evaluation form, with his home phone number, into his shirt pocket. He had an idea.

Petrov was raised in the part of St. Louis known as "The Hill", surrounded mostly by Italians. His parents had immigrated to America from Bulgaria in 1952 with their two young daughters. With little in the way of marketable skills, Boris Petrov relied on his work ethic to impress potential employers. While others were trying to show off their past work experiences, Boris simply showed up before everyone else at the Brown Shoe Company and started doing pushups in front of the foreman's office. By ten o'clock he was offered a job in the shipping department. "Work hard and you will survive," he would tell young Stoyan, years later. "Work harder than everyone else - and you will succeed." For Boris Petrov it was just that simple, and his only son took every word to heart.

Stoyan signed with St. Louis Busch at fourteen, due mainly to his athleticism. Big, strong, and fast, he was just what the staff was looking for and he was actually placed on the "YES" list before they even saw him play. *Hard-working, fast, strong as an ox, and fairly creative* was written on his evaluation form.

Petey, as he was known, did everything with maximum effort. His daily regimen of five hundred push-ups and one thousand sit-ups made him an awesome physical specimen. He had fantastic size and speed which allowed him to hang with the first-teamers at fifteen. But what set him apart was his competitive spirit. Petey played the game - every game - to win.

By the time he was nineteen Petrov was the starting defensive midfielder for Busch, and had already earned a reputation as a dirty player. He was initially upset by the designation but, after St. Louis beat Pittsburgh Steel 4-0 in Pittsburgh, he saw an interview with their head coach on the nightly news:

Reporter: "Coach, tough one tonight. Can you sum up your thoughts?"

Coach: "Well, you know, we try to go to Jenkins in the middle, and Petrov shuts him down. So we push him up to forward and the guy stays with him. Then I put the new kid, Stewart, in for Jenkins, and Petrov nearly kills him on his first touch..."

Reporter: "Ah... and no call?"

Coach: "No *foul*. Just the hardest tackle I've ever seen. Petrov...I....I really hate that guy."

Reporter: "A lot of coaches complain about his play, some call it dirty."

Coach: "You want the truth? We all wish we had a guy just like him. He's not dirty. He just plays at an intensity level six notches above the rest. He's amazing."

Stoyan Petrov slept well that night.

Even with the skill set that sixteen-year-old Jimmy Maxwell possessed, he could not be expected to compete with the likes of Petrov, or any of the other professionals at St. Louis Busch SC. He was four years younger than Petey; still a boy. And a small one at that. Gary Rickman knew this, but was sure this kid deserved a shot with a big club. The touch, the pin-point passing, the way he could dribble out of trouble and the field awareness were all years ahead of his counterparts. "Shoot," Rickman would tell his wife, later that evening, "this kid could be the best player I've ever seen."

Considering who Gary Rickman had played with and against, that statement was quite remarkable. As a member of the Busch squad in the early seventies he had been teammates with Pat McBride and Al Trost, and had personally marked Boston's Brandon Rafferty at least eight times (although it seemed like more). He had faced Johan Cruyff twice (against Ajax and Barcelona), and had even marked Pelé in an exhibition match against Santos in 1973.

"I'm not giving up on this one, Rita," he told her after dinner. "You should see this kid play." Gary knew she would appreciate Jimmy Maxwell's style, perhaps more than he did. She had an eye for the subtle nuances of the game - like the way some players could feel pressure before it arrived, or play the second- (or third-) option pass as others were just catching up to the first. Those little things brought her great joy, and she missed them dearly. The "style" employed by Busch Soccer Club was too direct, too fast, too physical for her taste, and she hadn't been to a match in years. With her health declining so rapidly, Gary had wished for something to cheer her up.

"He nutmegged two defenders in a row, one with each foot, with a third guy on his back – all inside the penalty box!" he offered to help her see what she had missed. "Stayed on his feet the whole time with these monsters trying to mug him, then lays of a little back-heel pass to the trailing midfielder. Who, of course, shot high over the crossbar," he added, with a laugh. Her eyes lit up when she heard Gary describe the play.

"Of course, Messina signed all three defenders, and the shot-misser, right?" she asked, only half-joking.

"No, silly," he replied. "Only *two* of the defenders," he hesitated for effect, "*and* the shot-misser." All they could do was laugh.

The drive home from St. Louis was long enough without the dark cloud of disappointment hanging over it. Three hours in the car with his older brother would normally be loads of fun, but this trip hadn't ended so well for Jimmy. Dale tried to console him but was, in this case, seriously ill-equipped. When the radio signal from KSHE-95 faded near Festus, reality set in: He had failed. To make matters worse, his favorite *REO Speedwagon* song was just starting when the static took over.

They had planned to stop in Poplar Bluff to see Coach Franklin before heading home. Ken Franklin managed the Mules of the Midwest Conference, in the Third Division, and had coached Maxwell since he was twelve. Ken would say that all he did was "let 'em play", but his coaching method was solid, and a few of his charges had gone to play professionally. He was certain Jimmy would join them someday.

The boys arrived at the Franklin home just after seven, hungry and tired of driving. As they crawled out of the cab of Dale's Ford F-150, Ken met them in the front yard and could immediately tell how the weekend had gone. It took all the strength he could muster, but Jimmy walked right up to his coach and gave him the confirmation.

"I didn't make it," he said. It was tough to look him in the eye, but he forced himself to do it.

"How'd you play? Did you leave it all out there?" Coach Franklin believed in the power of hard work. His charges were constantly reminded that often in life the difference between winning and losing is the tiniest bit of effort, and you never want to regret not trying hard enough. Skill levels and athletic ability would set some apart, but effort was something anyone could excel at.

"Yeah, I think so," Maxwell replied. His big brother was behind him, nodding in agreement. "It was weird, coach. They only picked the biggest guys. Some were so bad you would have cut them from the Mules!"

"Jimmy, I was afraid that might happen. You see, some coaches can only spot what's right in front of their eyes," Franklin offered his explanation, "and many of them are with the bigger clubs. They can't afford to take a chance on a kid who isn't already physically ready to play with the professionals."

"Do you remember Joey Baxter?" he asked both the boys. Neither did. "He played for us on the first team about nine years ago, left back. We went up to Kansas City for a match against the Spurs, back when the Winston Cup was still called the U.S. Open Cup. Anyway, Joey had a pretty good game even though we lost 3-1, and the KC coach wanted to talk to him after the match. I remember Joey's response when that coach offered him a shot at a tryout. He said, "No sir, I can't see playing for somebody who thinks *I'm* the best player on this team.""

"He knew what that coach saw, and it wasn't his skill. Baxter was about six-two, one-ninety. Sure, he had been working really hard to improve his game but he knew he was nowhere near most of the other guys," Franklin explained, "and that took guts."

"What's he doing now?" Jimmy asked.

"Last I heard he was in graduate school up at Mizzou - mechanical engineering, I think. He was a sharp kid." Coach Franklin continued, "Moral of the story is this: Soccer wasn't his future, and he knew it. You, on the other hand, were born to play this crazy game, and you shouldn't let this minor setback get you down. I'd bet good money we'll see you wearing the ten shirt for the national team one day."

"Thanks, Coach," Jimmy said. "We need to get going," Dale chimed in.

"Glad you stopped by, boys, and say "Hi" to your folks for me," Franklin replied. His wife handed them some sandwiches, hoping to provide some solace in her own way. Bologna and cheese never tasted so good.

As they made the short trip home to Fisk, Jimmy realized he felt better, and was trying to picture himself on the US National Team. Wearing number ten, of course. His life was about to change in ways he had never imagined.

The Maxwell's phone rang that evening at 9:20. No one ever jumped up to answer, since they had to wait for the familiar "ring.....riiiiiiiiiiiing" that signaled a call to their house and not the Kershaw's, with whom they shared a party line. Ma Bell had not made much progress in Southeastern Missouri. Jimmy was in the kitchen devouring a large bowl of Cap'n Crunch and reading a Spiderman comic book, when his mother entered and handed him the telephone handset. The twenty-foot cord came in handy, especially when the

55

older boys took calls from girls. Privacy was hard to come by in a five-room farmhouse with one phone.

Jimmy didn't ask his mom who was on the other end, in order to avoid potential embarrassment. Any time a girl called he had to endure the teasing from Dale and Bob, so it was easier to keep a low profile. He assumed it was Sara Sabulsky, the latest in a string of cute upper-classmen who had taken an interest in him. The feeling was somewhat mutual. She was athletic and attractive, but nearly four inches taller than him. He was still not entirely comfortable with the whole process, but it was being thrust upon him. Jimmy braced himself, and answered the phone.

"Hello," he said in a muffled voice, trying to seem uninterested. He was still tired from the tryout and the long drive, so he didn't have to fake it much.

"Jimmy Maxwell?" asked the obviously male voice.

"Yes, sir," he replied, sitting up in his chair, "who's this?"

"My name is Gary Rickman, I was at the tryout this weekend," the caller answered. "I am one of the assistant coaches for St. Louis Busch."

Jimmy thought he must have left something at the field, his new cleats maybe. *Oh, no.*

Rickman continued, "This may sound strange, but I called to find out two things: First, how tall are your parents? And second, are you serious about being a professional soccer player?"

"Uh...hold on," Maxwell replied. With his hand over the phone, the boy then called into the living room, "Mom, how tall are you and Dad?" He waited for the response, then answered, "Mom's five-eight, Dad's five-eleven."

"Good," Rickman was relieved. Before he could call his friend Ramon about a small sixteen-year-old prospect, he needed to be prepared.

"And YES, SIR!" Maxwell blurted out, upon realizing he had not answered the second question. "Sorry, but what is this all about?" he asked.

"I have a good friend who does some scouting for a different club," the coach replied. "Before I call him, I needed to know those two things. He will ask me about your size, and now I can tell him not to worry. Any older brothers?" he asked.

"I get it," Jimmy caught on quickly. "Tell him Dale is nineteen and six-foot-two, and Bob is seventeen and about six-foot-even. They were short when they were my age, too."

"But I'm a LOT better than they were," he added, since both were listening in.

"Great," Rickman laughed with Jimmy. "I'll see what I can do and call you back. It's sometimes hard to track Ramon down, so don't worry if it takes a few days. I will let you know either way."

"Can you tell me who he scouts for?" he had to ask.

Jimmy Ray Maxwell had just turned four years old when he got his first soccer ball. If the weather had been more cooperative, he probably would have gotten a bicycle (with training wheels) or maybe an electric race car set but, in the summer of 1964, drought had nearly decimated their watermelon crop and the income from the summer wheat barely covered their living expenses. Jimmy and his younger siblings were fine with whatever they received, but the older boys felt cheated with that year's diminished presents. Younger brother Jerry would have been satisfied with the box Dale's new socks were packaged in. Three-month-old Phyllis didn't care about Christmas yet.

Jimmy learned soccer from watching his brothers play at the field on Route 60 in Fisk, about twelve miles from Poplar Bluff. Since Dale and Bob were among the younger boys at the Saturday pickup games, it was accepted that Jimmy wouldn't play, but could come along to watch. Like most young boys, his attention span was similar to that of a puppy, so watching quickly became tiresome. Their pitch was mostly grass, due to the efforts of the Davis boys who lived nearby, but it was surrounded by a sand and crabgrass mixture that was annoyingly bumpy and slow. This was Jimmy Maxwell's playground.

Too rough to dribble on, the sandy soil ringing the field provided a bevy of problems for the older boys, but it was all Jimmy knew. He thought nothing of having to scoop the ball into the air and balance it on a thigh while looking for an imaginary teammate to make that far-post run. By the time he was nine, Jimmy could run the length of the pitch without letting the ball touch the ground. If you could call it running, that is. His curse as a youngster was his growth cycle – he would fill out to sometimes pudgy proportions, then shoot up three or four inches in height. As a child, Jimmy Maxwell never was comfortable in his own body. His teenage years were even worse - the same changes, amplified.

He would be nearly twelve before he was allowed to get into a game with his older brothers, and by then Jimmy was able to make his ball do pretty much whatever he wanted. Still too young to be much help with farm chores, he had hours of free time to play in the yard with his ball every day. An old walnut tree next to the house provided excellent target practice, since even the slightest error would cause a rebound that had to be chased. One-v-one games with Jerry, two years his junior, gave him the opportunity to play with his left foot to "make it fair". That didn't last long, since Jerry was a sore loser, and Jimmy never let him win. Playing with the older boys allowed his talent to shine.

Bob and Dale were exceptional players in their own right, and constantly challenged their little brother to try new moves, or juggle with a new body part. They were unknowingly creating the best soccer player in the country, but it would be years before all the work would pay off. By pushing him to improve, they thought they were just doing what big brothers did.

Allowed to tag along everywhere, Jimmy became sort of a mascot for the older boys. They would marvel at the little kid's ability to juggle for what seemed like hours on end. One of Bob's friends even got him a gig entertaining the crowd at halftime of the Poplar Bluff Mules' home games. Most times, he could keep his ball up for the entire twenty-minute period - not bad for a ten-year-old. Club management put a stop to his show when the supporters began to *boo* the home team when they would come out and stop him.

When he was finally allowed to play with the older boys, Jimmy was placed up top, away from the grinder that was the midfield. His brothers sought to protect him from the physical contact by giving him freedom to find open spaces. What they could not have predicted was the nature of their little brother, seven years younger than the oldest boy on the field and at least two years younger than anyone else, when he had the ball at his feet on a grassy field, thirty yards from goal.

Twelve-year-old Jimmy received a bouncy pass from one of his teammates, softly settled the ball, turned, and took it directly at the eighteen-year-old defender who was the closest opponent between him and the goal. The older boy was a little surprised, but dropped anyway expecting a pass. Jimmy kept coming, and the defender felt he had to go for the tackle before they got too close to his goal. The younger boy side-stepped his mark with the ease of a seasoned striker and laid a square pass to his teammate, who promptly slotted the ball into the goal.

Ken Franklin had a list of "Undeniable Truths of Soccer". Things like: 'The *more* defenders you have, the *more* likely you will be scored upon', 'Playing for the tie will *guarantee* the loss', 'Nothing bad happens when you are moving', etc. When he started coaching twelve-year-old Jimmy Maxwell, he added this one: 'Creativity comes from being aggressive'. The two of them would discuss this while watching *Monday Night Soccer* at the Franklin house. The coach believed most players that were deemed "creative" were better at performing tricks than getting results. He often said true creativity had more to do with forcing your will on the game. He knew one other player understood.

The Boston Patriots' new attacking midfielder, Brandon Rafferty, embodied Franklin's newest 'Truth'. Everyone in the park knew he was going to attack his rival, beat him, and, when a second defender stepped up to help, dish the ball to an open striker. He broke the mold of the holding central midfielder who played deep and sprayed long passes to his forwards. Twenty-five-year-old Rafferty led the American Premier League in assists his second season, and helped Boston climb out of the bottom half of the table, where they had been since the inception of the new league two years before. Jimmy dreamed of playing with the likes of Brandon Rafferty some day. Rafferty was a real Number Ten.

"Who, my friend Ramon?" Gary Rickman asked. He was reluctant to tell the kid, for fear of getting his hopes up. He knew he couldn't guarantee anything.

"Yes, sir, I guess. Who does he scout for?" Jimmy persisted.

"Real Madrid." Rickman waited for a response, but got none. "I'll call you later," he added, and hung up.

The boy put his cereal bowl in the sink, grabbed his soccer ball, and sneaked out through the back door. The juggles started that night with "Uno....dos....tres" and ended, a little over an hour later, with "dos thousand, ocho hundred, diez". He would need to work on his Spanish.

Chapter 5

CHOICES

The final buzzer at Assembly Hall was almost drowned out by the cheers from the Phillips supporters. Alfred Bauer could barely look up at the scoreboard from his seat at the end of the East St. Louis bench. His Flyers had been completely overmatched by the team from Chicago and, as if losing the state championship game by twenty-eight points and sitting the last six minutes after collecting a fifth personal foul wasn't bad enough, Johnny Jackson was fast approaching.

"Poo-ky!" Jackson called out, almost singing Bauer's nickname. He held out his monstrous right hand and Alfred took it, allowing his long-time nemesis to pull him to his feet. Johnny felt, and looked, ten feet tall. He was only six-six, but still five inches taller than Bauer. He had just finished his basketball career with a game for the ages: Thirty-six points, eighteen rebounds, nine assists, and MVP of the state championship. Not bad for a soccer player.

"Congratulations, Johnny," was all he could muster. Alfred tried telling himself that he didn't really care about basketball - that soccer was the important thing in his life - but losing was losing, and it was always hard. He was upset, but also relieved that he was finally free to focus on his future as a professional soccer player.

The Bauer family quickly made their way to the floor, with Alfred's grandmother, Effie, in the lead. Fourteen family members had made the one-hundred-seventy mile trip to Champaign.

"Poo-ky!" she yelled from across the gym. That's where Johnny got it. Effie Bauer tried to make every game that her Alfred played - soccer or basketball, rain or shine. His opponents had long ago stopped kidding him about her funny, high-pitched voice. (She was most famous for shouting "Shoot, Pooky, shoot!" as he was crossing mid-field – or half-court!) Word spread quickly that you teased Pooky Bauer at your own risk.

Jackson was in his second year as the starting goalkeeper for the Chicago Sting Reserves, having turned down a pro contract at seventeen so that he could complete his high school basketball career. Despite numerous scholarship offers, he had never considered playing college hoops, but wanted simply to help his Phillips teammates win a state championship. The 1975 season had been a dream come true for Johnny Jackson: Parade All-American in both basketball and soccer, Illinois' Mr. Basketball, and now a State Champion. He could finally sign that contract that would earn him the Sting's highest-ever rookie signing bonus.

Alfred Bauer chose to finish high school for different reasons. He also had the opportunity to turn pro at seventeen, when he was offered a contract by his club, St. Louis Busch. Alfred wasn't ready to quit school yet, or give up basketball, to train with the First Team.

In truth, lots of players quit school to sign with soccer teams now that the American Premier League, with its abundant cash, was in full force. To deflect criticism, the league had set up programs to ensure that young players had ample opportunity to finish school or obtain a G.E.D. diploma during their training.

While Johnny Jackson was a high-scoring power forward who had no interest in pursuing a career on the basketball court, Alfred "Pooky" Bauer wasn't always sure what he wanted to do. During his junior year at East St. Louis Senior High, Bauer led the Flyers to their first Regional Final in over thirty years where he caught the eye of Kansas University head basketball coach Ted Owens. The Jayhawks had just won the Big Eight title and had made it to the NCAA Final Four in 1974, and KU was the alma mater of Alfred's hero, Jo Jo White, who had grown up right across the river in St. Louis.

The Celtic guard had worked several camps in Bauer's neighborhood over the years, and the two had struck up a friendship. Alfred could see himself following in the footsteps of his mentor - first to Kansas, maybe the Olympics, then to a career in the NBA. Coach Owens told him he could be the starting point guard by the time he was a sophomore. For the first time in his life he knew what he wanted to do. Then his soccer coach found out.

Gary Rickman pulled double-duty with the Busch Soccer Club. In addition to his highly visible position as Tom Messina's First Assistant Coach, he also had sole responsibility for the reserve team. He loved coaching his reserve boys and truly enjoyed seeing them move up to the First Team. As Head Coach of the reserves his only task was to develop players, regardless of the team's success - he had made that clear to Messina when he was offered the job. "I will develop players, or win games. Which do you want?" he had asked rhetorically. His boss gave him all the rope he would need, he thought, to hang himself. Rickman used it to build a bridge from the reserves to the first team.

Bauer met with his coach after one of their summer practices. While most of the pro players took time off from mid-June to mid-July, many of the reserves stayed around to hone their skills and stay fit, just in case an opportunity arose. Gary Rickman enjoyed these smaller, more personal, sessions. It was a great place to get to know the boys.

Alfred showered, got dressed, and entered the coach's office. "Got a minute?" he asked.

"Sure, Pook. What's up?" Rickman replied. He had played 4v4 with the guys at the end, and was cooling off in front of a large fan with a wet towel on his head.

"I wanted to talk to you about my future," Bauer began his prepared speech. "The basketball coach at Kansas has offered me a scholarship, and I'm thinking about giving up soccer."

The coach removed the towel from his head and wiped the sweat from his face. "Really? You think you can give it up?" he asked, surprising his player.

"What do you mean?" Bauer was confused. Exactly the effect Rickman was hoping for.

"Pooky, look," he began. "You are a fantastic basketball player, but it's because of the soccer player in you. I've seen you play. You play point guard like you play center-mid. If you played football, you'd be the quarterback. That's who you are. *The guy in charge.*"

Bauer nodded in agreement, not sure of the intended point.

"The difference is that on the soccer field," he paused, then added, "you really are in charge. Do you know what I mean?"

"Sorta," he wasn't so sure of himself anymore.

"When you passed on that contract last month, I didn't think much of it. Lots of guys want to finish high school; for their family, for some girl, whatever. I was sure you had a good reason. Besides, we knew you would still be with the reserves," Rickman turned serious. "But if you are honestly considering quitting, think about this: How happy are you going to be when your coach is calling the plays? When you have to set a pick or make a cutting run even when you see a better option? Think about that because that's college basketball, and that's *especially* KU basketball." Rickman added, "I just want to make sure you've thought this through. You know you can call me if you need to talk."

That evening, after a few hours of deep thought, 17-year-old Alfred Bauer called his friend and mentor for advice. He dialed the long-distance number with no regard for the cost of a call to Boston, Massachusetts.

"Jo, this is Pooky. I need some help," Bauer jumped right in when White answered. The Celtic star knew right away who was calling. Only one Pooky had his home phone number.

"Hey, little brother, what's wrong?" White truly cared about the boy, and feared the worst. He knew of the temptations in the inner city.

"Which should I choose: Soccer or basketball?" Bauer blurted out before he could stop himself.

"Are you kidding? Is that why you called?" White was relieved it wasn't something serious. At least to him it wasn't serious.

Alfred explained the situation, and told Jo Jo White how torn he was. He felt like he was having to choose between his first love and pleasing his hero. White could tell he was fighting back tears.

"Pooky, listen to me," the Celtic guard was stern with his young friend. "I've seen you play soccer, and I've seen you play hoops. I think you are too good a soccer player to give it up."

Bauer listened, but couldn't believe the response he was getting from his friend.

"Besides," White continued, "at your height, it would be really tough to make it to the NBA. You know the average height in the league now is six-seven!" Then he took it to the hoop. "Little brother, basketball may have the tallest athletes, but soccer has the BEST athletes. That's where you belong."

Alfred was stunned. What Jo Jo said did make perfect sense, though, and it was coming from the only person who could have delivered the message.

"And you should know how proud I am of you," White said. "I can't imagine how cool it must be to have a professional contract waiting for me to graduate from high school!" Slam-dunk.

"Thanks, Jo. I'm glad I called you," Alfred suddenly realized he needed to call Coach Rickman. "Gotta go. See ya, bro."

"You're welcome, Pooky," Jo Jo White answered as the line went dead.

He made a mental note to ask his friend, Brandon, about the St. Louis franchise. Surely, he would have some contacts there, and he wanted to make sure his little brother was looked after. He would bring it up at the gym in the morning. The Celtics and Patriots shared a facility for off-season workouts, and Brandon Rafferty never missed a session.

High school graduation finally came two-and-a-half long months after basketball season ended, and both Jackson and Bauer were now free to pursue their new careers. A major development had occurred in the meantime.

One which would have a profound effect on both of their bank accounts.

Effective May 1, 1975, the American Premier League, itself only three years old, became the Texaco Premier League. The oil company had been looking to make a major investment in the soccer market since the mid-60's, but had been turned off by the poor performance of the NASL. Several teams had folded or moved. Few had their own stadiums and, if they did, most of those were in disrepair. The formation of the American Premier League in 1972 changed the way the business community looked at the sport.

Several large companies jumped in to sponsor their local teams, knowing full well that ABC's new television contract with the league would provide them with national exposure. Anheuser-Busch, Chrysler, IBM, U.S. Steel, and Coca-Cola were the first to jump in, which led to a feeding frenzy among those who were left. Many teams saw their sponsorship and advertising revenue increase three-fold over the 1971 figures. Added money in the coffers permitted higher salaries, better facilities, and a better product on the field.

The league was started with one rule that seemed, at first, destined to make it less competitive. For the initial three years of its existence, the American Premier League would keep the same twenty teams. This would allow all franchises adequate time to figure out what they were doing. Then, starting with the 1975-76 season, the league would begin a promotion/relegation system in affiliation with the United Soccer Leagues' 2nd and 3rd Divisions. Both Texaco and the league agreed that the time was right to make a bold statement, and signed the multi-million dollar deal on national television.

Since promotion and relegation were somewhat *foreign* to American sports fans, the league felt the

70

concept had to be sold to the public. The larger markets, it was assumed, would see less resistance than some of the smaller ones whose teams would have a harder time staying in the top flight. Texaco tried to help by running a series of commercials where a poor-performing service station owner was "relegated" to selling only Exxon gasoline. (They didn't last long.)

But American fans did not need to be sold on an arrangement where teams were rewarded for performance. If anything, it was a more of an *American* system than any other sport. Fans liked supporting a winner, even if it meant dropping to a lower division, and the possibility of being relegated made the regular-season matches that much more important. Each season, the bottom three teams would be booted out of the league, and replaced with that season's top three clubs from the lower division. The impact was huge and immediate.

Johnny Jackson signed his first professional contract at the Chicago Sting home office at Soldier Field. His family was on hand, as was his high school coach, Herb Mills. Coach Mills was the only one present who didn't have his picture taken with Johnny's giant bonus check. The real one was only 3½" by 8½" but, since it was worth $151,000, it was much more impressive. The unusual amount gave Jackson the distinction of being the most expensive rookie signing of the 1975-76 season. Los Angeles' Brad Mishigawa had held the title for just under twenty-two hours. The Aztec midfielder had signed for $150 thousand, which had been necessary to fend off his other suitors. Fortunately for the Sting, Johnny Jackson had maintained a relatively low profile.

The scene at Busch Memorial Stadium in St. Louis was quite different for Alfred Bauer's signing ceremony. Since their *other* season was in full swing, the club's owners were not overly concerned with the latest crop of newcomers to the soccer team. Cursory handshakes and photos followed the contract signings, then the whole group was invited to the owner's box to watch the Cardinals play a baseball game against the New York Mets. Bauer spent most of his afternoon explaining the rules of America's former national pastime to the new signees from Portugal and Italy.

Seven new players were added that day. None received more than a $20,000 signing bonus. Three months later, though, only Pooky Bauer would be on the First Team roster.

Chapter 6

CALIFORNIA BOYS

"Laundry?" He answered with a question.

"Sure," was the response. Brad Mishigawa never backed down from a challenge. His new roommate had just introduced him to *soccer golf,* and they needed something to play for.

"Loser does the winner's laundry for what, a *month?*" Juan Espinoza was confident in his skills, but didn't want to push the issue. Besides, he knew Mish would agree. A quick handshake sealed the deal.

The game was simple, just like real golf. Play your ball until it hits the pin; total the number of shots; lowest score wins. Espi never lost at soccer golf, and his new roomie was almost too eager to play.

Juan Espinoza had bought the house in nearby Glendale two years earlier, in May 1975, after he signed with the Aztecs. One of the few home-grown players on this Los Angeles squad, Espi had never thought he would be able to afford a home this nice. He had actually come up through the Lazers youth system and, even though he starred on their reserves, he was routinely passed over in favor of players from outside the area. Head Coach Martin Crown had a habit of pursuing expensive "foreign" talent, much to the chagrin of his supporters, and the local players in his club.

Juan could have signed with the more prestigious Aztec Academy at fourteen since their training facility was only six miles from his home in the Belvedere section of East Los Angeles, but bus fare was hard to come by. He decided to play for the Lazers because his uncle worked swing shift at the Navy Yard in Long Beach, where the club's stadium was, and had offered to give him rides to practice for free.

The long trips allowed him time to finish his homework and engage in conversation with his uncle, Carlos. Both were rabid soccer fans, and huge supporters of the LA Aztecs. Carlos understood the boy's predicament, but never missed a chance to rib him for playing for the "stinkinglazers". All one word. Always in English.

While the freeway discussions always revolved around soccer, Carlos was careful to sprinkle in plenty of important life lessons. He didn't want to see his little sister's son end up like so many of the youngsters from their neighborhood. Juanito had the tools, both physical and mental, to escape the cycle of the barrio. His father, Big Juan, had left when the boy was too young to remember and had wound up doing time in San Quentin for stealing a car in Anaheim. Carlos thought his continued absence was the best he could do for the kid.

House rules dictate that the host always tees off first in soccer golf. At least that's what Espi said, so he went first since they were playing at his home course. The groundskeepers at Wilson & Harding were used to

Juan and his teammates knocking soccer balls around on their courses and, since they usually stayed away from the *real* golfers, actually had little reason to run them off. They would normally approach him only for an autograph, or to introduce a friend. Espinoza often thought that the game had lost some of its excitement since the danger of being chased away by men on lawnmowers had virtually disappeared. As a boy, he had been run off the courses at Montebello and Monterey Park more times than he could remember. The new thrill was in the wagers, which sometimes reached hundreds of dollars per hole, although he felt this one was almost too easy. His new roommate was part country bumpkin/part hippie and hadn't said more than three words since his arrival this morning from Santa Barbara. To a gregarious personality like Juan Espinoza, quiet is often mistaken for lack of confidence. He didn't know Brad Mishigawa yet.

Average height, average weight. That's where "average" stopped when describing Mish. His straight black hair hung down just past his shoulder blades, obscuring most of the tattoos on his upper back. When not on the soccer field or in the surf, he was wearing jeans – giant bell-bottomed jeans that covered his feet, which may or may not be in sandals. (Usually not.) Having to wear *socks* with his uniform bothered him greatly, but he was willing to make that sacrifice for his chosen profession.

Bradley John Mishigawa was born in San Luis Obispo, on the campus of Cal Poly, where both his parents worked. His father, Ken, was a senior physics professor, while Barbara chaired the Music Department. Brad was their first son, and the Mishigawas would have two more boys to go with two older daughters before calling it quits.

Their farmhouse in Paso Robles, twenty miles north of the university, was built with education and competition in mind. "Family Game Night" was like *Jeopardy* and *Superstars* combined. The kids were fierce participants and no challenge was taken lightly. As a result, the Mishigawa children had excelled at nearly everything they attempted. Both of Brad's sisters were doctors; Susan was an orthopedic surgeon in Seattle, and Beth had a family practice in Santa Barbara. Younger brother Dan was studying pre-law at UCLA, and little Justin was an All-State wrestler and class president at Paso Robles High. The middle child was no exception.

After high school, Brad traveled to the Far East to explore his Asian roots. His soccer skills opened a few doors, allowing him to stay long enough to earn a black belt in karate before returning two years later. Then twenty, and an unknown in the American soccer community, Mish would need to prove himself in a hurry.

His amazing ascent started when he was playing with a bar team in San Diego, and they were asked to scrimmage the Pumas reserve squad in a preseason match in July. He had been back in the states for only four months, and was living with an old surfing buddy in Coronado. His friend had been a fixture on the bar squad for several years and was able to get Brad on the team. It was easier still because the bar's owner was also of Japanese descent. Mish was only interested in playing soccer. He was grateful his friend Jake had an empty spare bedroom and he assumed everything else would take care of itself. It was part of his new Zen philosophy.

The San Diego Pumas had finished the 1975-76 season in 17th place, barely avoiding relegation to the USL's First Division. Halfway through the next season, they were only two points from bottom-dwellers Cleveland, and were suffering through numerous injuries to key players. Jack Myers worried about his job if they were sent down to the lower division. Most USL clubs had no money for a full-time reserve coach.

Myers had no way of knowing how his fortunes would change, in the span of a few short months, because of a tattooed Japanese-American surfer.

New Year's Day 1977 marked the official kickoff of the second half of the season. The Pumas were hoping for some good luck when they hosted Washington, but knew they were in for a tough match. The Diplomats had beaten them 4-0 in October, and had picked up a new Spanish striker who was known for scoring on even the best defenses. After his third goal, twenty-two minutes in, Sergio was substituted and the San Diego crowd began to turn on the home team. At halftime the decision was made to fire the head coach and move Jack Myers into the position until a permanent replacement was found. Myers found out as he was leaving the field, with plastic beer cups raining down on him and his squad. Only a few were empty.

With nothing to lose, Myers called in favors from a few old friends, including the Los Angeles Aztecs' Head Coach, Terry Fisher. The Pumas and Aztecs agreed to play in a pair of exhibition matches, for charity, so the new coach could take a look at a few fresh faces against decent competition. He knew better

than anyone that their reserve team had been decimated, and he didn't have much time to waste trying to
negotiate trades with other TPL teams. He had to find
talent somewhere else - in a hurry.

After the first charity game, where he did see one
player worthy of a shot, Ben Wagner reminded him of
the bar team they had scrimmaged back in the summer.
Ben had started the season on the reserves, but was
called up when both central defenders were lost to
injury on successive weekends in November.

"Oriental-looking dude, long black hair. You remember, he scorched us down the right side at will," the
defender said. He was glad to be on the *other* side of the
defense that day.

"I *do* remember. He played most of the game in
the back but when he moved up to midfield we couldn't
find a way to stop him," Myers responded. "The clock
saved us, if I recall." Now he would have to do some
detective work.

Finding out who was in charge of Mishigawa's
team was relatively easy. Jake was home when the
phone rang, and the invitation was made with little
fanfare. Myers even offered to let his surfing buddy suit
up just to make sure he wouldn't back out. The guys
showed up with different expectations, although they
both enjoyed their instant celebrity status with the girls
in the crowd. Three phone numbers was enough for
Jake to call the experience a positive one.

Brad Mishigawa had a slightly different
objective. He knew his years of toiling in the obscurity
of Paso Robles weren't wasted. Far away from a proper
field, and more than thirty miles from the nearest club,

he had learned to make the most of his rural surroundings. Mish was always a hard worker, but his backyard training sessions were brutal. Had he known better, he might have been less inclined to push his body so hard, but he just incorporated his martial arts practice into his soccer. Ken had introduced him to karate when Brad was nine and he loved the disciplined training methods. His early soccer experience was limited to the high school squad and the occasional pickup games with college players at Cal Poly he was able to sneak into.

The trip to Japan after high school showed Brad how promising his soccer career could be, when he was regularly paid to be a guest player on several semi-pro teams. The extra cash enabled him to stay much longer than he had planned, and he came to enjoy the lifestyle of a professional athlete, Tokyo-style. He tried to imagine how his life would change once he became a star in the new Texaco Premier League.

Myers started seven of his top eleven, but they all knew this was an exhibition and ninety minutes wasn't likely. Mishigawa began out wide on the right, with his buddy Jake in front of him at forward. Newcomers filled in at the left and center back positions. When Jake asked Mish for any words of wisdom, all he got was, "When I have the ball, get out of the way." There was serious work to be done tonight.

By twenty minutes in, it was apparent that the best players on the field were the opposing right midfielders, Mishigawa and Espinoza. Each team ran their offense through them and, even though the Aztecs had a vastly more experienced squad on the pitch, San Diego was generating just as many scoring chances (Jake was doing a good job of staying out of Brad's way).

The halftime score was 1-1, and the Pumas were knocking on the door when the whistle blew. Hurrying to the locker room, the San Diego coach didn't notice the brief conversation Terry Fisher had with Brad Mishigawa as the players were leaving the field.

The halftime talks could have not been more different. While Fisher ripped his boys for allowing these "scrubs" a goal and way too much of the possession, Myers was almost speechless. He was wondering whether he should offer Mishigawa a contract right there, but decided it could wait until after the game. His only request was that they *keep doing what they were already doing.*

The second half started as the first ended, with San Diego controlling much of the play, but Los Angeles eventually wore them down and the match finished 3-1 in favor of the Aztecs. Jack Myers was oblivious to the score, and really just wanted to get to the business of signing Brad to a contract. One of the backs also looked promising, so the evening was going really well. The team owner was in the stands, and Jack couldn't wait to introduce him to his newest signings. He had no way of knowing that his coaching career would end tonight.

"Mishigawa, can I see you?" Myers asked after the player had showered and gotten dressed.

"Sure, Coach," Mish replied. He followed Myers to the training room, where they could have a little privacy.

Myers started, "You really impressed me out there tonight. I'd like to offer you a spot on the team."

Mishigawa was taken aback. "Wow, coach. Two offers in one night. This is more than I had hoped for."

"What do you mean, two offers?" Jack was confused. *Had his assistant already talked to him?* No one else had the authority to make an offer.

"Well, I've already accepted Coach Fisher's offer to play for the Aztecs so, I guess, thanks, but I'm sorry." He thrust the dagger deep into Myers' gut. "He spoke to me at half time, just before we came in to the locker room." And twisted.

Terry Fisher had simply beaten him to the punch. It didn't take a genius to know that Myers was going to offer this kid a contract, if he hadn't already signed him, so Fisher took the shot on the off-chance he was still available. Myers' mistake was due to his naiveté. He should have had the newcomers sign some sort of agreement prior to the match, but he couldn't have anticipated a scenario like this. He would never speak to Terry Fisher again.

The Los Angeles Times reported Mishigawa's signing the next morning. San Diego's owner read about it over breakfast and fired Jack Myers before lunch.

"You're not bad, for a *rookie*," Espinoza added after telling Mish how he should have approached the last hole. Juan had the gift of gab, and he knew it helped him get in the heads of most his opponents. He wasn't sure about this guy, though. After the third hole, his lead was only one stroke. *Beginner's luck*, he told himself.

Mishigawa liked Juan from the start. Even though they seemed like complete opposites, these two were sure to be good friends. "So," he asked, "game is *five* holes?"

"Yeah, just like we agreed. Don't try to change it just because you can't keep up," Espi replied with a smile. "You flew in from Santa Barbara - you from there?"

"No, just visiting my sister. I'm from Paso Robles, small town north of San Luis Obispo," Mish answered. "Been living in San Diego since I got back to the states last year."

The next hole had a sharp dog-leg to the left, around a grove of tall trees. Juan teed off with a drive that stopped rolling one-hundred-ten yards away, in the center of the fairway, perfectly placed for the ensuing shot which would surely place him on or near the green. His ability to drive a ball sixty or seventy yards in the air, with pinpoint accuracy, was what cemented his place on the Aztecs' starting lineup only a few months after signing. The LA strikers knew Espi would find them, given half a chance, whether he was whipping in a cross or launching a free kick.

Brad Mishigawa surveyed the landscape, looking for some way to get back the stroke that separated them. Then he saw the flag through the trees. "How far is it from here to the pin?" he asked Juan, thinking that it was about seventy yards.

"Two-twenty. You saw the sign," Espi replied, somewhat confused.

"No," Mish said, "From here to the pin, straight-line. I'm guessing about seventy." Then he launched his tee shot over the trees with some serious backspin.

"You want to concede, is this what you're doing?" Espi laughed at the unconventional shot, then added, "Hey, that's *my* ball you just lost. Dude, you are going to owe me big-time!"

Brad would keep his mouth shut until he saw his ball on the green, nine feet short of the pin. "Looks like I was off by a few yards."

After the fourth hole the score had been turned upside down. Mish had picked up two strokes and was now leading by one. Espi was temporarily speechless. "Back in the states from *where*?" he finally asked.

"Japan," Mish answered, with a typically short response.

"Playing professional soccer?" Juan needed to know more. He was thinking he may lose to this newcomer, and hoped he had some credentials.

"Nope." Brad Mishigawa smiled for the first time this afternoon, and said, "Professional soccer golf."

Chapter 7

QUALIFICATION

"Hey *raggazzi*, keep it down," Doc called out, in his usual half-English, half-Italian. Seven members of the United States National Team had been gathered in his hotel room, watching attentively for the last forty minutes, and they were growing restless. No one in this group could claim to be a big fan of *Dallas,* but Leslie King's latest commercial was about to debut and they had made plans to see it.

Spending their last Friday night in the country stuck at the Holiday Inn in Fenton, Missouri, was bad enough without having to watch JR and Miss Ellie plot to steal little John Ross from Sue Ellen. The team would be flying to Honduras the next morning for the final round of CONCACAF qualifying and the Tegucigalpa nightlife would, no doubt, be off-limits. A little partying was to be expected.

The opening scene shows a distant soccer field and what appears to be some kind of a tryout. Trialists are playing 3 v 3 to small goals, and as the camera zooms in you can make out the Brooklyn Dodgers' logo on some of their practice vests. One of the younger players, wearing a paper "126" on his chest, steals the ball from a veteran and slots the ball into the open net.

Background singers harmonize, "Bring OUT your best!" as an ice-cold bottle of Budweiser Light suddenly appears.

Narrator (presumably player 126): "I wasn't even drafted until the seventh round."

One-twenty-six pressures his mark and forces a bad pass that goes out for a throw-in. His team is on the attack - no time for congratulations.

Narrator (126 again): "They didn't even know my name."

The ball is rolling out, but "126" slides to keep it in bounds. His opponent traps him in the corner and he loses possession. Whistles blow, and he hangs his head as the players walk off the field.

A lone figure approaches and, as the picture becomes clear, you can see that it is Leslie King in all his glory. He smiles at "126" and says, "Schroeder, huh?" and offers the rookie a pat on the back.

Had King's teammates been paying attention after this point in the commercial they would have seen the Dodgers enjoying a few of those ice-cold Budweiser Lights, joking with their new buddy, while we are told once more to "Bring OUT your best!" Instead, they were laughing out loud and trying to figure out how best to tease King at the next training session. It was time to follow the Dodgers' lead and head downstairs for a few beers themselves.

Ten minutes later the guys met up with the rest of the team at the hotel lounge where they soon found out that the TV over the bar had been tuned in to *Dallas* and everyone there had also seen Leslie King's latest acting gig. King's endorsements had made him a household name and a major celebrity, but he could always count on this group to keep him grounded. Which explained why he was attempting to hide in a dark booth at the back of the bar.

As famous as King was (talk-show host Tom Snyder had described him as "more famous than rich – and he's VERY rich!"), these men knew him as a hard-working soccer player who would do anything to help his team win. Even though his Brooklyn Dodgers hadn't won any major trophies since the Winston Cup in 1979, and he was nearing thirty years old, Les continued to be among the league leaders in goals and points and his position as the US National Team's go-to striker was as solid as it had ever been. He was happy to be back with the team going into some games that really mattered.

"I swear they made his teeth sparkle," Brandon Rafferty said. "You know they can do that on television." He was trying to be serious.

"Les's teeth always spah-kle, Raff," Billy Ford replied, making fun of Rafferty's Boston accent, as usual. "Ask your wife, I'm sure she's noticed."

Rafferty would only take this kind of abuse from Ford. They were the team's "odd couple" – best friends from dramatically different backgrounds, who had hit it off right from the start when Billy had been called in to his first National Team Camp four years earlier. Raff had been a mainstay of Team USA since the failed campaign to qualify for the 1974 World Cup.

Back then, the CONCACAF Region (North & Central America and the Caribbean) only sent one representative, but there was still no excuse to be eliminated from the first round of group play with only one point! Rafferty and Marco DeSantis, or "Doc" as he was called by his National Team buddies, were the only members of that squad still with the full national team, hoping to qualify for their second World Cup. Leslie King should also have been on the '74 squad, but that coach had relied on his forwards from the previous campaign (also a non-qualifier) to the detriment of some of the younger players.

DeSantis was the backbone of this team's defense, just as he was at his current club Liverpool, in England, and had been at Fiorentina before that. As a boy growing up in Tom's River, New Jersey, Marco never would have dreamed his soccer career would turn out like this.

Marco's father, Luca, didn't think twice about moving his family to Italy when his mother became ill. He knew his son, fourteen at the time, would assimilate into the culture easily since kids always have an easier time than adults. His wife, Maria, was from Rome and also missed her family. His business was thriving and Luca's partners could handle it without him. The decision to move to Italy was easy, but where they would settle was a different matter.

Luca DeSantis grew up in Turin, in Northern Italy, and had supported Juventus since he could remember. He still had the black-and-white striped outfit he had worn as an infant and, of course, his mother was there. But Maria wanted to be close to her aging parents as well. Worse yet, they were all Lazio fans! A compromise was agreed upon that satisfied everyone. Well, almost everyone.

Marco couldn't believe the squad wore *purple*. As a member of Fiorentina's Under-17 team he quickly fit in with the other boys, and caught the attention of the coaching staff. His ability on the field brought instant respect from his teammates, and his outgoing personality helped him make friends quickly. Life in Florence was great, except for the purple uniforms. Both Luca and Maria could easily visit their parents, and neither had to see Marco play for the other's team. Luckily, Fiorentina was no threat to Lazio or Juve in the league standings.

DeSantis had developed first as a soccer player in New Jersey, and then had made the transition to central defense. That distinction was lost on many, but not Willy Schneider. As the head coach of the United States National Team, Willy looked first for soccer players. His style was often derided by the press, and had gotten him fired from seven coaching jobs, so far. He never seemed to care.

Schneider's approach was definitely not simple. He would collect the best soccer players (meaning that they were comfortable on the ball, could pass and shoot with both feet, and *saw* the game as he did) and he would teach them how to play positionally, as part of his team. Schneider used his background in psychology to place his boys in the best possible spots. He utilized a battery of tests he had developed as a graduate student at Princeton in the late 1950's to evaluate their personalities and skill sets.

His bosses in New York had had the patience to let him prove his worth, and the Cosmos' trophy case was proof. In his six years with the club they had won every prize possible at least once, including three of the last five league championships. His 1980 team had even won the heralded "double" by winning the Texaco Premier League *and* the Winston Cup in the same season. Schneider's critics would point to the wealth of talent he had at his disposal, but he was one of the few coaches in the world to win with a team full of international superstars while keeping them all happy. His appointment as head coach of the United States National Team was a fitting feather in an already large cap.

"Wake me *after* we land, not before," was the order. Marco DeSantis was in the aisle seat, speaking to the backup keeper, who was looking out the window of the Boeing 747. The flight from Lambert Field in St. Louis had been smooth and uneventful. The team had plenty of time to stretch their legs in Miami International before boarding for the second leg of this all-day journey. Everyone was looking forward to landing in Honduras and getting to the hotel. Two and a half hours to go.

"Didn't think *you'd* be afraid to fly," Johnny Jackson replied with a smile. He knew Doc had put in more air miles than anyone else on this team, by far. Actually, making the transatlantic flights had become routine for the defender, now in his ninth year with the National Team. This was something entirely different.

Marco DeSantis was still playing for Fiorentina when he got his big break. The National Team was in need of good defenders, and he was already in Europe. He had first been called up in 1973 for a friendly in Israel and had impressed Coach Gordon Bradley enough to secure a starting spot in the upcoming World Cup qualifying matches. Only twenty years old, he was paired with relative veteran Bobby Smith in the central defense. Smith was only two years older, but the two New Jersey natives formed a strong backline, which had little support elsewhere on the field. Even though this team failed to qualify for West Germany, the youth movement which began in the 1950's was beginning to pay dividends.

"You've obviously never flown into Tegucigalpa," Doc answered with a smile of his own. In fact, only Rafferty, Ford, King, Mishigawa, and DeSantis had ever made the flight into Toncontin Airport.

Jackson laughed nervously, and attempted to ignore the comment. Turning his attention to the *Life* magazine he had picked up in Miami, he soon forgot about Doc's ominous smile. Marilyn Monroe's pictures inside certainly helped, as did the gripping article about Irish hunger strikers. He was asleep midway through the third paragraph.

Every team has a practical joker, but Billy Ford was a legend. He had shown up at his first national team camp dressed like Apollo Creed from *Rocky*, complete with the red, white, and blue shorts and matching cape. He claimed he was there to challenge Brandon Rafferty for the title of Captain America, which *Sports Illustrated* had recently bestowed upon him. His million-watt smile allowed his new teammates to laugh with him, and he and Raff were instant best friends.

Ford had his pick of the newbies on this trip, but Doc had asked him to pay particular attention to Jackson. Ninety minutes in, Billy switched seats with another rookie in order to be directly behind Johnny. He told Jimmy Maxwell to sit in the aisle seat and keep quiet. The twenty-year-old barely had time to say "Yes, sir" before Ford was in position.

The approach to Toncontin Airport in Tegucigalpa is among the most dangerous in the world. Arriving aircraft must head straight toward the neighboring mountain range, then make a hairpin u-turn to the left *while* dropping altitude *and* slowing down. American Airlines has special training for their pilots who fly to Honduras, and many airlines would not risk it at all.

To make matters even worse, the runway is barely a mile long, making it one of the shortest in the world. All this was scary enough without Billy Ford's antics.

As the 747 flew directly toward the nearby mountain range, the experienced pilot proceeded to slow and decrease his altitude rapidly while banking hard to the left. He had made this approach almost a hundred times, and was among the best at this landing. This would be the worst possible time to wake up from a deep sleep, and Billy knew it.

With his hands over Johnny's eyes, Ford began to scream, "We're going down! We're gonna die!" at the top of his lungs. Jackson woke up to the sound of the massive engines whining as they tried to slow the plane and, when he opened his eyes, he was blind. Billy turned his head toward the starboard side window and removed his hands. Johnny could see a mountain fast approaching while the plane seemed to be in a death spiral. He could only shriek and re-cover his eyes.

Rafferty, King, and Mishigawa joined in with a half-hearted scream which included arms flailing overhead. You could tell they had ridden this roller coaster a few times before. Ford was laughing hysterically at the look on Jackson's face. Maxwell was petrified. Stoyan Petrov threw up in his airsickness bag, which made Juan Espinoza follow suit in his own lap. All the while, Marco DeSantis slept.

The 747 landed without incident and taxied to the designated gate while the flight crew helped clean up the mess in the cabin. Petrov and Espinoza were spared any more shame since most of the veterans had experienced the same fate on this flight. Fifteen minutes later, the squad was picking up their bags and heading outside.

Willy Schneider knew the local customs all too well and had planned in advance to minimize their impact. He was famous for going to extreme lengths to gain a tactical advantage. Two white vans with no windows were waiting to meet the team at the airport. He had the rental company paint "US Soccer" in large red letters on both sides, and "USA" across the back in blue. The veterans were concerned that the boss had lost his mind. They remembered the treatment they got the last time they were here to play Honduras.

"Coach, do you think we could be a little *less* obvious?" Brandon Rafferty verbalized what many were thinking. Two years ago the team was pelted with rotten fruit on the way to their hotel, after they had beaten the hosts 3-0 in a friendly match.

"Don't worry yet," Schneider replied, "we don't play the Hondurans until the twelfth. They won't hate us for almost three weeks." He seemed calm enough.

It was late by the time the team was checked in at the InterContinental and everyone was looking forward to a good night's sleep. Tomorrow was Sunday, but the day would start early with a run together, then breakfast at the hotel. Team USA would be training twice a day for the next week in preparation for their opener on November 2nd against El Salvador. It was the same routine they had had back at the National Training Center in Missouri for the last two weeks.

The CONCACAF Group Finals were staged as a round-robin tournament, with the top two teams going to next year's World Cup in Spain. This was the first time the region would send *two* entrants, since the Cup had expanded from sixteen to twenty-four teams. The Americans would face, in order, El Salvador, Haiti, Honduras, Mexico, and Cuba over the next month, with the winners wrapped up by November 22nd.

94

Chapter 8

CRUISING

"Any questions?" Coach Schneider asked the squad after laying out his game plan. He knew the Salvadorans would pack it in and try to frustrate the Americans. It was imperative that they stay focused for the full ninety minutes.

"We're playing for the win, guys. Nothing else matters," Brandon Rafferty asserted before they left the locker room for pregame warm-ups. And when Captain America spoke, these guys listened.

Raff knew the drill as well as anyone. These smaller countries would invariably play with only one forward, pack either the midfield or the defense, and hope for a counter-attack or free-kick goal. A scoreless draw would be a huge victory for El Salvador this afternoon, and Team USA was determined to disappoint them.

The United States National Team had been training in Honduras for a full week prior to their first match on Monday, November 2nd. As expected, they would play in their traditional 4-4-2 formation with Arnie Mausser in goal. DeSantis, Espinoza, Alexi Mayer and David Knott would man the backline, with Rafferty and Petrov in central midfield, Ford and

Mishigawa playing out wide. Leslie King and Rick Davis were the forwards.

Coach Schneider had several good options on the bench and planned to substitute liberally throughout the tournament. He was especially interested to see how the new players would acclimate to the increased pressure of the international game. Jimmy Maxwell and Johnny Jackson would get their first taste soon, and Willy was expecting big things from these two. Training this week had shown that they were more than ready.

It was no surprise when the Salvadorans started the game in a 4-5-1, with Luis Zapata as the lone forward. They would attempt to stifle the American attack by shutting down their midfield. Most scouting reports touted this US midfield as easily its best ever. Rafferty was well known as a gifted playmaker, even though he may have lost a step in the last few seasons. Petrov was the ball-winning engine behind Raff who played like two men, even on his bad days. Billy Ford's speed was amazing, but his speed *with the ball* was downright scary and, with Mish on the right side serving crosses with pinpoint accuracy, they were an awesome pair of wide players.

El Salvador's defensive posture kept them even until the 32nd minute when Leslie King headed home a cross from Ford. Billy had isolated himself to the left of the penalty area about five yards from the end line. His first move to the right caused the defender to slip and fall down and, instead of taking advantage of him, Ford pulled the ball back and waited for him to get up. He then faked right, stepped over the ball and touched it left, past the defender's planted foot. A split-second later he was in the box as King was making a far post run from the penalty spot.. The keeper almost reached the little chip as it sailed just over his outstretched hand, and Les buried it from six yards out. As usual, King just grabbed the ball and jogged back to his half of the field, mumbling all the way.

"Who's he talking to?" Jimmy Maxwell asked. He had just taken his seat on the bench after the brief team celebration. This group expected to score against every opponent, so a goal against little El Salvador was nothing to get too excited about.

"No one knows for sure," Steve Newton replied. Willy Schneider's assistant had been with the Cosmos since 1976 and King's secret conversations were constant fodder for the New York columnists. "Probably his dad – died when he was young and never got to see him play professionally." Newton had a pretty good idea, and he was sticking with it.

Maxwell made a mental note NOT to mention this to King.

Pete King had been a standout in a world of superstars. He had been hand-picked by Admiral Rickover himself to captain the Navy's newest nuclear-powered attack submarine, and he knew he was the best man for the job. His resume was impressive: Top of his class at the Naval Academy; Two-time NCAA wrestling champion; Master's degree from MIT; and twenty years of outstanding fitness reports. His time had come.

Being a submarine commander was everything Pete had dreamed about, with one exception. He had never thought about the toll it would take on his family and, because of his hectic schedule, he missed much of his son's formative years. Through his high school career, Leslie had only seen his father in the stands a handful of times. Both had looked forward to a less demanding civilian career after Captain King retired from naval service, and the government contractors were lining up with offers. Instead, Pete succumbed to a massive heart attack during a port call in Naples, Italy.

The USS Hammerhead was due to return home to Norfolk in four weeks and their CO was excited about finally seeing his son play professionally. Now in his second season with the Virginia Beach Mariners, Les had earned a starting spot and was scoring regularly. Rumors already had him linked with several NASL clubs, even though he repeatedly claimed to want to stay at the Beach. Leslie King was eighteen when his father died.

When Alfred "Pooky" Bauer was eighteen, he was labeled by the St. Louis Post-Dispatch as the "next Brandon Rafferty". He had all the tools Raff had (excellent field vision, superb passing ability, phenomenal touch) and some he didn't (speed and size). He was starting for Busch at nineteen, and he was a Texaco All-Star for the first time in 1978, at twenty-one, but Willy Schneider never thought of Bauer as a play-maker.

Pooky's first call-up to the National Team happened almost by accident. Schneider had been named coach in the summer of 1979, after an exhaustive search. After the poor showing at the 1978 World Cup, the United States Soccer Federation was looking for someone to shake things up and the New York coach fit the bill. Schneider's Cosmos were back-to-back TPL champions but, while no one questioned his knowledge of the game or his respect for the national team program, Willy marched to his own drummer. He also demanded total control of the team, with absolutely no interference from the USSF. "Fine," said the Federation President, "you're on your own, but you'd better produce."

A month after accepting the job, Schneider was in St. Louis to watch a pre-season scrimmage between Busch and the Chicago Sting. Twenty-three year old Stoyan Petrov was starting to make a name for himself and Willy wanted to check him, and a few others, out in person. Bauer played in the middle with Petey for the first half, with mixed results. Schneider was sold on Petrov as a defensive midfielder, but wanted to see him get forward more. He and Bauer seemed to get in each other's way too often. He had to remind himself it was just pre-season. Still, he had a feeling about Bauer.

St. Louis Busch started the second half with Petey's backup, Donnie Wilson, in the lineup with Bauer in front of him. Schneider decided to hang around and watch Bauer a little longer. Wilson was a rookie hoping for a spot on the squad when the season started and he ran relentlessly all over the field, trying to impress the coaches with his work rate. Pooky settled in at a deep midfield position and just let him run. Then Willy figured it out: Bauer had a unique personality trait. *Interesting*, he thought, and filed that bit of information away.

Normally, when a team is playing for the tie and they are scored upon, they will open things up and try for a goal of their own. Only makes sense, since they have nothing else to lose. Surprisingly though, El Salvador stayed in their defensive shell and seldom ventured forward for the remainder of the game. The match finished 1-0, even though the US had eighteen shots to El Salvador's four. But, like Raff said, the win was all that mattered. Schneider was pleased to get the first game in the books, get maximum points, and get the chance to see a few guys play in different positions. He was especially happy with Pooky Bauer's showing at center back.

At the sixty-minute mark, Newton had told Bauer to get warm. He assumed he would be going in for Rafferty, since they both played the same position for their clubs, but Schneider wanted to experiment. El Salvador's attack was minimal, at best, so he wasn't risking much, and he wanted to see how comfortable Bauer would be in the back.

"Pook!" Willy called out. "Go in for Knotty." David Knott was in central defense, with Marco DeSantis.

"Sure, boss," Bauer replied with a laugh, but the look on Schneider's face convinced him it was no joke.

"You can do it," the coach said. "Ask Doc if you need help." That was that.

Bauer played the last half-hour in a position he had never played before – and loved it. So did his coach.

On the ride back to the hotel, Bauer sought out the seat next to Schneider. The gaudy vans had more

100

than enough room and Willy always sat alone, so it was easy.

"How did you *know?*" He almost whispered the question. Pooky was now in complete awe of his head coach. He had never played in the back, and somehow this guy just knew he would thrive there. "It was like I was *supposed* to be there," he added.

"Simple, my boy," Willy replied like a college professor would. "I have been watching your behavior for two years now, and you have a pure defensive personality."

"No way, I've always played in attacking positions," Bauer didn't get it yet.

"That only means all your previous coaches were wrong," Willy stated, matter-of-factly, then asked, "Look around the bus. Who's making the most ruckus?"

"Well, Les and Grey are dancing; Rick and Billy are singing, as usual; new kid Maxwell is trying to get Jackson to wrestle with him. Seems normal enough."

"*Attacking* personalities," the coach pointed out. "They like being the center of attention, and they aren't worried about making mistakes. I remember the first time I saw you play, one of your defenders fouled a Chicago player just outside the box and both teams started shoving each other around. Do you recall what you did?"

"Not really," Pooky answered with a smile - he was intrigued.

"You pulled two guys out of the mix and set up a wall, just in case they tried a quick restart," Willy smiled back. "See, *defensive*. Your first instinct is to defend your goal."

"Did I really?" Bauer asked in amazement. "Wow."

"I would like to use you there some more," Schneider added. "Are you OK with that?" He had to make sure Pooky was on board. No need to keep him on the team as a backup center-mid. He had other players, better suited players, who could fill that role.

"I'd like that, coach," Bauer replied. "I really think I can contribute there."

Willy Schneider smiled. That was the answer he was hoping for. While there were several players in the American player pool who would be considered better defenders than Bauer, Willy was always partial to well-rounded soccer players - who could defend. Pooky was as comfortable on the ball as anybody else on the national team and with his size and athleticism he could be a formidable central defender. But first he would have to learn how to play *outside* back.

Training was light the next day, and several of the players visited local historic sites after practice. The team was treated well by the locals, but everyone knew that would change as they got closer to the match with Honduras next Thursday. Pooky Bauer and Marco DeSantis stayed after to work out defensive positioning on set plays. Jimmy Maxwell joined in to help with free kicks, while Johnny Jackson manned the goal.

102

"Johnny, how much if I score on you?" Maxwell asked, assuming Jackson had never seen him take free kicks. He still spent at least an hour every day practicing them and had finally been allowed to take some for his club. It was just the latest of many hurdles he had to clear with the Spanish giant. He seemed to take them all in stride.

"Fifty if you score on any spot kick outside twenty yards," Johnny was confident. He had recently led his Chicago Sting to the Texaco Premier League championship at the tender age of twenty-four. He was one of the youngest starting goalkeepers in the league, and Coach Schneider had just informed him that he would get the start against Haiti.

"Fifty it is, señor," Jimmy answered quickly, before Jackson could change his mind. He began placing practice balls in an arc roughly twenty-five yards from goal, between the corners of the penalty box. "Get your wall in place," he added.

Bauer and DeSantis would serve as Johnny's "wall", blocking the easy shot to the near post, while the goalkeeper would cover the rest. In a match situation, at this distance, he would have added two or three men, but this was good practice. Besides, he had never seen Maxwell play.

After ten attempts, Johnny was thinking he was $400 in the hole, and he was furious. "Is that what they teach you in Spain?" he asked, not quite sure what he was witnessing.

"Only that last one," Jimmy replied. "The others I learned from my brother, Dale." His tenth shot was one he had learned from Real Madrid's captain,

Santillana, only a few months ago. The Spaniard showed Jimmy how to strike the ball with the inside of his heel, instead of the forefoot, to get topspin on the ball and make it drop after clearing the wall. The approach on this one looked the same as his bender he could put around the wall, so this new shot made him doubly dangerous.

His specialty was one he had learned on the sandy fields of his childhood, perfected as a teenager with the Mules, and demonstrated to the world as a young professional with the Real Madrid reserves. While most free-kick experts liked to lightly place the ball high up on the grass, Jimmy would shove the ball down into the turf (or mud or sand) and strike it hard with the inside of his right boot. The resulting shot would come out of its little hole like a knuckling cannon-ball, driven over the wall only to dip dramatically on its way to the goal. He scored five of these on Jackson.

"Hey, I was impressed. You made two pretty good saves," Maxwell was trying to get under Jackson's skin. When Johnny just laughed, Jimmy made him an offer, "You said fifty per goal, right? That's four hundred *pesetas* where I come from."

"Oh yeah," was all Johnny could come up with. He was wondering how this could get worse. "How much is *that?*"

"About six bucks," Jimmy answered with a pat on the back. "Buy me lunch and we'll call it even."

Chapter 9

DISASTER

"Why'd you call me a *howler monkey?*" Knotty asked, somewhat confused. Alexi Mayer had just called him by his new nickname, inspired by the star of the jungle excursion he and a few others had taken the day before.

"Yeah, the tour guide said they are considered the *laziest* of all the primates," Mayer replied, making sure to be out of arm's reach, as both laughed at the joke. It was the only entertainment available at the moment.

Friday afternoon's game had become a little boring for the guys on the bench. For over forty minutes, Haiti had kept all their players in their half, never venturing forward except to apply marginal pressure to the American backs. Even then, no more than one Haitian would cross the midfield stripe.

Team USA had kept possession for almost seventy percent of the half, and had taken nine shots on goal, but still had yet to score. Situations like these always made Steve Newton nervous. He couldn't count all the times he had seen a lesser team sneak in a goal simply because their opponent lost concentration. Everyone knew this was a huge mismatch and a few of his players had even been overheard discussing next week's game during warm-ups. All the signs were there. And it was just too quiet.

The National Stadium, formally known as the Estadio Tiburcio Carias Andino, sits right in the center of Tegucigalpa and has a capacity of 35,000. Haiti had the edge in fan support, with about twenty-five thousand in the stands, but it sounded like ten times that when the referee blew his whistle and pointed to the penalty spot in the forty-fourth minute. The noise was deafening, and no one on the field was quite sure what had just happened.

A Haitian defender had launched another long clearance into the US half, but this time their lone forward gave chase and was challenging Bobby Smith in a foot race. No big deal, since the American defender was almost as fast - and had a much better angle. But Smith slipped when he got to the ball and he inadvertently knocked it out for a throw-in fifteen yards from the corner.

Haiti's captain, Andre Dumond, grabbed the ball and quickly tossed it into the space in front of a streaking Pierre Fontaine, who was being chased by Brandon Rafferty. The Haitian midfielder received the ball near the end line and immediately turned toward goal as Raff was backing up, trying to maintain a proper defensive stance while awaiting help.

When Fontaine flicked the ball into his ribs, Brandon Rafferty didn't think much of it. *Easy to handle; clear it out; get back up the pitch.* He never even heard the whistle.

Apparently, the referee's view was slightly different. The official not only gave Haiti a penalty kick, but he was reaching for his red card. After pointing to the spot, he looked directly at the American captain - card in his hand, high above his head.

106

Rafferty was speechless. Looking up at the bright red piece of plastic against the clear blue sky, he just couldn't spit out the words that were fighting to be heard.

"I didn't *handle* the ball, it hit me right *here!*"

"I was two feet *outside* the box. That was no penalty!"

"He hit me with it on purpose!"

But nothing came out. Brandon Rafferty simply handed his captain's armband to Doc and walked off the field, toward a spot on the bench. Despite his long career he had never been sent off before, and was initially surprised when a member of the stadium security detail asked him to leave the field. He felt like a criminal.

Dumond beat Johnny Jackson to the left post and put Haiti ahead, 1-0. The referee blew his whistle to end the half as soon as US forward Charlie Scott touched the ball and the teams headed for their locker rooms. Marco DeSantis and Billy Ford made sure no one approached the officials. They still had another half to play, and being *one* man down was going to be bad enough.

The referee thought Rafferty had purposely handled the ball, denying Haiti a goal-scoring opportunity, while inside the penalty area. Simple decision in his mind: Red card and penalty kick, just like the rulebook says.

Once everyone made it to the locker room, Willy Schneider called the team together. "Gentlemen, this," he began, "is why *you* were chosen to represent your country. Sort it out." He left the room in search of a cool drink.

Most coaches would be feverishly trying to devise a new game plan, or trying to pump up their players in the face of adversity. Schneider knew these guys well enough to know they were up to the task without him. That's why he had picked them.

"What the heck happened?" Juan Espinoza asked, not really knowing why Raff was sent off.

"He thought he hit it with his arm, in the box, intentionally," Barrett Grey replied. He had overheard the ref describing his decision to the linesmen as they walked off the pitch. Spanish was no longer his primary language, but he still understood it plainly enough.

"We will drop Charlie into the midfield and play a 4-4-1," Doc wrested control of the splintered conversation. He was the captain now, and it fell to him to take charge. He probably would have, anyway.

"Good call," Billy Ford was lending his support to help calm the team down.

Then a voice came from the seats near the lockers in the back of the room. "Wait. It's still *Haiti*, right?" Jimmy Maxwell asked, matter-of-factly.

"What do you mean?" Doc replied. "Of course it is."

108

"Well, why not go on the attack?" Maxwell asserted. "You know they can't handle us for long."

"Thanks for the input, but we're going with the 4-4-1 to start the second half." DeSantis shut the rookie down and it was settled. He was just doing what good defenders do.

The United States came out with the same squad that had ended the first half: Jackson in goal; Bauer, DeSantis, Bobby Smith, and Espi in back; Ford, Petrov, Scott, and Mishigawa in midfield; and Grey as the lone striker.

For the next twenty minutes the Americans dominated possession, but rarely tested the Haitian keeper. Their lack of numbers in the attacking third of the field caused problems they hadn't planned for, and Doc was hesitant to allow his backs to venture forward. He was pure defender at heart, and had his own priorities.

After twenty minutes of this, Schneider summoned Alexi Mayer to his side. Mayer was as strong a left back as the United States had ever produced, having solidified his spot on the National Team a little over two years ago. Although not as big as the rest of the defenders in this camp, Alexi made up for his size with amazing quickness, bulldog-like tenacity, and a left foot capable of whipping in amazing crosses. He was among the league leaders in assists each season - usually the only defender in the top ten - and he played for Willy in New York. The plan had been to rest him against Haiti. So much for plans.

"Hey Coach," he said. "What are you thinking?" He knew his boss was *always* thinking. He also knew it was odd that Willy would be considering a defensive substitution now. They definitely needed more in the attacking department.

"Lex, I think you should get warm," was Schneider's reply. "We will pull Bobby Smith and go with three in the back. Move Bauer to attacking mid, and push Scott back up to forward with Grey."

"Got it, Boss." No need for more. He entered the match at the sixty-eighth minute.

Mayer had been in the game for six minutes when Willy Schneider had a change of heart, though it wasn't Alexi's fault. Quite the opposite. After a quick give-and-go with Petrov, he was blazing down the left side of the field, looking for a crossing target. His pass was a little strong, and it sailed to the far side of the penalty area where Barrett Grey headed it back into the box and it dropped near the penalty spot, twelve yards from goal. No one was there. The goalkeeper scooped it up on the first bounce.

Charlie Scott had made the near-post run, drawing his defender away from the front of the goal, which was the right move. When Willy looked up to see Petey at midfield and Bauer only ten yards ahead of him, he realized what the problem was. Pooky.

"Maxwell," he called to the end of the bench. "Get warm."

"Looks like you're going to get some action, kid," Leslie King said. "Please don't embarrass us," he added with a smile. Then he rose and offered to help Jimmy warm up.

A few minutes later, Jimmy Maxwell was stretching on the sideline, preparing for his first cap, when he remembered what his coach in Spain had told him before his debut appearance with the first team at Real Madrid. It made him smile.

"Mags-vell," Boskov barked, in English. "In for Juanito." The Yugoslavian had been head coach for two years, and was famous (sometimes infamous) for making bold moves. This time, he would be pulling an in-form striker at a crucial time in the match and replacing him with an unknown American rookie. Thirty minutes left and, if this backfired, there would be hell to pay.

Maxwell warmed up and approached his new coach, looking for any last-minute instructions. He was only eighteen, but it had been quite a while since he had been a sub, having started every reserve match so far this season. He just assumed Vujadin Boskov would need to impart some words of wisdom.

"What do you want from me?" his coach asked. "You know how to do this job."

"Exactly," Jimmy thought, as he removed his track suit. *Exactly.*

The Haitians were playing with an extra midfielder and they had hounded their American counterparts for over an hour, stifling any creativity from the designated playmakers. Maxwell entered the match with a little less than fifteen minutes to play, and immediately took the spot between the Petrov and the two forwards. His first touch was painful.

Studs to the Achilles tendon always hurt, so the pain wasn't what surprised Maxwell. The fact that there was so much *space* in front of him was what struck him as odd.

The Haitian defenders had become complacent, which made sense since the American attack had dwindled to nearly nothing. Barrett Grey and Charlie Scott had been invisible since the substitution that had them paired together once again. Bauer never seemed to make the probing pass that they needed to force the action, and both forwards were tired of making runs for no reason. Enter Jimmy Maxwell.

Some playmakers like to stay central, some like to pick out a flank to operate from, and some (like Maxwell) prefer to roam laterally side to side, using short passes to pick defenses apart. His specialty was the type of pass he would provide Billy Ford in the eighty-eighth minute.

The foul was immediately called when Fontaine cracked Maxwell from behind less than a minute after he entered the match, and Jimmy realized he was going to be man-marked closely. There was really no other reason for Fontaine to be on his back like he was. No problem, he thought. That's why he preferred lateral movement − it kept defenders honest.

After a few minutes of possession in the midfield, Billy Ford saw an opportunity. He waited until Maxwell reached the far side of the field, received a pass from Brad Mishigawa, and turned toward him. He then began making a run down the left side of the pitch, staying wide so that his Haitian counterpart couldn't see both him and the ball at the same time. Jimmy saw him and accelerated to the center of the field with the ball close to his feet.

The defense had been focused on Grey and Scott and, when they saw Maxwell speed up, they naturally locked onto their marks. Jimmy stopped abruptly, just short of the center circle, and turned toward goal. His shadow, Fontaine, did his best to avoid a collision, and actually ended up on the wrong side of Maxwell for a second. That's all it took.

The ball played between the American forwards looked initially to be just another errant pass from the US midfield. But what the Haitian keeper thought was going to be an easy pickup at the edge of the box quickly became his worst nightmare. He saw Ford coming from his right side and sped up to beat him to the pass. He knew he would have to meet it outside the penalty area, and prepared for a sliding kick to send the ball into the stands. But the American Number Five was just a little too fast.

No other soccer player on the planet had Billy Ford's burst of speed. Had the United States not boycotted the 1980 Olympics, he would probably have added a gold medal in track to his personal trophy case, maybe two. Understandably, his mother was more upset than he was, since she had also missed out on Olympic gold.

The Haitian goalkeeper slid, but nothing happened. No ball; no contact; no tangled legs; nothing.

Billy had already come and gone, having blown past the keeper faster than he could have imagined. He rounded the corner with the ball on his right foot and tapped it into the empty net. Time expired a few minutes later on the 1-1 draw.

The mood in the American locker room was pure relief. No celebrating, no high fives, just an occasional pat on the back. Coming from behind with ten men was hard work, but they all knew they had squandered a valuable point. When they heard that Mexico had just lost to El Salvador they felt some consolation, but this was still a hard pill to swallow.

Willy Schneider summed it up in a brief meeting following showers and Gatorade: "You were dealt a tough hand," he said, "and you played it pretty well." As the players started to file out he added, "Oh, and dinner's on Rafferty."

Next Thursday's match against the host country would be interesting.

Chapter 10

REST

The team had not had a real day off in almost five weeks, and this Saturday morning most were engaged in exploring the possibilities presented by the hired Honduran guides. Willy Schneider had planned this recovery day regardless of the outcome of the Haiti match, knowing his guys would need a breather. He was right - especially now.

Several players were gathered in the hotel's restaurant, feasting on the breakfast spread laid out by their gracious hosts at the InterContinental Hotel. Brochures were plentiful, but written in Spanish. Grey and Maxwell were the most fluent, but neither of them was currently available. They would have to rely on the guides to help them see the sights, but none really worried about the tours. A day off was the real treat.

Barrett Grey finally arrived and, after pouring a cup of fine Guatemalan coffee, helped with translations. Jimmy Maxwell was in his room enjoying Saturday morning cartoons with Alexi Mayer. Watching the *Smurfs* speaking Spanish was normal for Jimmy, but Alexi could only laugh.

"How long did it take for you to learn the language?" Alexi asked, during a commercial break.

"Not long, maybe six months," Jimmy replied, "I've always been pretty good at picking up stuff like that."

"How'd you do it?" Mayer asked. "Did they send you to classes or something?"

"Ha, no classes," Maxwell laughed at the idea. "Well, every day was a class, I guess, every minute really. I just got out there and tried to meet some people. That helped."

"I know what it's like when you don't speak the language," Alexi said. "My Mom's Greek and we have visited her family a few times in Athens. I could read some of the street signs, but I couldn't understand anything they said. Lucky you found some "people" to help you out – who were *they?*"

"Let's see," Jimmy thought about it, "Maria, Carmen, and lovely Lucia."

"That's what I thought," Alexi laughed, "some tough classes!"

The Madrid tabloids had already made Jimmy Maxwell a minor celebrity. While the sports writers at *El Pais* had dubbed him "el pequeño asesino", the front page frequently showed him exiting downtown clubs with one of his shapely acquaintances. He had recently been photographed with several popular starlets, whose attention wasn't due solely to the multi-year contract Maxwell had just signed with Real Madrid. Billy Ford had started calling him *Leslie King's long-lost son*, based on the attention he received from the female fans

116

and, even though he was bigger than her husband, Lisa Rafferty said he was a little hunk.

Despite his status as one of Madrid's most eligible young bachelors, Jimmy would rather spend this afternoon off kicking a ball around on the beach with his buddies.

"Now that you've mastered Spanish, what's next?" Alexi asked, while juggling a ball in the warm mid-day sun.

"Portuguese," Maxwell answered, without hesitation. He balanced a soccer ball on his forehead while answering.

"Really? Why? Are you planning a move to *Portugal?*"

"Nope," Jimmy replied, "Brazilian supermodels. Madrid's crawling with 'em."

Alexi just shook his head and laughed. He also made a mental note to visit his new friend in Madrid.

Leslie King hired one of the Honduran guides to take him and Brad Mishigawa to visit some of the ancient ruins outside the city, but the plans changed shortly after the trip began. Mish had asked the guide about the local wine culture, and the Honduran native abruptly stopped the car and began describing his family's traditional wine made from the sap of one of the indigenous palm trees.

The local man offered to take them to his village for a taste, and both players were intrigued. King was always up for a new drink, but Brad was genuinely interested. The Mishigawa family vineyard in Paso Robles had become a hit in the California wine industry, producing award-winning varietals each of the last three seasons.

The editor of Wine Weekly magazine had to amend his rule about animals on wine labels when he tasted their '79 Cabernet Sauvignon. He had long held the belief that if a label had animals or babies on it, the contents must not be worth drinking. *The Smiling Dog* wines featured a portrait of Brad's Border Collie, Buster, on every bottle.

Brad Mishigawa had helped his parents expand the family wine-making operation with his first signing bonus, and a large portion of his pay had initially gone to the family business. His parents had become interested in viniculture when Brad was in Japan, and they approached their new hobby in typical Mishigawa fashion. His father, Ken, had recently retired from the university and was working the 80-acre vineyard full-time. Brad was now the majority share-holder, and was starting to see his investment pay off. Since he made a good living as a professional athlete, he could plow all his dividends back into the vineyard, helping the whole family.

"Interesting," Mish said, as he sipped the pale yellow liquid from an old Mason jar. It had a peculiar taste, but was only mildly alcoholic.

"I'm not gettin' it," King quietly whispered to his teammate. He didn't want to offend their host, but the old cab driver heard him. He was used to trendier drinks – with more kick.

"You drink more," he said. "Then you like!" They couldn't argue with that.

Fortunately, the drinking started before noon. That would allow the guys to be back in the hotel by dinner time and, after quick showers, sound asleep by nine o'clock.

Leslie King was always the life of the party, but with a few drinks in him he was a one-man variety show. He was disappointed that his host didn't know who he was, but he did his best to explain his immense popularity in the most humble of ways. Brad laughed at his frustration, which only made him try harder.

"I hosted SNL in '77," he said. "I was the first athlete to do so."

"What is *S-N-L?*" Jose the cabbie replied. He had no television.

"Saturday Night Live!" King couldn't believe it. This little man had surely heard of him, and he was going to prove it. Mish was really enjoying this.

"Ever heard of Donna Summer?" This would be easy. "Queen of disco?"

"No, sorry," was the answer. He was going to tell Jose how he had joined Donna on stage for a duet before the Winston Cup final in 1978. Their version of the *Star Spangled Banner* was actually replayed on the radio nationwide and reached number six on the Billboard Top 100.

"I dated Mariel Hemingway," King boasted. "And I escorted her to the Oscars in '79, when she lost to Meryl Streep."

The cabbie's confused smile made Brad laugh out loud. Even though Jose spoke fairly good English, Les was speaking a foreign language to him.

"Shannon Tweed?" he asked, with his eyebrows raised. King had been linked to the centerfold model for several months. The New York paparazzi absolutely loved the possibilities.

"Who?" Jose replied. *Ahhh, this was impossible!.*

"Have you heard of *KISS?*" he was grasping.

"Oh yeah, *Detroit Rock City!*" Jose finally woke up. He had indeed heard of KISS. "Are you in that band?" he asked excitedly, wailing on his air guitar.

"Well, no, but I did jam with them a few times," Les had to confess, now that he had gotten his host's attention. Gene Simmons was a friend of his, but he was so much bigger than this. Why couldn't this little cab driver understand that?

"You are not a musician or an actor," Jose asserted. "Then why should I know who you are?"

Les finally relented. "You a futbol fan?"

"Si, of course"

120

"Well, I'm Leslie King. I play for the Brooklyn Dodgers," he just said it.

The cabbie knew all along, but had enjoyed toying with his celebrity guest. He replied, as seriously as possible, "Sorry, I'm more of a Cosmos fan." Then he laughed, and offered them another round.

Sunday morning training started at 8 o'clock sharp. Everyone was there in body, though many were barely present in mind. Willy knew the guys would go out and have some fun, so this early practice was meant to be more of a bonding experience than a productive session. He thought they could use a common enemy, to make sure they were all on the same side, and to quickly forget about Rafferty's mistake. It worked - they all hated their coach.

He knew it wouldn't last long.

Chapter 11

BACK ON TRACK

Tournaments always posed unique challenges. With the added pressure of World Cup qualification, this one was especially trying. Four weeks living together in a foreign country, hotel food, daily press conferences, an unfamiliar training ground, and five determined opponents should have combined to maximize Coach Schneider's stress level. Somehow, he never seemed to be troubled by it. He had a secret and only Doc knew what it was.

Training with Willy Schneider was never boring. The US National Team coach was constantly looking for ways to test his players: Mentally, physically, and psychologically. This week would be no exception.

Monday's training session was designed to be intense. Willy had set up a series of individual and team challenges for the guys, and was famous for measuring everything. His intent was to rekindle any competitive sparks that may have faded. The players all knew that the draw against Haiti was a huge letdown, and were somewhat surprised to find a smiling Willy Schneider greeting them at midfield when they had completed their warm-ups. A few noticed there were no soccer balls, and thought that was odd.

"Boys," he began, "today is Test Day. Let's see what we are made of, shall we?"

The first half of the day's session involved nine individual physical tests, each lasting five minutes. With no time for discussion, the coaches quickly assigned the players to the designated areas for each exercise, two men to each space. When Willy's whistle blew, they would start doing whatever the sign said in their area and continue until the next whistle, when they would switch areas. No rest needed. Simple.

The signs told the players to do the following: Pushups, situps, jumping jacks, leg raises, jump rope, 10-yard sprints, 40-yard sprints, laps around the field, and "Peteys". Do as many as you can (or, in the case of leg raises, as long as you can) in the five minutes allotted. Again, simple.

The coaching staff was busy writing down the results at each station, apparently keeping track of the outcomes in meticulous detail. After the first three stations, players were beginning to enjoy themselves. The comments flew like the sweat.

"Hey, Les," Brandon Rafferty called out during his leg raises, "do you need a sub?" King was busy with 10-yard sprints, and didn't hear his pal's comment. Or if he did, he ignored it. He was still in peak condition at twenty-nine, and Raff knew it.

"Long way down, ain't it Johnny?" Jimmy Maxwell teased the keeper. Jackson was doing "Peteys", which were especially tough on the taller players. A "Petey" is done as follows: Start upright; drop to a pushup position-down, up; Legs apart, then together; Hop up and do a jumping jack. That's one. Named for Stoyan Petrov, of course, because he introduced them to the team when he was called up for his first National Team Camp. He alone *liked* them.

124

"Shut up, Gringo," was Jackson's reply. Jimmy could hear the pain in his voice - and laughed. He was jumping rope, which he could do for hours if necessary. This was a piece of cake. Petrov wasn't the only guy on this team who worked hard to stay in top shape.

The half-time whistle came after forty-five minutes of grueling physical tests, and the players were quickly gulping down Gatorade and trying to cool off in the shade. Twenty minutes later the second half would start, and none of the players knew what to expect.

While the team rested, Coach Schneider and his staff were busy setting up the second phase of Test Day. Small grids, approximately ten yards square, were laid out on one half of the field. The other side of the field had three 20 by 40 yard mini-fields set up. Teams were established during half-time when the equipment manager passed out practice vests in six different colors.

The second half of Test Day consisted of small-sided games to goal - either 2v1 or 3v3. Teams of three would alternate between the smaller grids, where the game was 2v1 and the goals were foot-tall cones, and the larger mini-fields where they would take on another 3-man team in a game to small goals. Nothing too radical. Willy had used these drills often, and the guys were familiar with them from their club teams. Then Coach Schneider introduced the fruit.

Schneider held a large sack of produce, and commanded, "Get your game ball, gents. Play starts in ten seconds!" Then he dumped the contents on the grass. The four grapefruit were snatched up first, then a few oranges. When play started, the pile of fruit was half its original size. It now consisted of four more oranges, four mangoes, a dozen or so limes, and a

125

pineapple - which Willy began working on with the Swiss Army knife he pulled from his pants pocket.

While each of these players was a unique individual with his own set of talents and skills, and they all enjoyed competition, they could never be described as *normal*. What set them apart from most of the rest of the human race was their intense, burning desire to win. Even when their coach presented something as strange as playing with fruit, they immediately started looking for a way to get some sort of advantage. Maxwell was the first to figure it out.

The first set of matches was on the small grids, and Jimmy Maxwell, Arnie Mausser, and Rick Davis made up the red team. They would play three games of 2v1, each lasting five minutes, with no break in between. Once again, Willy's staff was close by with notebooks, taking down copious amounts of information.

Play started on all six grids when the whistle sounded. Those with grapefruit adjusted quickly – it was more like a small soccer ball. The two with oranges took a little longer, but the level of play still improved rapidly. Especially on the red team's grid.

Davis and Maxwell began together with Mausser going it alone. Arnie was a pretty good field player, as goalkeepers go, but couldn't be expected to hang with these guys. After five minutes, and many goals, the whistle blew and Mausser joined Maxwell. Jimmy quickly kicked off his cleats to start the second game. Whenever Arnie had the orange, he would remove a sock or shinguard until he was finally barefoot. Then he started having fun.

Jimmy Maxwell would keep his "ball" off the ground, balanced on either foot or juggling from foot to thigh and back, while Rick Davis applied pressure. Willy never called fouls in practice. His players knew they could complain if someone was a little too rough, but none ever did. "If you can't stand the heat," Schneider would have said, "get out of my kitchen." But he never had to actually say it.

As a forward, Davis was known to be a tenacious defender because he would harass opposing backs relentlessly. Too bad that kind of *defense* didn't work against someone like Maxwell, who was enjoying this game at his expense. Davis would push Jimmy in the back, knee him in the thigh, or pull on his jersey, and in return the playmaker would lure him away from the goal, lob a pass to Mausser, and they would score easily. If Rick tried to back off and play the pass, Maxwell just flicked the orange into the goal himself. *That's OK*, Davis thought, *we'll get him back soon*. The whistle blew and the third match started.

Five years earlier, the Maxwell brothers could have been found playing a similar game in the cellar of their farmhouse. Dale would craft a ball out of old socks, sewing the last one closed with his mother's yarn. The ball was usually about the size of a softball, but was sometimes bigger, sometimes smaller, depending on the availability of socks or rags for stuffing. The game was always some kind of keep-away, with no rules other than *try not to get into trouble*. That meant three things: 1. Nothing gets broken (hence, the cellar), 2. No one cries about any pain that may be inflicted, and 3. Chores get done first.

127

As the youngest participant, Jimmy had to learn to hold off older, bigger opponents while keeping possession of the rag-ball as they pushed, grabbed, punched, kneed, and pinched him. All in the confines of a dark, dank basement with a hard concrete floor and rough, cinder-block walls. His elbows were constantly scraped up from the walls, and his skinny legs typically had bruises as big as his kneecaps. He would try to dish it out as well, but the older boys were just too strong to dispossess without a good punch to the kidneys or a kick in the calf. Fortunately, Dale and Bob could handle his abuse without retaliation. He was still a boy, and they surely could have killed him.

Now, at six feet and one-hundred-seventy pounds, he could easily hold an orange without losing possession to these two. Maxwell just held off his teammates the entire five minutes, without even letting them touch the fruit. To frustrate them more, he never stopped smiling.

The 3v3 matches started next and Mausser and Davis were relieved to be playing *with* Maxwell. The teams were quickly assigned and, without rest, play started. Matches would last six minutes, and every team would play each of the other five teams once. Scores were recorded by the staff.

Brad Mishigawa and Billy Ford had removed their footwear, and immediately noticed the improvement in their touch, but the fear of being stepped on kept the others from joining in. Mish always practiced barefoot at home, so he was already aware of the advantages. Billy was too quick to hack when he had his boots *on*, so he saw no reason not to try it.

When the five 3v3 matches were complete, the players gathered at the midfield circle to rest, re-hydrate, and listen to their coach. The results of the day's competition were already in dispute, although none of the players even knew how the event was being scored.

"What do I get for winning, Coach," Barrett Grey asked, flashing a confident smile. He was certainly a contender. Willy tossed him a chunk of fresh pineapple, and returned the smile.

"Jake, got the results?" Schneider asked his equipment manager, who had gathered all the notebooks from the staff. "Yes, sir, here you go."

"Hmmm," Willy appeared thoughtful. "According to the results of the various tests performed here today." He stopped and looked them all in the eyes, for effect.

"*I* am in better shape than all of you!" He looked serious for a few seconds, but couldn't hold in the laugh. "Well done today gentlemen, I was impressed with each of you." He spoke more solemnly now, "And I'm proud to be your coach."

He knew he asked a lot of these guys, and they never complained. Their club teams had been in season for over two months when this camp began, so a few might have to temporarily ride the bench when they returned. Everyone missed being with their teammates, their families, and their friends. Schneider was pleased with the professionalism, and the dedication to the cause this group displayed. More importantly, he knew how tight they had become as a team.

"But, Willy, what about the scores?" Leslie King was as curious as anyone. They all wanted to see how they ranked, but Les was the first to ask as he hopped to his feet. Huge bragging rights were at stake. Willy handed him the stack of papers.

"What is this?" The pages were filled with depictions of the players – some quite bad, others very good. "You guys were drawing pictures – of *us*?" King asked.

"Sure," Steve Newton replied, "we had nothing else to do while you were goofing around." He offered to autograph his rendition of King playing 2v1.

Sunday's training ended on a high note, with everyone exhausted, but happy. The next two days would reflect a newfound focus in the team as Thursday's match against Honduras was becoming the most important yet. The hosts were on top of the table following shutout wins against Haiti and Cuba.

Always full of surprises, Willy Schneider had two more in store for Thursday.

Chapter 12

SURPRISES

When Wednesday's training session ended, Schneider posted the starting eleven for the Honduras match on the bulletin board outside the locker room. After the players showered, then dressed, they exited and studied the lineup sheet. That was where they saw the first surprise of the day.

Everyone assumed that Pooky Bauer would start in Rafferty's place, since their captain was suspended due to his red card against Haiti. A few jaws dropped when they saw Jimmy Maxwell's name in the usual Rafferty spot. Of course, no one knew that Schneider had already talked with Bauer about his decision. Pooky would be starting on the bench, but would be inserted at center back for the second half. His assignment for the first forty-five was to watch how DeSantis and Knott covered the middle of the defense. The learning curve was steep, but Willy had faith in his new defender.

When they gathered outside the locker room, a few of the guys noticed that their usual transportation was not waiting for them.

"Willy! Where's the wheels?" Leslie King asked. He had never liked the gaudy vans before, but the thought of *walking* back to the InterContinental was definitely worse than a ten minute trip in the red, white, and blue "Yankee-mobiles", as they were called by the locals.

"Stay in here!" Schneider demanded. The players were outside the locker room, but still in a passageway that led to the parking lot. Their coach was about to expose surprise number two.

The white vans had come and gone while the team was still in the showers, loaded with half the kitchen staff from their hotel - dressed in USA training gear. Willy had directed the impostors to cover their heads as they made the short trip from the vans to the hotel entrance, but a group of Honduran fans was waiting to pelt them with spoiled tomatoes, making the request unnecessary. Mission accomplished.

The calm, friendly demeanor of the locals was about to change. Thus far, they had been wonderful — smiling faces, helpful guides, and gracious hosts. But, tomorrow's match would pit the Americans against their beloved "los catrachos". Suddenly, the amiable Hondurans saw their guests as the enemy. Fortunately, Willy Schneider had a plan, which was not a surprise.

Just then, a bus pulled up to the passageway leading to the locker room. It was a charter, complete with tinted windows and signage announcing tours of the Honduran beaches. The players were confused.

"Kinda late for a tour, don't you think?" King asked. He was speaking to no one in particular, and his frustration was starting to show.

"Load up the bus, gentlemen," Willy took charge. "We need to get on the road." He had planned to let them in on his elaborate ruse once they were en route.

After five minutes, they were rolling and he rose from his seat in the front row and turned around.

"Coach, I left my swim trunks back at the hotel," Billy Ford announced. "I guess I'll have to go *au naturel!*" The groans were expected - and delivered.

"Keep your pants on, Billy," Schneider replied. "No one wants to see that!"

Brandon Rafferty immediately attempted to cover Billy's mouth, since he knew what would come out of it next. His right hand went for the face, while the left poked his best friend in the ribs, preventing Ford from getting anything out that resembled *Raff's wife!* As usual, they both laughed.

"OK, guys," Willy got their attention with one raised hand. "Now I can let you know what's going on." He began by describing the team's last trip to the Honduran capital, as well as several other away games, when the local fans made the US team feel less than welcome. *Came with the territory*, he said.

"So, we will be staying at a different hotel tonight, away from the city," he said. "The vans were carrying some friends of mine who, hopefully, fooled our detractors into thinking we are still holed up at the InterContinental."

"Is this really necessary?" Johnny Jackson whispered to his seat-mate. "I mean, it's just rotten tomatoes, right?" He was new at this national team stuff, so Mish just smiled. "Necessary? Not really," he replied. "But a *very* good idea."

The last time the US National Team visited Tegucigalpa, for a *friendly* match, a small but well-organized group of locals made sure the Americans knew they were in hostile territory. Somehow, they arranged to have the air conditioning turned off to the entire third floor, where the US team was staying, and each room received multiple wake-up calls during the night, ensuring a miserable stay the day before the match against the home team. Sometimes these situations got out of hand, but usually it was just gamesmanship - international soccer style.

"We will stay in Comayagua the rest of the week," Willy continued. "The Plaza Victoria has all the amenities we've been accustomed to - and no one knows we are staying there."

"How does he do it?" King quietly asked Doc, who was seated next to him. "I mean, does he really *know* all these people? I never see him out in town, or hanging out with anyone. It just doesn't make sense." DeSantis smiled at him and said, "You don't know?" It was both a question and a statement.

"I've also had our match time adjusted, so we can take part in something special tomorrow morning. Then, we'll re-board the bus and head for the stadium at noon. Breakfast is at nine, match is at two o'clock. I know that isn't our normal routine, but it will be worth it." Then Willy turned around and sat back down.

The bus arrived at the Plaza Victoria Hotel just before six o'clock, and the players were relieved when they were escorted to a side entrance – away from the lobby. No one noticed the American contingent as they went upstairs to their rooms.

"Good number," Billy announced when the elevator doors opened on the fifth floor. He was the most superstitious member of every team he had ever played on.

"Why's that?" Alexi Mayer asked, not knowing the complete life story of his new roommate. Rafferty would have stopped him from asking, if he had been on the same floor. Instead, Alexi heard him laughing as the elevator doors closed.

"Well, son," Billy began. He would have put his arm around the younger (by six months) player, but both hands were carrying bags. "*I* was born on the fifth day, of the fifth month, of the fifty-fifth year of this century."

"That's why I wear number five, and why Willy puts me on the fifth floor, and..." He stopped for a moment when he saw the room number, 523. "See, two and three is five – good one." Alexi rolled his eyes as he entered their room and grabbed the dinner menu. Willy had also instructed them all to stay in and order room service, just to be safe. He wanted them to get a good night's rest.

On the way to his room on the third floor, Marco DeSantis was stopped by Leslie King, who pulled him aside and asked, "*What* don't I know?" It was killing him, and Doc could see it. He never thought Schneider's secret was something only he had known about. This was suddenly fun.

"Willy is working undercover for the CIA," he whispered, trying to be as serious as possible. "The coaching thing is just a cover, to get him access to sensitive areas in foreign countries." He was a pretty

135

good actor when he wanted to be, but King wasn't buying it. "OK, really," was his terse response.

"All right, come with me." He dumped his bags in the room he was sharing with Petrov and, after King did the same in his room, they took the stairs down to the ground floor. It was dinner time, and Doc knew where his coach could be found.

Les didn't ask any questions, and assumed they were going to find Schneider in the hotel's restaurant, probably eating alone. As they made their way past the maitre d', then through the mostly unoccupied dining room, he realized they were heading for the kitchen. Before he could ask, Doc opened the swinging doors and there was Willy Schneider, chopping onions with three other line cooks, swapping stories in Spanish.

"Hey, guys!" Willy greeted them with a big sweaty smile. "What's going on?"

"Nothing, coach," Leslie King replied, his mind racing. *This was how he arranged the impostors at the InterContinental – he was working with them! Probably how he got the secret rooms here, too. This was actually better than the CIA!*

"Just wanted to see what the dinner recommendation was," Doc added.

"The sea bass is excellent, right Rico?" Willy asked the sous chef, who was responsible for tonight's menu. "Si, Willy. She is excelente!"

"So, Willy works in the hotel kitchen," Leslie King stated, after they were heading back to their rooms. "Why?"

"He calls it his stress reliever and I guess it works. He never seems to be upset about anything."

"Easy for you to say," King said. "You're not an onion!"

Chapter 13

A STAR IS BORN

Breakfast in a hotel restaurant always posed certain risks. For most of the players, the basic *bacon and eggs with toast* was first choice, with some kind of Danish as a backup. Being in a foreign country usually increased the odds against your typical American morning meal. Sometimes though, the local cuisine called for some experimentation.

This morning's feast was certainly different. A few of the pickier guys could be seen looking for options, but when Willy entered the dining room from the kitchen, they felt relieved. They knew he would be looking out for them, and assumed he had been checking out the facilities.

"Morning, gentlemen," Willy called out. "We've prepared a meal fit for kings here, so dig in!"

"*We?*" Mish asked what several others were thinking. Leslie King smiled at Marco DeSantis.

"Sure, I helped a little," Schneider replied. "This is a traditional Honduran breakfast: Scrambled eggs, beans, dry cheese, fried bananas, and toast." Then he added, "Oh, and some of the best coffee in the world. Enjoy!"

By ten-fifteen, the dining room was empty and the players were gathered in the hotel's most secluded conference room. Rafferty had been tasked with ensuring everyone was ready to leave directly from there for the twenty minute bus ride to the National Stadium. There would be no time to waste, and the team still had no idea why their coach had deviated from the standard game-day routine.

Willy Schneider arrived just after ten-thirty, wheeling a 27-inch Sony color television behind him. No one knew what to expect, but he had told them it would be worth it. *We'll see,* was the prevailing thought.

After plugging the set in, turning on the power, and adjusting the rabbit ears for maximum reception, Coach Schneider turned and faced the team.

"First, let me say that I hope this works," he smiled as he began his semi-prepared speech. "Next, I'd like to thank you all for the dedication you've shown this past few weeks. I know you all understand the enormous honor of representing your country, and today we get a rare chance to see another one of the amazing accomplishments made possible by the ingenuity of the American people.

"Gentlemen, in a few minutes we will watch the liftoff of the space shuttle *Columbia*, marking the first time a craft has ever been re-used for space flight. It was seven months ago, exactly, when she lifted off for the first time and many of us missed the live broadcast since it happened on a Sunday game day!"

Schneider turned up the volume, and the players gathered closely to watch the small television. The narration was in Spanish, but the visual was what

140

caught their attention. They had all seen the old Saturn V rockets take off during the Apollo missions, and were instantly amazed when *Columbia* literally blasted off the launch pad. A collective "Wow" filled the room.

Willy had only one more thing to add. "We are here to represent the greatest country God ever gave mankind. Let's not forget that." No one did.

As the charter bus pulled into the stadium parking lot, it passed their old white vans on the way to the side entrance reserved for visiting teams. They weren't white anymore. Willy's plan had worked perfectly, and his informant at the InterContinental Hotel told him that the crowd had numbered nearly two hundred at its peak around midnight. Noisemakers, fireworks, wake-up calls, and the chants of "Yankee, go home!" filled the night, and would have kept even the heaviest sleepers on edge. Instead, the US National Team slept like babies - thirty kilometers away. Willy's impostors kept up the act and made the trip to the stadium just to entertain the hostile crowds - and use the tickets Schneider had bought for them, as payment. Of course, he understood they would be supporting the home team today.

Warm-ups were rushed, but efficient. These guys were professionals, and each knew how to get himself ready to play, both physically and mentally. During the pre-game action, Willy and Steve Newton discussed last-minute details with the players, and gave the two new starters a chance to ask any questions they might have before the game began. Frank Price was very nervous, even though he had played in nearly every qualifier this year. Willy calmed him down, and moved on to find Maxwell.

Jimmy Maxwell's last conversation with Coach Schneider, two days earlier, was short and sweet. Willy had asked, "Ready for the start?" and Maxwell said, "Yep". It was time for another of their heart-to-heart talks.

"Any questions?" he asked. The midfielder was dribbling in and out of imaginary defenders near the center circle. "Nope," was the answer.

"He sure seems confident," Newton noted, as they walked toward the bench. "Are you *really* OK with him, in a situation like this?" Willy's assistant had never seen Maxwell play with his club team, but he knew they needed a win to stay in contention. Worrying was part of his job description. Willy didn't believe in it.

"Steve, I saw him play against Atletico last year, in a derby match, when the fans were hurling insults that would make *you* blush," Schneider reassured him. "He knows pressure – and I think he actually *enjoys* it!" Willy had seen him play a few other times, too.

His assessment, as usual, was right on. Maxwell was a "gamer" - one of those rare talents who seemed to be able to perform closest to his peak when the stakes were at their highest. Willy had first seen him play on a videotape sent to him from Spain in September, 1979. Real Madrid had just won the Santiago Bernabeu Trophy with wins over Ajax Amsterdam, Bayern Munich, *and* AC Milan. Maxwell was voted tournament MVP - at eighteen! The Madrid press called it his coming-out party. The farm-boy from Missouri called it "Pretty cool".

That performance solidified his starting position on his club *and* caught the attention of his home country's new head coach. By the time he turned twenty, the young American was wearing the heralded number ten jersey for *los blancos*. His national team career, though, began slowly. Due to the logistics involved with trans-Atlantic travel — and Schneider's desire to let him mature as a player.

The starting lineup for the Honduras match had a veteran feel to it, even with the additions of Price and Maxwell. Arnie Mausser would be back in goal; Mayer, DeSantis, Knott, and Espinoza in back; Petrov at defensive mid, with Mishigawa wide right; King and Grey at forward. Frank Price would be at left midfield, giving Billy Ford a rest; with Maxwell, of course, in Rafferty's usual spot, just behind the front-runners.

National soccer styles come from many different sources. A cold climate tends to cause a more direct, physical type of play, while warm weather causes others to slow down and play a short-passing game, typically with lots of possession. Many countries have a standardized national style of play, where youngsters see their heroes play the same formation and positions as their youth teams. Other clubs are molded to fit their coach's preferences. The United States National Team was the latter.

Due to America's large geographic size, diverse weather, and varied cultures, the Texaco Premier League had virtually every style represented. This posed a unique problem for the national teams, since most head coaches did not have the skills required to pick a group that could work together in his preferred system. This problem didn't really exist in the early days of US soccer, since the game was only played in a few cities and all the players would be chosen from a relatively small population. For example, the 1950 World Cup team that beat England had five players from St. Louis, and two from Fall River, Massachusetts. Three were actually born outside the United States.

The increased player pool of the last twenty years had, until now, caused more problems than expected. Willy Schneider was the solution.

As soon as Rafferty was sent off against Haiti, Jose de la Paz Herrerra changed his game plan and decided his team would play a 4-4-2 in their next match against the Americans. The Honduran coach would have played it safe and gone with an extra midfielder but, with Captain America suspended, he thought he could afford to play the US straight up. That would prove to be a big mistake.

The first ten minutes was typical of recent CONCACAF matches. The United States had become the superpower of the region in a relatively short time, and many of the smaller countries resented their new status. Most of the region's teams had enjoyed dominance over the US for decades, until the last few years. Willy had enough veterans out there to handle the high-pressure start, which he knew wouldn't last long. His boys would weather the storm, and then force the Hondurans to play *their* game.

Maxwell was doing his usual job in the middle of the pitch: Moving to support the ball; keeping possession; probing the defense with passes to King and Grey. The three of them had been working on something and now, with the ball at Jimmy's feet near the left side of midfield, the time was right to try it.

Grey would frequently push up into an offside position, just to see how his defender would play him. He did it again, this time crossing into the penalty area, then he checked back toward the center of the field and Maxwell played a sharp pass into his path. Always looking to *pass-and-move*, Jimmy then made a run toward goal.

Leslie King was holding his position five yards from the eighteen, appearing to be a casual observer to the interplay of his teammates. When the ball reached his strike partner's path, King saw him let it run between his legs. The pass was actually meant for Les, with Barrett Grey providing the dummy run. King stepped toward the oncoming ball and quickly considered his options.

Maxwell was making the run toward the left side of the penalty box and King's left foot redirected the pass right into his path with one soft touch. Grey had continued his run, circling around to the right side of the area. All eyes were on Jimmy Maxwell, who was running into the Honduran penalty area, unmarked, with the ball on his right foot. Three defenders quickly converged on him, leaving no one watching Barrett Grey.

With no clear shot, Jimmy scooped the ball over the center back to his right, into the path of Grey, who calmly headed it into the back of the net.

13th minute: 1-0 visitors.

The problem most coaches had with trying to impose their style of play on a group of grown men was that they would be constantly out-voted by the players. Even if most bought into the system, it only took a few to disrupt the whole team. Willy Schneider was able to convince his players that *they* were actually in charge, while placing them in positions that maximized the *team's* overall performance. He was sure enough of his abilities that he didn't need to seek accolades, or spend time with the press discussing his brilliant moves. He understood that soccer was a player's game. And he let his results speak for him.

Twenty minutes later, Team USA had possession deep in their own half. After knocking the ball from side-to-side a few times, Marco DeSantis launched a fifty-yard pass over the Honduran defenders, who were tightly marking King and Grey about forty yards from their goal. Neither of the center backs saw Maxwell make the run past them.

The long pass arrived over his right shoulder and the midfielder reached out and cushioned it with his toes, while still running toward the Honduran goalkeeper. As the keeper came out to close down the angle, Jimmy drove directly at him while maintaining close control with his right foot. The goalie was tempted to come out of the box, but decided it better to stay just inside the eighteen – he may need his hands to stop this. Maxwell kept coming.

The "step-over" was commonly used in this scenario to fake in one direction – then go in the other. A good striker only needed a little room to slot a shot past a stranded keeper and put it into an empty goal. Most would be looking for it, but it was still effective since the defender had to respect the first move. Maxwell thought that would be too easy.

Left-right-left. Three rapid-fire step-overs froze the Honduran goalkeeper like a statue, and Jimmy Maxwell passed the ball between his legs before he could regain his composure. The twenty-year-old American was already on his way back to midfield when the ball crossed the goal line.

35th minute: 2-0 visitors.

The mistake previous coaches made when selecting a national team was to look for the "best" player at each position, and attempt to combine them into a cohesive unit. In a country as diverse and vast as the United States, this was doomed to fail. There were simply too many variables, Schneider would explain, to control it properly. He had a different plan.

His method revolved around a series of personality profiles, character assessments, and personal interviews. *After* watching them all play, of course. Supreme confidence on the ball was a given. Physical attributes were important, but Willy knew that they were often misleading.

147

He had heard dozens of coaches discuss their philosophies: *The fastest players must play forward, or outside midfield. Height was always necessary in a striker, or a center back, or both. Left-footers had to play on the left side of the field. Blah, blah, blah.*

Schneider needed his players to operate on a higher plane. He knew that size, speed, and strength were important, but he could see past the physical attributes. He was often critical of American football because of its reliance on physical measurements. "How can you call it *football tryouts* when no one touches a *football?*" he had asked while at Princeton. (The fact that some colleges were giving scholarships based solely on height and weight bothered him greatly.) Athleticism helped make the player who he was, but it rarely told the whole story.

The half-time whistle brought welcome relief for the Hondurans. The home team had been reduced to chasing the ball for most of the last ten minutes, and they looked forward to some rest and time to regroup. Making it to their locker room, though, was not going to be easy.

A large group of local fans had gathered at the area near the tunnel where both teams were headed, attempting to get as close as the security guards would allow. Both squads were hesitant to make the approach, but it was quickly apparent that the Hondurans were the target of the most vicious attacks. The Americans realized they were only in danger if they got between their opponents and the crowd. They still hurried just in case.

Jose de la Paz Herrerra had made a second mistake regarding this game. He had guaranteed a victory over the US in a newspaper interview, going so far as encouraging his countrymen to bet as much as they could on the match. He called it a *gift to his people*. Many in the angry mob had done just that, and saw their meager savings disappearing. The head coach did not pass by until he was surrounded by police with riot gear, protected from the various items being thrown his way. He was in need of a miracle, but none would come this day.

The second half began much like the first ended. The US players were energized by their lead and the local fans' anger, and wanted to make a statement. Pooky Bauer replaced David Knott, and was paired with Marco DeSantis in the center of the defense. The rest of the lineup remained the same, and the Hondurans were again chasing the ball while the Americans re-established their rhythm.

Six months earlier, Real Madrid had met Liverpool in the European Cup final in Paris. Even though the English team won, 1-0, Maxwell stole the show. He was simply the victim of some bad luck: Two of his shots hit the woodwork and three others were swatted away by Ray Clemence, Liverpool's decorated goalkeeper.

Marco DeSantis made sure to introduce himself to his fellow American after the awards were presented. He had heard of the kid, but was not expecting this.

"Does Willy Schneider know about you?" Doc asked, after some small talk.

149

"Yeah, we've talked a few times," Maxwell replied. "He said I might get called in to camp later this year, before the final round of qualifiers."

"I'll guarantee it," DeSantis told his future teammate. "Make sure you are ready."

"No sweat," Jimmy replied, and then he laughed. "I get it now. Why they call you *Doc*. That's funny." He pointed to the initials on Marco DeSantis' tracksuit.

As the Hondurans began to tire, the US launched multiple attacks down the flanks with Mishigawa and Price serving crosses virtually uncontested. The home team was able to hold them off, but could not mount any semblance of an attack of their own. The final dagger came in the 60th minute.

Brad Mishigawa had the ball wide on the right, just across the midfield stripe. His defender was trying to force him to the inside where he could get help from his central midfielders, and discourage any more of those crosses. Mish took the bait and charged diagonally, full-speed at the heart of the Honduran defense. Jimmy Maxwell backed away and set himself up to support the run, if necessary. King and Grey were even with the last defenders, each waiting for their mark to lose his concentration. One of them would have to step up and try to stop Mishigawa - soon.

Gilberto Yearwood was not about to let go of Leslie King, but his fellow central defender could not resist. As Mish approached, unmarked, Jaime Villegas left his man to deliver a bone-crunching tackle – his specialty. Unfortunately, for Villegas, the American midfielder released the ball just before their shins met. Both crashed to the turf as the ball rolled to Jimmy Maxwell, standing six yards away in the middle of the field. Frank Price was making the overlapping run on his left as the ref allowed play to continue, due to the American advantage.

Grey waited patiently. His marker had taken himself out of the play (perhaps the game) and had left him all alone twenty yards from goal. He couldn't believe his eyes when Maxwell turned to his left – *he was going to play Price!* Barrett Grey was still even with the last defender, Yearwood, and began preparing for the cross from Price. Plan B was still acceptable.

As Maxwell was about to pass the ball out wide to the streaking midfielder, he stopped and simply slotted it behind King and his Honduran defender. Neither was able to turn before Grey got there. First touch to prepare, second to bury the twelve-yard shot in the back of the net.

60th minute: 3-0 visitors.

Grey grabbed Maxwell by the shirt on the way back to the center circle.

"I thought for sure you were going to play Price," he said.

"Yeah, so did everyone else," he replied with a wink. Both laughed.

The match ended 3-1, with Honduras grabbing a late goal on a deflected shot from just outside the penalty area. Mausser was helpless, and was especially disappointed to lose his shutout. It was a good win, though, and the mood was upbeat in the locker room afterwards.

The United States would face their next-door neighbors in just three days and they had to stay on track. Mexico had been struggling, but would definitely be ready for this one. It was always a street fight when these two met.

Willy Schneider sought Maxwell out before they left the stadium. He was especially pleased with his young playmaker's performance.

"Good game, Jimmy," he said. "Looked like you were enjoying yourself."

"Yep, must've been that breakfast."

Chapter 14

BLOODBATH

After three matches, the United States was on top of the group with five points – the only team without a loss. The host country was one point behind, their only blemish being the recent loss to the Americans. Mexico and El Salvador were tied with three points each, and Haiti had two. Cuba's only point came from their draw with El Salvador. Since the top two teams would go to the World Cup, there were still four countries with a legitimate shot. The pressure was not off yet, especially with the Mexico match still to come.

Almost twelve months had passed since the Americans had played Mexico in the first round of qualification. Expectations were high on both sides.

The CONCACAF Region was divided into three Zones: Northern, Central, and Caribbean - which was split into two Groups, called A and B. Mexico, Canada, and the United States made up the Northern Zone and the top two teams from each of the various Zones advanced to the Group Finals in Honduras. Then, after a five-game tournament, the two teams with the highest point totals would advance to the World Cup Finals in Spain. A win earns two points, a draw gets one.

The first round games were also played in a round robin setup, but with each team playing the others at home *and* away. Because Mexico and Canada tied both of their games, the United States ended up in an enviable position, where they could control their own destiny. They had Mexico at home, in Ft. Lauderdale, for the last match of Group play.

Team USA had suffered a 5-1 loss in Mexico City three weeks earlier, but a draw or a win in Florida would get them through to the next round. Even though the Mexicans knew they were already in the Group Finals, they had no intention of rolling over for their neighbors to the north. Canada, meanwhile, had to hope for a US loss in order to stay alive.

Willy Schneider never believed in playing for a tie. He had seen too many teams end up losing to inferior opponents while trying to achieve a draw. Besides, if asked, he would have said there was no honor in that.

The Americans won that game 2-1, and the bad blood was evident from the opening whistle. The match set a record in CONCACAF qualifying - twelve yellow card cautions were issued - and both teams advanced, knowing that they would meet again in Honduras a year later. The Mexicans would be seeking revenge, and the familiarity between the teams only made it worse.

Four of Barrett Grey's former teammates from Club America played on the Mexican National Team, and his old boss, Raul Cardenas, was the Head Coach. Most of the US defenders had played against Hugo Sanchez, when he played briefly in the Texaco Premier League. The San Diego striker had scored on most of the Americans while on loan from UNAM Pumas.

154

Personal and national prides were on the line - but Willy was confident in his squad.

"Gents," he said, in the locker room before the game, "a lot has been written about this match. The talking heads have given Mexico the edge – mainly because we won the last time we played." He knew his guys read the papers, and most knew about the stories circulating back home. A few prominent sportswriters had predicted a US loss – for no good reason. Willy knew they liked to "stir the pudding", as he would say, but it was still frustrating. The Mexican press had jumped on the bandwagon, which just helped fuel their team's conviction.

"I believe that players will *run* for their club or their country – but they FIGHT for their teammates," he said. "That's why we will always have the advantage over the Mexicans." He knew that, as Americans, his players were used to not just tolerating, but living with and accepting, people from all walks of life. Bill Murray's line from *Stripes,* released just five months earlier, rang true with these guys: They *were* mutts. A TEAM of mutts.

And Willy knew they would fight for each other when necessary.

Sunday, November 15th, started clear and warm, but by match time the weather had taken a turn for the worse. A fast-moving cold front had caused some minor damage on Mexico's Yucatan Peninsula that morning, and was expected to bring high winds and plenty of rain to central Honduras all afternoon. Light precipitation greeted the players as they arrived at the National Stadium.

Juan Espinoza and Brad Mishigawa were the only US players who openly complained about the temperature. It was in the mid-40's at kickoff, well below the norm, and the two Californians were already miserable. Barrett Grey didn't like it either, but he was bundled up on the sidelines, nursing a twisted ankle from Friday's training. As usual, Espi was starting so he had to make sure he was adequately warmed up. Maxwell was taking Mish's place at right midfield, so Brad joined the other Eskimos on the bench. Johnny Jackson said the cold rain and wind made him miss home, and the others weren't sure if he was joking or not.

Team USA would be wearing their white (away) jerseys, with blue shorts and white socks. Alexi Mayer, Marco DeSantis, and Bobby Smith joined Espinoza in the back. Arnie Mausser was between the pipes. Billy Ford was rested and ready, Brandon Rafferty and Stoyan Petrov were central, and Jimmy Maxwell got the start on the right. Leslie King and Rick Davis were the forwards.

Mexico had a few players to be reckoned with, most notably their star striker. Hugo Sanchez had just joined Atletico Madrid after his short loan period in San Diego. The former Pumas man scored goals wherever he went, and was excited about proving himself in Spain's *La Liga*. Club America's goalkeeper, Pedro Soto, was a formidable presence for the National Team, and his club-mate Cristobal Ortega was a gifted playmaker. Ortega was a true Number Ten and Petrov would be responsible for shutting him down. It was the traditional green – white – red strip for the Mexicans.

The crowd was decidedly pro-Mexico, due mainly to geography, but the ever-present *Sam's Army* filled a section with nearly a thousand supporters wearing red and flying their colors in the downpour. By the opening whistle, the rain was falling in sheets and it looked like it would never let up. This game was going to be ugly.

Thick grass alone wouldn't have caused too much disruption in the playing style of either team, but the combination of the uncut turf and the steady deluge meant *Plan B* was in order. For the Mexicans, it meant instead of utilizing their skilled midfield to keep possession and move the ball up the field, they would try to play long balls over the defense. The American plan was similar, but they would attempt to utilize the flanks and play in crosses when they could.

Both coaches were dismayed by the referee's decision not to postpone the match, but they understood the nature of the schedule - and neither thought the other had an advantage in this weather.

Twenty minutes into the match the players had mostly figured out how to handle the elements, but the wind still caused problems. It would blow steadily at 10-15 knots for long stretches, then suddenly gust to twice that with no warning. One of Arnie Mausser's goal kicks had stopped in mid-air thirty yards outside his penalty area and just dropped, fortunately for the US, to Alexi Mayer's feet. Lesson learned: Keep the long kicks down.

A few minutes later, the Mexican attack nearly struck pay dirt when a long pass caught Doc and Bobby Smith off guard. Sanchez had been drifting out wide in order to lose their attention and, when a ball was played behind the American center backs, they both assumed it

157

would be an easy pickup for their keeper, who was calling them off. When the ball splashed in a puddle – and stopped – the Mexican striker got there first. He seemed a little surprised to be so close to goal without a defender harassing him.

Perhaps Hugo Sanchez had too much time to think about what to do, and instead of ripping a hard shot past Mausser, he tried to place the ball in the upper-right corner of the goal. It struck the goal post and bounced back into the field of play, two yards from the American goalkeeper, who calmly picked it up and punted it back downfield. Hard – and low.

Billy Ford received the long pass from Mausser and raced down the left side of the field, trying to avoid the growing pools of water. As he approached the end line, Billy attempted to cross the ball into the box, but he lost his balance when both he and the ball hit a deep spot. The errant crossing pass hit Alfredo Tena in the knee and went out for a corner kick. Both players were disappointed in the result.

Willy Schneider had a few hard-and-fast rules. One was that corner kicks should be in-swingers driven to the edge of the six-yard box. Always.

That meant that on a corner from the left-hand flag, a right-footed player would play the ball so that it would curve toward the goal. Nothing special, since a normal inside-of-the-foot strike would make it happen anyway. Jimmy Maxwell would come over for this one, and Billy Ford would take corner kicks from the opposite flag with his left foot.

Set plays were especially important in bad weather. The field conditions made it increasingly difficult to sustain any decent possession or generate much of an attack. These chances could not be squandered.

As Maxwell played the ball to the near corner of the goal box, Leslie King was trying to break free of two defenders. They had him boxed in and were not allowing him to move. The Mexican backs were so focused on keeping King from getting away they didn't see the ball coming directly at them. The American striker did.

The only direction Les could move was up, so he jumped and redirected the corner kick to the far post. His glancing header put Team USA up 1-0. It was the 26th minute.

Twenty more minutes of sloppy play just frustrated everyone. Fans of each side were as concerned with staying warm and dry as they were with the match. The coaches tried to stay engaged, but the conditions made it difficult. At one point, Cardenas was seen with his back to the field simply because the rain was blowing so hard it stung his face. Willy Schneider normally complained about his glasses on wet days, but this time they actually protected his eyes from the blowing rain. For the players, it was getting worse by the minute. Water was piling up everywhere, and the wind made playing an airborne game nearly impossible. Fortunately, better weather was on the way.

The stadium's grounds crew was ill-equipped to handle the situation they found themselves in, but they felt they had to try something. Had the rain not looked like it might let up, though, they probably would have surrendered. The showers were now merely steady, and the wind had diminished to a stiff breeze.

Half-time activities were identical for both teams: Get dry; get warm; get some rest. The players all knew what they needed to do. Both head coaches spent the time changing their clothes - socks and underwear included.

An enterprising young member of the stadium staff was dragging a rolled-up tarp across the field, pushing much of the standing water off to the sides. He had rigged it up to a golf cart, whose nearly-flat tires wouldn't cause any gullies to worry about. It worked surprisingly well, and the field was in better shape when the second half started than it had been for the opening whistle. When the players came out from the locker rooms, the rain had slowed to a light shower.

The United States started with the same team that ended the first half, but Mexico made one substitution. Jesus Martinez replaced Tena in the defense, allowing him to join the long list of outside backs Billy Ford had run into the ground.

The second half began with both teams somewhat surprised about their new playing environment. It took ten or twelve minutes for the players to get reacquainted with a proper soccer pitch. Some aspects of the game would not change, however.

Stoyan Petrov had been harassing the Mexican central midfielders all day, and his hard tackles had nearly forced Ortega out of the match - twice. The playmaker had complained to the referee several times, but his pleas fell on deaf ears. At halftime, he asked his old friend Pedro Vela for help.

Twenty-four minutes into the second half, Vela saw an opportunity to exact revenge. The Americans had another corner kick and Vela chose to mark Petrov, who normally took up a position right in front of the goal, about ten yards out. His primary objective was to prevent a second US tally, but he would try to send a message, if he could. The Billy Ford in-swinger was going over their heads when Petrov felt the contact.

Pedro Vela had planted his elbow just above Petey's right eye as the American midfielder jumped for the ball. The skin parted and blood flowed instantly from the inch-long gash. Luckily for Vela, the official's attention was with the ball and he missed the intentional hit. His luck was double when he realized that Petrov himself hadn't noticed who had caused the damage to his face. Petey didn't like it when people broke the rules.

The referee stopped play after noticing the bloody American, and called for the medical staff to enter the field. Petrov tried to wave them off, but the official made them escort him to the sidelines and administer treatment. Blood flowed steadily from the cut and the team doctor recommended stitches, but Petrov wouldn't allow it. He wasn't scared – he just didn't want to miss any more of the game.

In order to appease the official, Stoyan Petrov allowed the staff to wrap his head with gauze, which looked like an extra-large version of Leslie King's trademark white headband. He promptly re-entered the game and fouled Cristobal Ortega - hard. He got mostly ball, but the ref thought he was seeking revenge and pulled him aside for a discussion, and a yellow card. Petey's glare was focused on Vela as he received his caution, letting the Mexican know *he knew*.

161

As the blood continued to flow from Petey's head, the rain washed it down his neck and shoulders until his white jersey was transformed into a lovely shade of pink. On anyone else it would have been funny, but Stoyan Petrov even made pink look scary.

The conditions on the field made the match more interesting, but only marginally. Mexico was reluctant to push up too much, fearing a second US goal if they were spread thin in the back. Most of the second half was played in the midfield, with both teams trading possession - until a moment of brilliance by Hugo Sanchez.

Ortega played a long pass to the striker, who received it on his chest. He was about twenty yards from Mausser's goal, with his back to the American keeper. Bobby Smith was attached to him like a Siamese twin, and DeSantis was only two yards away — just in case.

Sanchez dropped the pass from his chest toward his right foot, with Smith all over his back. He couldn't turn, so he flicked the ball backwards over his, and Smith's, heads. As the American defender glanced upward, Sanchez saw his chance. He quickly spun away from his marker and struck the falling ball before it reached the ground. Doc attempted to block the shot with a sliding tackle, but missed by an inch. The Mexican struck this one with all he had, and it bulged the net well outside Arnie Mausser's reach. 1-1, 82nd minute.

Despite a few frantic last-minute attempts, Team USA couldn't penetrate the Mexican defense, and the match ended in a draw. For his ten saves, goalkeeper Pedro Soto was named "Man of the Match". The Americans felt like they had lost – while Mexico celebrated. Each team earned one point.

The draw meant they would have to make sure and beat the lowly Cubans to win the group. It was getting close.

Chapter 15

TICKETS TO SPAIN

It had been a week since the disappointing result against Mexico. Practices had been focused, serious, and very businesslike. No one felt like going out in the evenings or enjoying the sights during the day. They all knew a huge opportunity had been squandered, and their collective mind was only concerned with getting the win against Cuba – and going home. Nothing else mattered.

Willy Schneider didn't mention it to anyone, but he was immensely proud of the way this team had pulled together during the time in Honduras. The local newspapers were constantly running stories about the in-fighting between players on the other teams, or between players and their coaches.

So far, his guys had been able to resist using the press to launch any verbal attacks on each other, and had actually begun playing a game with the local journalists to amuse themselves. Alexi Mayer had started it when he was approached by a reporter after the match against El Salvador. He was just continuing a game he learned with his club team in New York. It was a lot more fun with foreign journalists, and soon the whole team was in on the act.

A cute Honduran reporter got Alexi's attention as he was heading to the locker room after the team's first match. As he had hoped, his interview appeared in the paper word-for-word.

Reporter: *I'm with Alexi Mayer, USA defender. Tell me Alexi, what did you think of the result today?*

Mayer: *Well, we just tried to go out there and give 110%, you know. I think it was a total team effort, and we kept our focus throughout.*

Reporter: *Any thoughts on the next games?*

Mayer: *We're just trying to take it one game at a time, you know. Trying to dig deep and give it all we've got.*

Leslie King was the first to see the article before breakfast the next morning. He immediately went to Mayer's room to congratulate him.

"Absolutely the worst post-game interview ever!" King proclaimed.

"Why, thank you, sir," Alexi replied with a bow. "That *was* the idea."

And the competition was on.

The Cuban Soccer Association had hired Hungarian coach Tibor Ivanicz to get this squad into the World Cup. His task was daunting, but he took it seriously. Ivanicz was actually the second Hungarian, and the fourth foreigner, to lead the Cuban team's attempt to make it into the Finals. None of his predecessors had qualified, but the pressure was real, nonetheless. Previous foreign coaches had taken this job knowing that it was a low-risk, high-reward venture.

While few expected tiny Cuba, primarily known as a baseball country, to qualify for soccer's biggest tournament, the CONCACAF region was not immune to surprises. Small countries in the Caribbean and Central America, namely Haiti and El Salvador, had qualified for past Cup Finals and the potential rewards for a coach who could pull it off were huge. The expansion of the tournament to twenty-four teams had added another CONCACAF spot, effectively (if not realistically) doubling their chances. Most honest analysts knew the top qualifiers would be the United States and Mexico but, as Willy Schneider liked to say, *the analysts weren't playing the games.*

Sunday, November 22nd, was the last day of this qualifying tournament and two very important games remained. USA-Cuba would be first, at noon, and then the final match between the second- and third-place teams would decide it all. Honduras and Mexico trailed the United States with five and four points, respectively. Since the Americans had six points, all they needed was a tie to qualify, but they were intent on winning the group. A loss to Cuba, combined with a Mexican win, could possibly keep them home, depending on the scores.

The Americans were confident, rested, and eager to take the field for their final qualifying match. They knew that twenty-two tickets to Spain were waiting. Willy Schneider knew the team was anxious to play, and was toying with them the day before.

167

When Brandon Rafferty asked about the starting lineup, he simply smiled and said, "I haven't decided yet. What do you think?"

Raff's response was predictable. "Seriously, who's starting?"

"We'll see – tomorrow." Another smile and that was that.

The locker room was a little tense when Willy came in with his assistant, Steve Newton. They called the players in for a quick pre-game talk. Schneider and Newton were firm believers that a coach's work was done in training, not during games. If a player needed to be *pumped up* by a coach prior to a match, that player could never play for Willy. The lineup was announced with little fanfare.

"Jackson's in goal," Newton began, "Roberts, Bauer, DeSantis, and Mishigawa in back." Ben Roberts was the oldest field player on the squad, but could still run with the youngest. He was an inspiration and a loyal teammate, but Willy knew he wasn't good enough to play on this team. Other national team coaches had all said he was, quote - *A great guy to have in the locker room* – unquote, whatever that meant. This would be his last chance to represent his country and, for his service, he would wear the captain's arm band.

"Ford and Espinoza out wide," he continued, "Maxwell and Price in the middle." Juan Espinoza and Brad Mishigawa were virtually interchangeable anyway, so Schneider wanted to see how they worked together from different starting positions.

The two Californians had been sold on the "Total Football" style of the Dutch even before Johan Cruyff joined them in 1979. The Aztecs could only keep him for one season, but Cruyff's influence was felt by the team for years. After winning the Texaco Premier League in '79, LA followed it up with a Winston Cup title in 1981. The '81 team was made up almost entirely of players who had played with the Dutch Master. For these men, changing positions during the course of a game was the norm. Mish and Espi had become so accustomed to it they hardly noticed the difference in Newton's lineup.

"Scott and Grey are the forwards." Barrett Grey was back to full strength after missing the Mexico game with an ankle injury. Charlie Scott was happy to be back in the lineup after the Haiti debacle. He knew the result wasn't his fault, but that match left him a little uneasy about his position on the team.

Cuba fielded the same squad that had beaten Haiti 2-0 in their last match. They were out of contention for the World Cup, but took this game very seriously. National pride was at stake every time they faced the mighty Americans, in any sport. Too bad, for them, this wasn't baseball or boxing.

Twelve minutes into Team USA's final qualifying match for the 1982 World Cup, Charlie Scott scored the "Goal of the Tournament".

It started with a long ball played by a Cuban defender, to no one in particular, that Johnny Jackson scooped up and threw to Billy Ford, who was waiting near the midfield stripe. He faked inside, cut to his left and took the ball out wide, where there was more space.

169

Jimmy Maxwell provided support ten yards away, between Billy and the goal. Juan Espinoza filled in the central space, where Maxwell had been, as Brad Mishigawa took off down the right flank - unmarked.

Ford's pass was played with enough weight that all Maxwell had to do to redirect it back into Espinoza's path was apply a well-timed touch. Juan received the pass on the inside of his right boot and immediately played the ball downfield, toward the corner flag, with his left – leading Mishigawa perfectly.

Brad's first-touch cross was whipped in from ten yards outside the penalty area, and was heading straight for Barrett Grey's head. Grey had started his near-post run from just outside the area, and he had a step on his defender. The American striker was definitely going to get to this one first, which was bad news for Cuba.

During his four years in Mexico, Barrett Grey was the most prolific header in the league. Accuracy and power, combined with the height and athletic ability to reach most crosses, earned him the title *El Cabeza Grande* - The Big Head. What really made him special, according to Willy Schneider, was his courage. Grey wasn't afraid to stick his head in the mix – and he had the scars to prove it. He would put this one low, inside the near post, just out of the keeper's reach. No problem.

Grey's head met the ball just as he was tripped from behind by the Cuban who was desperately trying to prevent his mark from scoring. The contact caused the American's shot to go high, but it still had enough power on it to beat the goalkeeper. The Cuban keeper saw the shot sail over his head as he was frozen on his line, and he was momentarily relieved to see the shot glance off the crossbar.

When Espinoza played his pass to Mishigawa, Charlie Scott had begun his run - ready for a cross, or to crash the goal after a shot. He started out wide on the left, curling his path toward the center of the field, a few yards outside the penalty box. Brad's crossing pass was going near-post, so the striker slowed down, waiting for the next opportunity. He was prepared to make a dash toward the Cuban keeper, just in case he fumbled a save, and was already leaning that way. Then the ball hit the woodwork.

The deflection sent Grey's shot back into the field of play. While it was heading directly for Charlie Scott, the ball was two feet too high to reach with his head. Without thinking, Scott turned his back to goal, leaped, and executed a perfect overhead bicycle kick, meeting the ball firmly with the instep of his right foot.

The fifteen-yard blast nearly ripped a hole in the net, and the landing nearly broke Charlie Scott's neck but, surprisingly, both survived.

United States 1, Cuba 0, 12th minute.

While the match had started with a distinctly pro-Cuba crowd cheering on the underdogs, that goal took most of the wind out of their sails. It would have been hard for anyone watching not to appreciate such a strike, evidenced by the smiles on the Cuban bench. The Honduran fans also appreciated quality, regardless of the side the goal-scorer played for.

On the way back to their half for the ensuing kickoff, Charlie and Frank Price high-fived and noticed

171

the song coming from the *Sam's Army* section. The group was known for their inventive chants, typically used to harass opposing players or fans, but this was their special cheer - designed for the rare, truly spectacular play.

We're not wor-thy. We're not wor-thy. All while bowing in mock deference to the hero of the moment. Surprisingly, many of the Honduran fans in the stadium joined in, as did the entire US bench, led by Leslie King.

"This is kind of embarrassing," Scott said to Price, trying to take it all in. The thirty-year-old had scored many goals during his career in Tampa, but none as remarkable as the one that just put the United States National Team in the 1982 World Cup.

"How many like *that* have you scored?" Price asked, assuming that this was a somewhat normal occurrence for the striker.

"First one," Scott replied. "Never even *tried* it in a game before."

"I'd say you picked a good time to experiment, bro," Frank said, with a pat on the back. "That was awesome!"

Charlie Scott's national team career would be defined by that bicycle kick, and it would be the last goal he would ever score.

The Cuban "attack" was almost non-existent. A few errant passes sent toward the US goal, only to be grabbed by Jackson, added to their frustration. Team

USA was able to keep possession for long stretches, forcing their opponents to chase the ball while they looked for their next scoring chance. It would come in the twenty-fourth minute, after a surprisingly good run by the Cubans.

Five passes in a row, for the first time this match, allowed Cuba to progress into the American defensive third – with numbers. A decent cross was met by a leaping Johnny Jackson, who immediately sprinted to the edge of the eighteen yard box and threw the ball sixty yards downfield. He knew the Cuban defenders had pushed up to the midfield line, and Billy Ford would be lurking out wide – anxious to get into a footrace with them.

Jackson's athletic abilities were obvious to everyone, but Willy Schneider saw something in the young goalkeeper that made him consider making him the permanent starter, at only twenty-four. Maybe it was because of his basketball background, but JJ was always looking for attacking opportunities. He would routinely opt for a well-thrown, or rolled-out, pass instead of the typical punted ball, most of which were won by the opposing side. His play actually reminded some of that of a seasoned NFL quarterback, prompting *Monday Night Soccer* announcer Howard Cosell to offer a mock warning to the Sting front office.

He was so impressed by Jackson's ball distribution during a game in 1979, against Atlanta, he joked that the Chicago Bears should sign him.

"Coach Armstrong, Chicago Bears," Cosell intoned, midway through the first half. "Are you seeing this?" He knew that the Bears were having quarterback troubles, again, with starter Vince Evans out with a staph infection, and no established backup to take the reins.

"Do you *really* think Johnny Jackson would make the switch to *football?*" Don Meredith asked incredulously. The two were constantly bickering and their arguments were legendary. The lawyer from Brooklyn trapped in the booth with the retired midfielder from Dallas. "Besides, there's no way the Bears could afford him, anyway," he added.

Except for a love of soccer, the two had absolutely nothing in common, but both could agree on one thing. "Ladies and gentlemen," Cosell announced after a long pause, "as difficult as this is for me to admit, I believe that my feeble-minded broadcasting compatriot has finally uttered a statement that I can agree with."

"Well, thank you, Howard," Meredith feigned humility, which was hard for him.

"I'm just telling it like it is," was Cosell's predictable response.

Jackson's long pass caught the Cuban defenders off guard and, as they turned to chase it, Billy Ford raced past them with a full head of steam, heading for their goal. Ford took the ball in stride on his right foot after its first bounce and drove straight at the Cuban keeper. The plan was simple: He would freeze him in place, fake right, then go left and slot the ball into the empty net – just like he had done so many times before. But something happened on his way to goal.

Cuba's goalkeeper, Jorge Molina, wisely chose not to be a sitting duck, and sprinted away from his goal – directly at the American. Molina was very quick, for a keeper, and the two met just outside the penalty area, with Ford unsuccessfully attempting to hurdle the Cuban's sliding tackle.

The referee's whistle surprised most of the players, since the contact appeared legal, and the ball hadn't yet rolled across the end line just wide of the post for a goal kick. A free kick was awarded to the Americans, twenty yards from goal, lined up with the left post. This was Jimmy Maxwell territory, and Johnny Jackson made sure their Captain knew it.

"Benny," he called out to his left back. "Make sure Jimmy takes this one."

"Who else?" was the reply. Roberts was no fool, and he *had* seen what the Real Madrid playmaker could do with a dead ball. With Brandon Rafferty on the bench, and an angle best suited to a right-footed player, this was a no-brainer.

Six Cubans formed a wall covering the near post after ensuring their goalkeeper was fully recovered from his collision with Ford. Billy was rattled more by the goalie's decision to attack him than by the contact with his shin. Physically, both players were fine.

Maxwell placed the ball on the spot as directed by the referee and pushed it down into the soft grass. He then took four long steps backwards and waited for the whistle. Molina covered the far half of his goal and was confident that his wall could cover their half. Besides, he knew that it was virtually impossible to strike a ball hard enough to make it dip under the crossbar from only twenty yards out. He was sure this shot would be coming at him – probably directed at the upper corner on his left. He leaned that way, just a little bit, to be ready.

Two seconds after the first whistle, which prompted Maxwell's shot, came the second whistle, signifying a goal. By the time Molina saw the ball clear the wall, dipping with topspin, it was too late. The power, technique, and accuracy were simply too much to believe - let alone stop. The keeper was stunned, and he knew that this game was over. His eyes briefly met Maxwell's with a look that said, *Well done, señor.*

United States 2, Cuba 0, 24th minute.

The Cubans had lost what little confidence they had left after the second goal. Team USA controlled the possession and peppered their goal with ten more shots before halftime. Only one would score, though, with five minutes left.

As often happens when a team goes down 2-0, Cuba tried to force the action by sending one of their defenders into the attack. Left back Jose Baro was an effective crosser and had the speed to recover defensively in most situations. He was conscious of the American tracking with him as he made the run forward, so he wasn't worried about being hung out to dry on a counter-attack. He actually thought he was helping his team out by dragging one of the US mid-fielders into their defensive third of the field. Normally, that would have been true.

What Baro didn't consider was that, as Juan Espinoza dropped to cover him, Brad Mishigawa headed forward and took over the midfield duties. Mish was certain his roommate could handle the job, and quickly pushed up as high as he could. With Scott and Grey, the Americans were three-on-three against the Cuban backline. Now they just needed the ball.

Marco DeSantis saw the Cuban defender's run and he patiently waited for the pass. When the ball was played he stepped in and made the interception, continuing forward into the empty space behind the opposing strikers. His momentum, and the fact that most of the Cubans were racing forward, allowed for a quick counter. Doc played a short ball to Jimmy Maxwell, and sprinted ahead. He was eager to get into the attack, partly to make amends for his two missed headers earlier. He was Billy Ford's favorite target on corner kicks, but he felt he had let the team down when he put the last one over the crossbar. *At least the first miss had been on-goal.* Every Cuban defender saw the American racing toward their goal. Unmarked.

Maxwell allowed Doc to get ahead of him and headed for the right side of the field, ten yards into the Cuban half. Mish was wide right, hugging the touchline and staying even with the last defender. Charlie Scott had taken up a position near the penalty area and Barrett Grey was drifting out to the left, trying to lose his mark.

Everyone watching, players included, knew Maxwell was going to play a through-ball to Mishigawa so he could attempt to whip in a cross. That's when Jimmy Maxwell showed why he was wearing the Number Ten for one of the most respected club sides in the world.

177

From the stands, or on television, it is easy to see passing options as they emerge from the run of play - often before they even happen. A defender forces the action; the player on the ball changes direction; space opens up; someone makes the run away from the ball; two passes later, magic happens. Many fans would admit to having seen the play develop before it actually did, and they would be right. But seeing it from above was simple compared to seeing it at field level.

Mario Kempes was able to do it. Argentina's Number Ten from the last two World Cups had all the tools of a great playmaker, *and* he could score! France's Michel Platini could see three moves ahead of mere mortal defenders, and had excelled in the 1978 World Cup even though his side was eliminated in the first round. Both would be back, but Spain '82 would introduce the world to two new world-class playmakers, Jimmy Maxwell and Diego Maradona.

Maxwell saw Mishigawa making the run down the line, *and* Doc sprinting toward the Cuban goal. He took the ball wide to the right, quickly turned up field, and launched a hard diagonal pass just out of DeSantis' reach, toward the left corner flag. Charlie Scott saw the ball coming but couldn't quite get his foot on it as it cut between him and the keeper.

"What the..?" Willy Schneider grabbed Steve Newton's arm and interrupted his question. The Assistant Coach just saw a decent opportunity wasted, and was already anticipating the resulting goal kick. The Head Coach was more patient. "Wait," he said.

As the ball slipped through the penalty area, untouched by everyone, Willy saw Barrett Grey approaching from the far side. The striker's run had begun seven seconds earlier, when Maxwell glanced his way. As usual, the American midfielder received the ball on his trailing foot, letting it run across his body first. His head was constantly turning, looking for defenders, or an attacking opportunity. His first club coach, Ken Franklin, called it "Head on a swivel" and all his players knew that if you wanted to play in the Mules' midfield, you'd better master it. Jimmy Maxwell had.

Grey's path covered nearly sixty yards, starting out wide on the left side of the field. Initially traveling away from Maxwell, he then turned up field and headed straight for goal. By then, all eyes were on the ball coming from the opposite side of the pitch, which was somehow eluding everyone.

The easiest goals are often the result of many players doing several things right in preparation for the final shot. The third goal of this game was one of those. Barrett Grey tapped the ball into the Cuban net with little effort, and calmly saluted the US supporters in the stands. For those who saw the pass from above - from the stands or on television - it was a thing of beauty. That's how magic happens.

USA 3, Cuba 0, 40th minute.

As the players entered the locker room for halftime, the mood was still very serious. No one wanted to seem overconfident or premature, but they all knew this match was over. They also knew what that meant, but someone needed to break the ice. One member of this team was a specialist in ice-breaking.

"Well, I never been to Spain," Leslie King started with his best rendition of the popular *Three Dog Night* song. "But I kinda like the music." Smiles could no longer be suppressed.

"Say, the ladies are insane there," Billy Ford led the group in the second line. "And they sure know how to use it." Singing was apparently the only talent missing from Billy's vast repertoire – not that *he* knew it. The entire team was up, singing in the middle of the cramped locker room.

"They don't abuse it," Johnny Jackson wailed. "Never gonna lose it!" Schneider and Newton wished they had a video camera. This was priceless.

Then, for some reason, all eyes turned to the only member of this team who actually lived in Spain. The kid who had arrived at training camp in Missouri less than two months ago, unknown to nearly everyone, had emerged as the big story of this tournament. His teammates were acknowledging him, and it felt good.

Fortunately, Dale had all of *Three Dog Night's* albums, and Jimmy knew the words to this one. Not that anyone doubted it.

"I can't re-FUSE it!" Maxwell sang from his heart, because it was fun – and because it was true.

The match ended 4-0, with both teams subbing liberally in the second half. The second game ended with no score, sending Honduras to their first World Cup Finals. Mexico's failure to qualify was the big news but, in Tegucigalpa, no one cared about that. *Los Catrachos* were going to Spain! The party would last for days.

The American contingent stayed around to watch the Mexico-Honduras game, planning to congratulate the home team and wish them luck at the Finals. Twenty thousand fans filled the pitch when the final whistle blew so Team USA decided it more appropriate, and much safer, to send a telegram to the Honduran Federation instead.

Now it was time for the players to get a little rest, a few days anyway, and re-join their clubs. Most would have a game in a week.

It was 203 days until the World Cup.

Chapter 16

CLUB TIME

Thanksgiving at the Rafferty household was always a joyous occasion, but this year it seemed a whole lot better. The qualification process was behind him, and it felt good to know he would be going to his second World Cup Finals. Fortunately, Brandon's Patriots were among the majority of the TPL teams that took the holiday off, and he always had a full house. Most of his family still lived within an hour of Boston and the big house off Minuteman Road was the perfect place to host a holiday dinner. Still, he had an uneasy feeling.

As usual, Leslie King was present, having arrived a few days early for his team's weekend match against Boston. He told his coaching staff he needed to rest up after the qualifying tournament, and he really just wanted to spend a few days relaxing – needed or not. He and Raff were old friends who rarely got to spend any time together, and Brandon had specifically asked if he would be coming this year. He said he needed to talk. About what, he didn't say.

The "most eligible bachelor in New York City" was more at home in this converted 19th century farmhouse, playing hide-and-seek with the Rafferty kids, than he was in his Manhattan penthouse. Lisa desperately wanted to see him settle down, and was constantly trying to set him up with her single friends. Of course, Les always went along with Mrs. Rafferty's plans, though none had panned out. *Yet,* she would always add.

The Tampa Bay Rowdies were in Detroit to take on Billy Ford's Chrysler squad at one o'clock Eastern, and Dallas would host the San Jose Earthquakes at three. Charlie Scott and Ford were both starting, and expected to go the full ninety minutes. Three days rest was plenty. ABC-TV had been promoting the Thanksgiving Day double-header for two weeks, as usual.

Lisa Rafferty's kitchen was bustling with activity. The smell of fresh-baked bread filled the house, and turkey with all the trimmings was ready at half-time of the first match. Detroit was leading 1-0, but Tampa Bay had squandered several opportunities. Everyone was looking forward to watching the second half — as soon as they finished eating. Jack Rafferty was the only one who actually saw the injury happen.

Captain America's eight-year-old son was refusing to eat at the kid's table while a game was on in the living room. Leslie King had caused the necessary diversion that enabled the boy to sneak out when he grabbed Lisa and tried to dance with her in the tight confines of the kitchen. As expected, she just laughed and pushed him away. Les pleaded with her as his eyes motioned for Jack to make his escape. Brandon watched the whole scene from his spot at the head of the table with great amusement. A few minutes later, the dinner conversation was interrupted.

"Dad! Uncle Les! Come quick!" Jack Rafferty called out from the living room. He was no longer worried about being caught. Something very serious had happened, according to the announcers, and he could tell it looked bad.

184

"What is it, buddy?" Raff asked as he and King arrived. His son just pointed. The scene on the television told it all.

"Oh, man," Leslie King said, "is that Charlie?" They could see a player down, in obvious pain, being tended to by a team of medical staffers. The only clue was a green-and-gold striped jersey sleeve, with what looked like a "9" on the front.

"Could be," Raff said. "Jack, go get your mom. Now!" He knew it was Charlie Scott - and he knew it was bad. Bad enough that the announcers were refusing to show a replay. They just kept reminding the viewing audience of their unprecedented decision, and you could hear it in their voices.

"Jack told me Charlie Scott broke his leg. Is that true?" Lisa Rafferty asked as she ran into the living room. Brandon's effort to shield his son from the carnage had obviously not worked. The boy was the only one in the room who had actually seen it, and he was right. "Yeah," was King's hushed reply. He felt sick to his stomach.

Twenty minutes into the second half John Gorman had launched a long pass into the Detroit penalty area, looking for the head of his striker. The collision between Scott and the Chrysler defender wasn't all that bad but it caused both of them to lose their balance and, because he kept trying to get a foot on the loose ball, Charlie's leg got trapped under the pile of bodies. Everyone in the stadium heard the "CRACK".

It was immediately obvious that something had gone terribly wrong. Detroit's goalkeeper was first on his feet and he began yelling at the medical staff to come quickly, before the referee knew what was happening. At this point no one cared about the ball (which the keeper had tossed into the stands). The players and officials all had a new priority.

"I'll call Ang," Lisa said, as she left the living room. She knew that Charlie Scott's wife never watched the games, and she wanted to be the one to tell her what had happened. Lisa Rafferty took care of everyone, or at least she tried.

The Rafferty's phone rang as Lisa was about to pick it up. It was Carolyn Ford, calling from the owner's suite in the Silverdome.

"Lisa," she started immediately. "Can you call Angie? I'm on my way to the hospital with Charlie." She was all business, as usual. The yin to Billy's yang.

"I was just going to call her," Lisa said. "She will be happy to know you're there. Do you know where they'll take him?"

"Pontiac Osteopathic Hospital, it's only a few minutes away, but tell her to stay by the phone and I'll call when we get him settled in."

It was nearly fifteen minutes before the match resumed. Scott's leg had been immobilized and he was stretchered off the field to a standing ovation from the Detroit fans. The combination of adrenaline and endorphins did their job of numbing the pain and allowed the Rowdies' striker to wave to the crowd in relative comfort as he was carted down the tunnel to a waiting ambulance.

Highlights from the United States' qualifying matches were being shown on the broadcast feed and on the JumboTron in the stadium during the delay in lieu of the standard replays and advertising. Charlie Scott heard cheers from the crowd as he was being loaded into the ambulance and asked if Detroit had scored again. *This just keeps getting worse*, he thought.

"No, son," his coach answered. "They just showed your goal against the Cubans. Brilliant!" He left for the hospital with a smile on his face.

Forty minutes later X-rays confirmed what the doctors, and Charlie, already knew. Scott's tibia and fibula were both fractured six inches below his knee. He was slightly comforted to know that shin guards, which he never wore, wouldn't have prevented his injury. He appeared to be in good spirits when he received the news, only because he had already come to terms with the reality that he would never play again. His career was over at thirty years old. "Let Chuck know," Scott told his wife on the phone later, "I'll be able to coach his team." Their five-year-old son would be starting pee-wee league in the fall. He was always looking for the good news.

The mood at the Rafferty home was somber. The elephant was in the room, but no one wanted to acknowledge it. The subject of injuries, especially *career-ending* injuries, was something all athletes' wives wanted to talk about – but none of their husbands would. When Brandon walked in on Lisa's phone conversation with Carolyn King later that afternoon, he just turned around and walked out. She knew. They had been together a long time, and some things were better left unsaid.

187

Les asked him what it was he wanted to talk about, but Raff wasn't in the mood. "Not now," he said. "We've got time." But they would never get the chance to discuss Brandon Rafferty's fear that he was no longer fit to lead the National Team.

The crowd around the Rafferty's television saw Dallas beat San Jose 3-1, with Barrett Grey bagging two of the Tornado's goals. After the match, Grey sought out the on-field reporter from ABC. She had played his game before, and was hesitant to stick her microphone in front of him. This time, though, he surprised her.

"Suzie, I'd like to say something to a good friend who is watching from the hospital," he started very seriously. She thought she could see tears in his eyes.

"Um, sure," was all she could say. *This has to be a trick.*

"Charlie," Grey said, looking directly into the camera, "the few games we got to play together were the best of my career. You are, without a doubt, the best teammate I ever had. Get well, buddy."

Eighteen other members of the United States National Team agreed.

He smiled at Suzie, thanked her, and walked away. It had never bothered her that he was married — until now.

The next day, Willy Schneider dropped twenty hand-written cards in the mail. One, to Charlie Scott, expressed his sadness in what had happened to a wonderful man, and wished him a quick and successful recovery. The other nineteen, sent to cities from Los Angeles to Madrid, said the following:

Gentlemen,

Charlie's little mishap serves to remind us that every game, every play, every practice, could be your last. Remember that when you are out there on the field, and you find yourself dogging it, or only giving 98%, and ask yourself, "Is this how I want to go out?"

Regards,

Willy

P.S. We know Charlie will be happy with his last play, even though he didn't score.

. . .

Christmas "break" in the Texaco Premier League was something of a joke. Sure, the teams all got the holiday off, but the schedule was anything but a break. This year, Christmas fell on Friday which meant the next three matches would be Sunday-Wednesday-Saturday. Three games in a week's time, then back to standard league routine – weekend matches with the occasional mid-week Winston Cup game thrown in.

At the halfway point of the 1981-82 season, three of the top four teams were as expected: New York Cosmos, Los Angeles Aztecs, and Chicago Sting. The surprise was that Atlanta was in fourth place, currently two points ahead of Tampa Bay. The Chiefs had barely avoided relegation last season, and a few pundits had expected them to fare even worse this season. Their lineup was virtually unchanged, with the extra year's experience appearing to make all the difference.

The Cosmos appeared to be back in the form that won them the league and cup titles only two years before. As the richest club in North America, and one of the top three most-expensive on the planet, New York had resources most of their TPL opponents could only dream about. The wealth of talent from all over the world included Giorgio Chinaglia, Roberto Cabanas, Rick Davis, and Vladislav Bogicevic. They looked unstoppable again this season, but they still couldn't get the "trophy" that had eluded them for so long. Their quest started almost ten years earlier.

The Virginia Beach Mariners were not prepared for the attention their young striker would generate in the spring of 1972. In his third season with the team he had grown up supporting, Leslie King scored thirty-two goals and led the USL in scoring. The scouts from New York had been in the stands several times that spring and everyone knew the twenty-year-old striker's contract was about to expire. It was time to pounce.

The Cosmos front office had given their men the authority to offer King $300,000, which was more than ten times his current salary and would make him one of the highest-paid players in the first division. Then they made a fatal mistake. They told him he would probably even see some playing time in his rookie season.

"What do you mean by *some* playing time?" King asked. It had sounded good so far, but this little detail bothered him.

"Surely you didn't expect to start on the *Cosmos*," the scout laughed at the young star, and sealed his fate.

"No, sir," Leslie agreed. "I don't ever see that happening." He offered his hand, but the New York Cosmos' Director of Personnel didn't reciprocate.

"Well, thanks anyway," King turned and walked away. He let Coach McIlvenny know he would be around for another season, if he was OK with that. Surprisingly, no one else was prepared to offer King a contract since they all knew the Cosmos were in the hunt – and, of course, they would be offering the most money.

Leslie King stayed in Virginia Beach one more season and set the league's single-season scoring record, with thirty-six goals. His decision to stay in his home-town one more year made him a local hero and, after the Mariners won the USL Championship, he was offered another contract by a team from New York. This one was considerably more lucrative.

With the additional money available to the teams as part of the new Texaco Premier League, the Cosmos suddenly had some competition for the top players. A bidding war, of sorts, was about to make Leslie King the first million-dollar man in American soccer.

The Cosmos opened the bidding with a $500,000 offer, knowing they could go as high as $700,000. Los Angeles' big club, the Aztecs, knew they were a long-shot, but needed a striker badly – and had plenty of cash. They quickly upped the bid to $750 thousand, and assumed they had it in the bag. New York management was furious since the Aztecs were their arch rivals, but were somewhat relieved that King would be 3000 miles away – out of the daily media grind which would hound them mercilessly for losing the star striker. Then it got even worse.

A last-minute offer was made by a mid-sized club that had not *publicly* expressed any interest in King. The Brooklyn Dodgers had been working in the background, though, for six months. In a package devised by Leslie's agent, his mother, Dodgers' management, and the marketing executives at Puma, King would earn $1.1 million his first year in New York City.

Leslie King had achieved his goal, set in the third grade, of being the first American soccer player to break the million dollar mark.

• • •

The draw for the World Cup Finals was held in Madrid on January 16th. Most of the TPL teams held light workouts or *kick-arounds* on Saturdays, the usual day before a match, but they were glued to television screens all over America on this day. The event was shown live at eight o'clock local time, which was 2pm on the East Coast.

This was the largest World Cup to date, with twenty-four squads representing the best of the 109 countries that had entered the competition. Six groups of four would each include one of the "seeded" teams: Argentina, Brazil, West Germany, England, Italy, and the hosts, Spain.

The format was also new. The top two teams from each of the six groups would move on to the second round, which consisted of four groups of three. The winner of each of these would move to the semi-finals. The final was scheduled for July 11th.

Team USA was drawn into Group III with Belgium, Hungary, and defending World Cup champions, Argentina.

The rest of the field was as follows:

Group I – Italy, Poland, Cameroon, Peru

Group II – West Germany, Algeria, Chile, Austria

Group IV – England, France, Czechoslovakia, Kuwait

Group V – Spain, Honduras, Yugoslavia, Northern Ireland

Group VI – Brazil, USSR, Scotland, New Zealand

There was less than five months until the start of the World Cup.

Chapter 17

PREPARATIONS

"No pressure there," Steve Newton said, referring to the draw. "Let's see, defending champions, and two European teams that won their qualifying groups!"

"You worry too much," Willy Schneider said. "This is exactly what we wanted – to be tested in the first round." Newton shook his head. Sometimes he thought his boss was crazy. Sometimes he was more right than he knew.

Willy went to work immediately with his plan to prepare for the finals. They had precious little time to train and squeeze in a few warm-up matches with club duties in high gear. Thankfully, most of the hard work was already done and he could concentrate on the few remaining, albeit important, issues.

He needed to arrange a series of exhibition matches that would test his squad, and help decide who would play in Spain. Some national team coaches tried to replicate their first-round opponents as closely as possible. Willy knew that, if he made the right personnel decisions, the opposition would have to adjust to Team USA. He knew his guys could play with the best – as long as he didn't screw it up.

Actually, the US Soccer Federation staff would make all the arrangements, but Schneider got to pick the teams he wanted to play. He knew that, with all twenty-four countries trying to do the same thing, he had to hurry to get quality matches scheduled. His short list was prepared before the draw was completed.

"Mexico, definitely," he told the Federation's Planning Chair. This one was easy, since there was no such thing as a *friendly* USA-Mexico match. "Then, in this order: Holland, Uruguay, Denmark, and Romania. I'd like to play Denmark and Romania in Spain the week we arrive there. The others we will fit in during the international breaks." Most of the leading professional leagues scheduled *breaks* for their players to join their respective national teams a few times each season. FIFA, the world governing body, assisted by laying out their tournament schedules a few years in advance. It worked most of the time.

The Federation already knew where the team would stay while in Spain. Schneider insisted that reservations be made before they had even qualified. *Lloret de Mar was perfect,* he told his boss. *Make it happen.*

Next up was to work on a final roster. He would have until May 17th to pare his list of potentials down to twenty-two players who would represent the United States. For most coaches, this was the hardest job of all.

As is usually the case in these situations, Willy knew his time now would be spent on a few *bubble* players. Since taking over the national team, Schneider had called fifty-six different men into camp. He had seen all of them perform for their clubs, and each had had a chance to play in at least one international match for him. He knew what he had to do, and he also knew that many of his counterparts would wait until the last minute to make this decision. Not him.

"I'll spend my time on the top fifteen," he told Newton. "You can decide on the rest." He was joking, of course, but his assistant wasn't sure. "Seems more than fair – that's only seven for you."

"But you probably have yours done already."

"I've got the whole roster done, Steve." He smiled and handed him a hand-written list of twenty-three players, broken down by position. The only visible change was a line through Charlie Scott's name. Alfred Bauer had been added to the *DEFENDER* group. This obviously wasn't a new list. "What do you think?"

"You've had this done since Honduras?" Newton asked, amazed again at his boss' efficiency.

"Sure, it's not like we don't know these guys. Besides," he added, "we both know the bottom three or four won't play anyway. Let's focus on the ones that will."

"This is a secret, right?" Newton asked, just to be sure.

"If you tell anyone, I'll deny it – and fire you," Willy smiled his *crazy* smile.

It looked like Willy would get everything he had asked for, but it was still early. He seemed to have it all under control, but one question lingered in the back of his mind. *Was Brandon Rafferty still the man to lead this team?*

The USSF staff's requests were well-received and they had a plan in place in just over two weeks. On February 1st, a tentative schedule was announced with great anticipation:

DATE	OPPONENT	LOCATION
3/26/82	Holland	Los Angeles
3/31/82	Mexico	TBD
5/12/82	Uruguay	New York
6/2/82	Romania	Girona, Spain
6/5/82	Denmark	Girona, Spain

Schneider had noticed the difference during the first round of qualifying matches. When Rafferty was on the field the team held possession more, took fewer chances, and attacked less. Statistically it was fine, and they *were* winning, but he felt something was missing. It wasn't the Raff of old, who never met an opponent he didn't try to beat first. Something had changed and Willy thought he knew what it was. Rafferty's legs were OK, but his *brain* was too old.

Willy's research had led him to a simple truth: We are influenced more by our mistakes than by our successes. Makes sense since we will try to prevent further disappointment, but this little feature of the human brain caused Schneider to realize something very important. Soccer players will become less averse to loss (i.e., losing possession, missing a shot, etc.) as they age. Therefore, certain positions (like defenders and goalkeepers) were better suited to older players. And some were best filled by younger, less "experienced" people – especially attacking center midfielder!

It wasn't Rafferty's fault he had become a *safe* player, it was just his brain trying to prevent him from making mistakes. By contrast, Maxwell's orbitofrontal cortex simply hadn't grown tired of losing the ball yet. *Then again*, Willy thought, *Maxwell's brain didn't actually see much loss.* Still, he wasn't quite ready to hand over the reins to a twenty-one-year-old kid. Not just yet.

Of course, lots of other variables worked together to make one player better than another at a given position, or caused a certain player to perform at his peak at one position rather than another. But Willy knew that his attacking maestro had evolved into a benign option – and that didn't appeal to him. The problem was that you couldn't make other teams fear you with safe players.

The next few matches would surely help him decide, but he would have to wait seven weeks for the first one, and he had something else to prove.

Most of the thirty players called in to national team camp in LA arrived on Monday, with a few showing up Tuesday morning in time for training. Jimmy Maxwell and Marco DeSantis landed at Los Angeles International at 8 o'clock Tuesday evening. Both were frustrated by the delays they had endured, but Willy understood and didn't hold it against them. "Get used to it," Doc said to the younger player. *Nice compliment*, Maxwell thought. *I will.*

The Friday night match against Holland was highly anticipated by the media and was billed as a huge test for the US heading into the World Cup. Sure, this Dutch team was talented, but they were not the caliber of the teams from the seventies. Two years earlier they had been knocked out of the European Championships in the first round, and they had not even qualified for this World Cup.

Still, Willy thought this squad would provide a suitable benchmark for his team and he had a few surprises in store, as usual. He was interested to see how the newcomers would mix with a few old stand-bys, and looking forward to the media's reaction.

Much to the chagrin of the established soccer press, Schneider had left several experienced players off the team that had gone to Honduras for the qualifying tournament. Once again, they had called him arrogant, stupid, inept, and even unpatriotic! Until Team USA won the tournament – then, of course, all was forgiven.

For the Holland match, Willy called in five players who had been curiously left home in November. All were in their early thirties, but still performed well for their clubs. Church and Carmassi were forwards; Hagar, Montrose and Furnier were midfielders. Three would be in the starting lineup.

Church and Grey would start at forward. Montrose, Price, Rafferty, and Furnier would fill out the midfield. The back four was Mayer, Smith, DeSantis, and Espinoza. Arnie Mausser manned the goal. This was the oldest, or *most-experienced*, United States team Willy Schneider had ever put on the field. *We'll see what my critics have to say about this*, Willy thought.

The 62,000 fans in the Rose Bowl were stunned by what they saw in the first half. Holland seemed to be able to do whatever they wanted, and Team USA looked like they were lost. The Dutch won every loose ball, completed almost all of their passes, and shot without pressure. The four-nil score could have been much worse.

At half-time, Schneider made three changes: Rick Davis for Church, Carmassi for Grey, and Hagar for Frank Price. He had a plan.

The game ended with seven goals – all scored by Holland. The second part of Willy's experiment was the most important. It was in five days. In Mexico City.

The United States National Team boarded the plane for the flight to Latin America's busiest airport immediately after the match in Los Angeles, since Willy wanted them to experience the altitude and air quality Mexico City was famous for. Club America had offered to let the squad use their practice field for training. Barrett Grey still had connections there.

Willy also wanted to get the team out of the country for another reason. He knew the press would hound them, and him, mercilessly if they stayed in LA. It was a distraction he didn't need at this point. The Mexican Federation had even requested that the match be played in LA, but Schneider was adamant. His experiment wasn't complete.

For Wednesday's match at the cavernous Azteca Stadium, Schneider put his older players on notice – he was going with the kids against Mexico. Several private meetings later, Willy knew his plan had hit a nerve. Nearly all the most-experienced members of the player pool protested. He heard it all:

"They'll get killed here."

"*We've* got to get ready for the World Cup."

"This isn't the time for tryouts!"

"You're gonna get yourself fired!" That was his favorite.

Schneider posted the starting lineup in the locker room after Tuesday's training, and a few heads were shaking when they saw it. Jackson in goal. Mayer, Bauer, Doc, and Espi in back. Ford, Maxwell, Petrov, and Mishigawa in midfield. Grey and Davis at forward. This was the *youngest* team Willy had ever fielded, and he was going to use them to prove his point. At least he hoped they would.

Since the American soccer boom began in the 1950's, each decade had introduced a new type of player. The early days were dominated more by pure athletes since there just weren't that many technically adept players to go around. The sixties saw the introduction of more technical players, and the US team became much more enjoyable to watch, though they still couldn't compete on the world stage. The younger players were starting to show promise, though.

As the game spread throughout the country, bigger, stronger, and faster became the chosen traits once again, and athleticism won out in many regions, although this time everyone had at least a minimum skill level. The 1970's opened with a nominal pool of national team players and ended with an explosion of talent.

The Texaco Premier League was finally becoming what its founders had envisioned at the beginning. It was a profitable, entertaining, nationwide league - and it was helping to produce a very talented crop of American players. From Leslie King and Brandon Rafferty to Bobby Smith and Billy Ford, the United States National Team saw an influx of outstanding athletes who could play soccer with the best in the world. The trend was very promising.

The eighties had introduced Willy Schneider to the future of US soccer, and its name was Jimmy Maxwell. In decades past, an American with his skill set would always have been too small or too slow to shine on the international level. He would languish in obscurity while hearing *if you were only a little bigger, or faster, or...something.* Not with this guy.

While everyone agreed that Maxwell was easily the most technically gifted player they had ever seen, he was also deceptively fast and strong. This combination, plus his incredible field vision, made him a game-changer that US Soccer had never seen. Schneider hoped Maxwell was the harbinger of things to come and not just a fluke, but he had to concentrate on the team he had right now. His master plan was about to be tested.

Five days after the Mexico match, Willy Schneider was the half-time guest in the booth of *ABC's*

Monday Night Soccer. His popularity had been restored after the last friendly, but many in the media were confused about his ultimate plan.

"Coach Schneider," Meredith started the grilling, after some pleasantries, "exactly what *were* you trying to prove last week?" It was the question every reporter had on his mind, but none had been granted an interview since the team had returned from Mexico. *Dandy Don* got right to the point.

"Well, Don," Willy smiled and answered, "I wasn't trying to *prove* anything. We just needed to get some games in before the World Cup." Willy didn't think highly of his questioner. "But, Coach..." Meredith drawled.

"Surely, you know what my partner here is getting at," Cosell interrupted. He sensed Schneider's contempt, and thought the National Team coach would be more likely to relate to another highly educated man. "You played Holland and suffered a Promethean defeat with a roster of grizzled, mature veterans in the friendly confines of an American stadium, then you took a troupe of relative novices into the formidable cavern of football madness known as *El Azteca,* and soundly thrashed a Mexican side that was virtually unchanged from the one that nearly defeated the US in Honduras only a few short months ago." He took a breath. "In the span of six days you have both exposed the soft white underbelly - and shown the razor-sharp teeth - of the United States' ever-expanding player pool."

Willy sat, mouth closed, for half a minute. He was waiting for a question.

"Was that your plan?" Meredith asked, inserting himself back into the interview.

Schneider leaned forward to the microphone on the desk and took a deep breath before answering.

"Yes."

There were a few seconds of silence while the professional talkers waited for more from the professional coach, but Willy made them wait.

"But at the end of the day," he finally continued, "I need to find twenty-two warriors who are going to give 110% for their country. Guys who will take it one game at a time, and leave it all on the field."

Cosell rolled his eyes and concluded the segment before being reminded that there is no "I" in team.

Around the world, several members of the United States National Soccer Team were giving their coach imaginary high fives.

The four-nil drubbing of Mexico had done both things Willy Schneider had hoped for. His young guns were more confident than ever knowing that they had the support of their coach, and some of the veterans were finally convinced that their services were no longer needed on the National Team. His final roster choices would be judged in a new light, with much less outcry – public or private.

There were seventy-two days until the World Cup.

205

Chapter 18

READY

The overnight flight from John F. Kennedy International Airport was designed to allow sleep, or at least some rest, before arriving in Spain. The spacious accommodations on board the Lockheed L-1011 also provided plenty of running room for the younger members of this trip. TWA had tried to seat the families with small children in one section, near the rear, but the attendants were unable to harness the energetic offspring of the fathers who were supposed to be the main attraction.

Making matters worse, Leslie King and Billy Ford were actually officiating the footraces down the parallel aisles of the airplane. The *Coca Cola*-fueled kids finally ran out of gas around ten o'clock, New York time - about three hours after takeoff. They would arrive in Barcelona in seven hours, where it would be a little after eleven in the morning. From there, they would take a bus to Lloret de Mar on the Catalan coast.

Willy Schneider had been married once, for two years, shortly after he began his coaching career. His longtime girlfriend thought it was finally time to settle down, and he just couldn't find a good enough reason to disagree. She assumed his schedule would calm down now that he was taking a *real* job. His playing days behind him, Willy could finally focus on his real passion. Gillian assumed it would be her, but she was wrong.

As a player, Willy had to devote lots of extra time to his craft. Physically average, he was almost always the least-athletic member of the teams he played for. Willy Schneider just *worked* harder than everyone else. He was the kind of guy who ran every sprint in practice as hard as he could, and didn't care if he came in last (which happened frequently), or first (usually late in the day when his teammates were spent). He hated the fact that he couldn't practice more, workout more, or run more. His mind would push his body as far as it could go – but there were always limits. Physical limits.

But, as a coach, Willy could work much longer. The limits imposed on the player (fatigue, pain, exhaustion) were almost non-existent to the coach. Even as a junior assistant, Schneider was always the first to arrive and the last to leave every practice or match. He watched videos until late at night, and scouted other teams and players in detail unknown to the profession. That was how he developed his unique outlook on personality characteristics – and ruined his marriage.

Both would say it *just didn't work out.* Gillian Schneider took some consolation from the fact that the "other woman" in this case was Willy's job, and they remained friends. She and her new husband would be his guests at the World Cup.

While Willy Schneider had no family of his own, he certainly understood the importance of the concept to his players. He was genuinely interested in the happiness of the men who played for him, and they all appreciated it. The *Hotel Rosamar Maxim* in Lloret de Mar was designed to make everyone as happy as possible during what could be a very stressful month and a half. The beautiful resort was less than a goal kick's distance from the beach, and all the players' families were on hand, or soon would be, to share the experience. Carolyn Ford couldn't take the whole month off from her job as co-anchor at WXYZ, but she would try to join them for the first game on June 15th.

Even the single players liked having the wives and kids along, since it lightened up the whole environment. They felt sorry for some of their opponents, whose coaches would prohibit any contact with spouses, children, or girlfriends during the World Cup. A few would eventually regret their strict mandates, but they thought it would help their players stay focused on the task at hand. Willy knew better.

The bulk of the team arrived at the hotel on Saturday, May 29th. Several players were involved in the final club match of the season, the Winston Cup Final, and were scheduled to arrive late on Monday the 31st. Schneider was glad his players were having success with their clubs, but he was a little anxious about having four potential starters show up two days before their first friendly in Spain.

The Los Angeles Aztecs made it interesting, coming from two goals down to tie the game with less than a minute of regulation time remaining, but New York dominated the overtime period and Giorgio Chinaglia scored the winner, as he famously predicted. A 4-3 sudden-death thriller was the perfect ending to a season that had had relatively few surprises. Willy had hand-picked his replacement to make sure.

Prior to the start of the 1981-82 season, most sportswriters had picked the Cosmos to win the double like they had two years earlier. Only one club had ever won both the Texaco Premier League *and* the Winston Cup in the same season – and New York had just done it for the third time! Since the US Open Cup was renamed for the popular cigarette in 1971, only five different teams had lifted the trophy presented by the President of RJ Reynolds, and the New York Cosmos had now achieved that feat three times in the last six years.

Alexi Mayer, Rick Davis, Juan Espinoza, and Brad Mishigawa arrived, by taxi, at the training facility in Girona just after the charter bus dropped off the rest of Team USA for Tuesday's practice. Traveling halfway around the world didn't always go as scheduled. Their twelve-hour trip had turned into a two-day fiasco. The friendly match with Denmark was the next day, and Willy had to adjust his roster accordingly.

The rest of the squad had been training at the Girona FC facility since Sunday, two days earlier, and were getting comfortable with each other. Most had been on the field together in Honduras and, of course, they were still fit from the club season – some more so after a few days of rest.

Girona had just finished the season in 18th place (out of twenty teams) and were dealing with the sad reality of relegation. After two years in the Third Division, Franc Fabregas' team had self-destructed during the last ten matches and was now on the way to the Regional Catalan League. He had sworn to stay on, as had most of his starters, to get them back to the national level. Willy Schneider knew Fabregas from an internship he had done at Barcelona several years before.

Franc bled Barca red-and-blue from birth. He had grown up down the coast in Arenys de Mar, played his entire career for the Catalan giants, and now lived in Lloret de Mar and coached at Girona FC. While Willy admired his soccer-playing abilities, they actually became friends while attending a Christmas party in 1972.

Fabregas was an investor in a very popular, and profitable, restaurant in Barcelona where the team held all its holiday festivities. Midway through the Christmas dinner, he was surprised to find the American coach in his kitchen helping prepare the paella. Being a closet chef himself, Franc joined in and before long the two were grilling sausages and lobster, and sharing a bottle of fine tempranillo.

Nearly ten years later, they remained good friends and the Spaniard had offered his team's facilities before Schneider had even asked. Perfect. It also allowed Willy to share some recipes, and fine wine, with his good friend who lived on the hill overlooking Lloret de Mar.

Denmark had never qualified for the World Cup Finals despite having several world-class players. This squad had defeated Italy 3-1 in qualifying, but finished third in their group and would have to wait four more years for another chance. They were among the teams in this Cup's *too good to not be there* group, joining

Holland, Bulgaria, and Mexico. But, as Willy Schneider liked to say – *That's why we play the games.*

Diminutive forward Allen Simonsen led the attack for the Danes like he did for FC Barcelona, where he had been named European Footballer of the Year in 1977. The twenty-nine year old striker was joined by team captain Morten Olsen, who anchored the defense. The center back plied his trade with Anderlecht in Belgium, and was highly regarded in Europe. This squad would give Team USA a run for their money. There was a great deal of pride at stake for the Danish players and the Americans were playing for starting spots. Motivation would not be a problem on either side.

Schneider changed his roster around a little to accommodate the players who showed up late. Making adjustments was what he was paid to do, and Willy didn't give it a second thought.

Arnie Mausser was in goal. Steve Garvey, Marco DeSantis, Pooky Bauer, and Paul Molitor across the back. Billy Ford, Brandon Rafferty, Stoyan Petrov, and Frank Price in midfield. Leslie King and Barrett Grey at forward. A pretty strong lineup, with considerable talent on the bench.

Two additions to this lineup had missed the qualifying tournament in Honduras for different reasons. Molitor had strained his right knee only a week before Willy had announced his roster for training camp and was left home to recover. Garvey was among the group of veteran players that Schneider still liked, along with Ozzie Smith. They had been left off the qualifying roster, reluctantly, to allow a few new guys to get a shot. The risk was paying off.

The only other change to the roster was the addition of Marcus Allen, a talented young striker from California who had impressed Willy during his first few months as head coach. He hadn't seen much national team action in the last year, but Charlie Scott's injury - and a flurry of goals just before the end of the TPL season - made him a suitable backup forward. His age also convinced Willy to bring him along, if just for the experience.

Closed-door matches are rarely something a national team coach takes part in on purpose. This one, and Saturday's match with Romania, was designed to be just that — a practice game viewed by families and coaches only. Willy wanted to be able to control as much as possible, and right now his priority was preparing his boys for their opener with Hungary on the 15th. He still had a few spots to sort out.

By halftime, he had decided on a starting lineup for the Hungary match. He would use the Romania friendly to finalize his 18-man roster.

After two days of very intense training, Team USA held their second scrimmage and Willy had his squad picked by the time they had played the first thirty minutes. Things were going smoothly until Johnny Jackson punched David Knott in the head.

The Romanian attack consisted mainly of long, high passes played to the head of their six-foot-seven-inch striker. Willy was more interested in trying to figure out how to break down their defense - something the Hungarians had barely managed to do in qualifying - and his attention was elsewhere when Jackson came out to clear a cross from his box.

213

As the American goalkeeper attempted to parry the ball away, he was *nudged* by the big Romanian and missed the ball completely. Unfortunately for David Knott, Jackson caught him square in the face with a knockout punch. The concussion would keep him off the field for at least a week, and he would surely miss the Hungary match. Schneider was forced to find another starting center back.

This decision was easier than most, since he had had a difficult time choosing who would be Doc's partner anyway. Willy knew either Knott or Bobby Smith could do the job and he was satisfied with his new lineup. He had ten days to prepare for the Hungary match, and he already had his starters chosen. Of course, he would keep that to himself until the last minute.

During a mid-week scrimmage against Girona FC, Willy appeared to be trying out different combinations every ten or fifteen minutes. He didn't like what happened when he subbed Maxwell in for Rafferty. Willy Schneider had never second-guessed himself before. *This may be tough*, he thought.

He had no idea.

Chapter 19

HUNGARY

"Finally!" Steve Newton was thrilled – and relieved. The package was late, and he had been worrying non-stop for the last two days. A quick inventory, then he could present his prize to the team. In style.

Willy Schneider had gathered the team for their standard debrief after the final training session before the match with Hungary when Newton made his entrance. "Ta-da!" He announced himself to the surprised crowd.

"Gentlemen, behold your new uniform!" Even with the extra twenty pounds their assistant coach was carrying, the red-white-and-blue strip looked fantastic.

"At last," Billy Ford said with a smile, "a *red* jersey." The Federation had unexpectedly switched the National Team to a blue home jersey for the 1974 World Cup campaign, and players and fans had been complaining ever since. Sam's Army actually refused to change to blue, even though they could have cashed in on the sale of new jerseys and t-shirts. "We're *supposed* to wear red," Billy added, for effect.

Newton had been working behind the scenes with the team at Adidas for months, and was proud of his secret accomplishment. He never imagined how hard it would be, but now he was enjoying the payoff.

"What happened to the stripes?" Leslie King asked. Among the ideas floated from the designers was a vertical red-and-white striped top, meant to be worn with navy-blue shorts. The nylon prototypes even looked like denim.

"Yeah, and that blue jersey with the stars?" Brandon Rafferty asked.

"No stripes, no denim shorts, and," Newton answered emphatically, "NO BLUE JERSEYS!" Adidas had built a blue home jersey with white stars in the pattern as a joke, just to throw off the players. Steve Newton was determined to create a kit the team would be proud of, but wanted it to be a surprise. His timing was perfect.

"This is our home strip: Red jersey, white shorts, and blue socks." Newton made his formal presentation. "And we'll wear all white for our away matches."

"Jimmy, I'll bet you like that," King said to Maxwell, since his Real Madrid club team wore an all white uniform. "Might look good on you."

"Unlike you, old man," Maxwell replied with a smile, "I look good in anything."

The team was ready for tomorrow's match and now they had new uniforms to show off. It had been a long road, but everyone was glad the day was finally here. Willy's planned starting eleven had remained healthy through the last few training days, and he was confident his boys could get the job done. Let the games begin.

In summer, daytime highs normally hovered around 90°F in Elche and Tuesday, June 15th, was no exception. Both teams had arrived the day before and were given ample time to train on the lush turf at the town's stadium, which seated 19,000. Luck of the draw had put the Americans in a tough first round group, but it had also sent them to a relatively low pressure location for their first match.

Two days earlier, in Barcelona, Argentina had been embarrassed by Belgium in front of 95,000 fans, becoming only the second cup holders to lose the first match of their defending campaign. The one-nil result at the Nou Camp proved that Group III was up for grabs, and that even the defending World Cup champions were not immune to having a bad day. It was a small blessing to be away from the most glaring media, especially for the first match of this tournament.

The United States began the 1982 World Cup with Arnie Mausser in goal; Alexi Mayer, Marco DeSantis, Bobby Smith, and Juan Espinoza across the back; Billy Ford, Brandon Rafferty, Stoyan Petrov and Brad Mishigawa in midfield; Leslie King and Barrett Grey at forward. Willy Schneider had a few subs in mind, but was more than willing to let the game decide the changes he would make. He was one of the few coaches who didn't plan out his substitutions before a match – it just didn't make sense to the man who planned everything else in minute detail.

This Hungarian squad was confident, experienced, and rested. Head Coach Kalman Meszoly was a veteran of two World Cups as a player, and had assembled a team that won the most competitive group in Europe on their way to the finals. Like Willy Schneider, he knew his boys could play with anyone. Consistency was the problem for Hungary, though, and Meszoly hoped his team would be ready for the challenge today. He feared his players were looking ahead to Friday's match with Argentina and may underestimate the Americans.

If the Hungarian defense was discounting the American attack, they didn't show it with softness. For the first fifteen minutes, Grey and King were kicked and elbowed mercilessly. The United States held the edge in possession and goal attempts, but hadn't created a good chance until Leslie King was tripped up just outside the penalty area in the sixteenth minute.

Billy Ford's pass to King's feet had enough pace on it to allow the striker to hold his ground without having to step to the ball, and the Hungarian defender was surprised by his quick turn. Leslie King was going around him as the ball passed between his legs, so the defender did what came naturally – since he couldn't stop the ball, he stopped the man.

King face-planted well inside the box, but the Danish referee decided the foul was committed a yard outside and, as usual, Brandon Rafferty stepped up to take the free kick. He was still the captain and everyone knew he was going to take this, but some doubts were starting to creep into the picture.

It was no secret that a new playmaker had arrived on the scene in Honduras. Seven months earlier, the soccer world had taken notice of the brash young American who had already become a star in Spain. Pre-World Cup opinions from many of the US-based sports "experts" centered squarely on the question of who should be pulling the strings of the Team USA attack. Unfortunately, for Rafferty, he had to read or listen to most of those pundits – and few were on *his* side.

The five-man wall was set, protecting the left side of their goal, and Raff stepped up to take the shot. The right-footed blast caught a Hungarian midfielder square in the forehead – he was in the middle of the wall – and deflected straight up. A defender headed it out and Hungary was off on a quick counter-attack. On the field, there was no time to reflect.

On the bench, though, three different sets of eyes glanced at Jimmy Maxwell when Rafferty's shot smacked into the wall. He tried to ignore them, but he knew he could do better – if he got the chance.

As if Hungary's strike force of Andras Toroksic and Gabor Poloskei wasn't potent enough, they could call on Laszlo Kiss, if needed. Meszoly would routinely rotate these three through the forward spots - and any combination could produce goals. This counter-attack almost produced the first of the match.

Poloskei had beaten Juan Espinoza down the left side and was headed for goal. As the American defender recovered, the Hungarian striker cut the ball inside and quickly blasted a shot to the near post with his favored right foot. Arnie Mausser dove to his right and got enough of his fingertips on the ball to deflect it out for a corner kick. Crisis averted, but the Hungarians smelled blood and were finally attacking with the fury the American defenders had heard about.

Doc knew how to handle these situations as well as anyone in the world and he quickly assessed the environment. His mates were on their heels, and they were scrambling to find their marks before the corner kick was taken. Their opponents were eager to get into the penalty area, sensing a goal – or at least a good chance. This would likely be a turning point in the match. One way or another.

"Billy, stay high!" DeSantis tried to be discreet, but the crowd noise forced him to yell his instructions to the speedy midfielder. "And take Les with you!"

Both were veterans, and knew how to play this right. Instead of running up to the midfield stripe before the corner was sent in, they meandered around the space between the penalty area and midfield until the ball was played. The back who was marking King noticed that he hadn't gone all the way back to help defend, drifting instead out near the right touchline. None of the Hungarians saw Billy Ford slip out wide left, fifteen yards into his own half, even though three defenders stayed central, near midfield. All their other players were in the box looking to score the first goal.

Doc was confident in his team's abilities and resisted the desire to call extra players back to defend just because the momentum had shifted slightly. He knew times like these afforded great opportunity. Willy Schneider had summed it up with a quote from Sun Tzu: *Pretend inferiority to encourage your enemy's arrogance.* Lure them in by pretending to be scared, appearing anxious and disorganized. All while setting up the attack that would catch them by surprise.

220

Despite his frantic screams to "Pick up your marks!", Marco DeSantis was orchestrating Team USA's first goal of the 1982 World Cup.

By the time the corner kick was played into the penalty area, all the American players were on the same page. Arnie Mausser leapt high and snagged the ball with both hands at the edge of his goal box. His next job was to find Brandon Rafferty streaking downfield, straight down the middle of the pitch. The keeper tossed a twenty-five yard pass to Rafferty, who took it on stride and played a long ball toward the left corner flag.

Billy Ford was behind the Hungarian backline before they knew what was happening, charging directly toward their goal with the ball on his left foot. Two of the defenders tried to cut him off as the third dropped back to cover the space in front of the goal. He didn't see Leslie King's run to the far post until Ford's pass went between him and his goalkeeper.

At the end of a sixty yard sprint, King simply tapped the ball into the net. As usual, he jogged back to the center circle as if he did this every day. A few words to his father, and he was ready to go again.

20th minute: United States 1, Hungary 0.

The American attack didn't produce another chance in the first half and most of the remaining time was spent in the middle third of the field. Hungary's forwards squandered two near-chances, and both teams went into the locker room at halftime knowing this one was far from over.

The US lineup was unchanged for the start of the second half, but Hungary made one substitution. Laszlo Kiss, the young striker Meszoly had discovered playing for his old club, replaced Toroksic. Kiss had scored two goals in his national team debut against Norway a year earlier and he was being called upon more and more to put the ball in the net for his country.

Willy Schneider was curious to see how his midfield would respond to the directions he had given them in the locker room. At times, he felt some of his guys got lost in the rhythm of the possession game and forgot to look for attacking possibilities. The Hungarians had kept ample pressure on Rafferty and, while his *pass completion rate* was always high, he wasn't looking forward enough to satisfy his coach. Willy was worried that his tiger lacked teeth, and he knew what he needed to do if the problem persisted.

Eight minutes into the second half, Laszlo Kiss made his presence known. He took a pass from his center back, turned, and quickly chewed up the space in front of him. Petrov was occupied with his mark, and no one stepped up to pressure the striker. He struck the ball with all he had from thirty-two yards and caught Mausser completely by surprise.

The American goalkeeper was ten yards off his line when the ball went over his head and clanged off the crossbar. Luckily for Team USA this one went out for a goal kick, but Kiss had caught their attention. Doc made sure he knew where the striker was for the rest of the match. This guy didn't need a second chance.

At the fifty-five minute mark, Willy called out to Rick Davis and Jimmy Maxwell. After a brief discussion of desired tactics, both warmed up and checked in with the sideline officials. Both would be playing in the World Cup for the first time, and reveled in the moment while waiting for the referee's signal to enter the match.

"Five bucks for first foul," Maxwell said to Davis, who wasn't sure what he meant. He slowed it down for his confused teammate.

"I'll bet you five bucks I get a foul before you do," the playmaker challenged the striker. Davis was as competitive as anyone else on this team, so he accepted the wager. He also knew that forwards tended to draw more fouls than midfielders, so he thought he had an edge.

The subs were called on during a stoppage in play at the sixty-first minute. Hungary had a throw-in near the US bench, and Maxwell waited until the ball was in the air before plowing into the back of his midfield counterpart while attempting to get his head on the ball. The whistle blew; the American helped his opponent up; and the referee signaled for a free kick.

As Davis ran back to help defend, he noticed Maxwell's smile.

"Cash only, please," he said.

"But you fouled HIM!"

"Yeah, what did you *think* I meant?"

Ten minutes went by with more midfield possession and a lack of attacking opportunities for both teams. With time running out, the Hungarians were desperate for an equalizer but were afraid to leave their backline exposed. This was just the first match of the round, and goal differential may be important in deciding who moved on to the second phase. After the seventy-fifth minute, it wouldn't matter.

When Brandon Rafferty felt pressure in the midfield he routinely turned away from it and played the ball back or square, relieving the pressure and keeping possession. Jimmy Maxwell had a different way of dealing with pesky opponents.

Maybe due to so many years of being man-handled by older brothers and their friends, or maybe just because he could, Maxwell took a great deal of pleasure in punishing defenders. It was never enough to simply beat someone with a nice move or a bit of trickery – those were nice, but Jimmy wanted to inflict pain.

A year earlier, he had been asked about his personal goals during an interview with a Madrid sports reporter.

"I've been told," she began, "that you approach each game with the goal of making your opponents cry. Is this true?"

"Yes," he stated for the record. "And to have their girlfriends asking for my phone number." The reporter wasn't sure if he was kidding.

He added, "I know it won't *always* happen, but that's my goal each game." And he flashed her *the smile*.

By the end of the interview Maxwell had her number.

A good attacking player always knows how much pressure is being applied, where it's coming from, and where his teammates are. Great attackers know the same things – but don't have to think about it.

When Brad Mishigawa made the pass to Maxwell, the American playmaker felt his opponent on his left shoulder, trying to step in front and intercept the ball. Mish had directed the pass to Jimmy's right foot, farthest from the defender, so the Hungarian had virtually no chance of getting to it. When the ball arrived at his boot, Maxwell stepped back, away from his opponent, causing him to lunge forward.

He could only try to grab the American's jersey as the ball went between his legs, momentarily regretting that he would surely get a yellow card for his actions. Instead he got a stiff-arm to his chest, which knocked the wind out of him and sent him toppling back onto the turf. As the ref yelled "Play on!", Maxwell was off to the races. *Just because someone wants to foul you doesn't mean you have to let them.* Coach Franklin's words echoed in his head.

Jimmy Maxwell was forty yards from goal with Mishigawa racing down the right side and Grey and Davis jockeying for position at the edge of the penalty box. He knew one of the central defenders would step up to try to stop him, and he also knew they would regret it. The one marking Rick Davis was the first victim.

Since Maxwell was charging ahead unobstructed, someone had to do something. The defender left Davis at the eighteen and attempted to force the midfielder to the right, towards Mishigawa. Jimmy chopped the ball with the inside of his right boot, behind his left foot, and barely broke stride as he eluded the defender. He was one-on-one with the keeper and twelve yards from the right post.

Barrett Grey stayed wide on the left, waiting for the right time to move. When Maxwell entered the penalty box, the striker stayed even with him, watching all the defenders turn to watch his teammate. It was almost too easy to sneak in and tap the ball into the net when the playmaker whipped the pass between the last defender and the goalkeeper. Three hands went up, hoping for an offside call that would not come. Grey and Maxwell high-fived and jogged back to the center circle.

75th minute: United States 2, Hungary 0.

Two points secured and a place on top of the Group III table.

The team would travel back to Lloret de Mar after showers, take tomorrow off, and begin preparations for the next match. Saturday's contest with Belgium, between both first-match winners, would be crucial. The winner would certainly be moving on.

Chapter 20

BELGIUM

Breakfast was sparsely attended, due to the late-night arrival from Elche. While most of the team slept in, Johnny Jackson and Alexi Mayer were in front of the television in Jimmy Maxwell's room, watching tapes on the video cassette recorder they borrowed from the hotel. Alexi had come through with a half-dozen tapes of MTV, which wasn't yet broadcasting in Europe.

Maxwell hadn't been exposed to the new video music network when he was back home over Christmas break – the farm still didn't have cable. It was probably better that he *didn't* have access to the 24-hour cable channel, since he could barely pull himself away from videos of the Go-Go's, Prince, and Joan Jett. He was always a big fan of *Don Kirschner's Rock Concert* and *The Midnight Special,* two shows where you could actually *see* the artists performing, but this was different. These little films set to music were very cool, and he was thrilled when Alexi presented him with the tapes.

"Now I'll have to buy a VCR," Maxwell said, after opening the box. "You know, they're pretty expensive."

"Shouldn't be much of a problem," Mayer replied, "on your salary."

"Thanks buddy. I suppose I owe you something for this?"

"Nothing really," Alexi smiled, "I'm just staying with you in Madrid for two weeks after the World Cup." He couldn't think of a better place to spend his off-season.

"Done," Maxwell agreed without hesitation. "We can watch MTV together."

"Uh, I was hoping for a little more than that!"

"Just kidding," Jimmy said. "We can hang out with some of my friends – *and we'll party like its 1999.*" His high-pitched *Prince* voice made both of them laugh.

"Good idea, I've seen some of your friends in the tabloids."

"Careful," Jimmy added with a wink, "you may end up in there, too."

I'd be OK with that, Alexi thought, as he bit into a delicious room-service pastry.

Wednesday proved to be a great day off, if only to watch the matches in other groups. Algeria stunned West Germany in the opening game of Group II, winning 2-1. Bryan Robson scored the fastest goal in World Cup history, and his English squad went on to defeat France 3 to 1. Even Honduras, who was seriously out-gunned by Spain, played to a 1-1 draw. It was good to see a fellow CONCACAF team fare better than expected.

Training was focused and intense on Thursday. Friday's session, in Elche, was just as focused but not as physically demanding. Everyone knew what was riding on the next match.

Saturday's meeting with Belgium had become more important than anyone had imagined. Prior to the tournament, the focus was on the first match with Hungary – and, of course, the big game against Argentina. Now it seemed likely the group would be decided *before* the Argentina match – and Willy looked forward to resting some players, if possible. They would have to get past Belgium to make it work.

As the unlikely winners of Europe's Group 2, Belgium had *scored fewer* goals than both France and Ireland, and had *allowed more* goals than France and Holland, but they had been disciplined enough to pull out wins when they had to. Schneider knew he couldn't take this team lightly, and decided to go with his *original* starting lineup. David Knott had fully re-covered from his concussion and would resume his spot next to Doc in the center of the defense. Willy felt he and Smith were interchangeable and liked going with fresher legs when possible.

Weekend games were scheduled to be played in the afternoon, allowing for a larger television audience. It also made for a less pleasant soccer environment, with the kickoff temperature at 94°F – fifteen degrees higher than their opener. Fortunately, the small stadium in Elche had decent air circulation and didn't hold the heat in like some of the cavernous big-club arenas. The Americans arrived in town the day before, as they had for the Hungary match, and held a light training session on what had become their new home pitch. It felt familiar, which was always good, but players sometimes mistake the feeling for lucky. It was definitely not lucky on this day.

229

Team USA began the game dressed in their all-white strip, just as they had against Hungary. For all Steve Newton's fanfare over the new uniforms, the Americans were drawn as the Away team in each of their three first-round matches. *Just another reason to get to the second round*, he thought. Their opponents wore all red.

Belgium took possession at the kickoff and immediately dropped the ball to their backline. Erwin Vandenbergh was drifting as high as he could while his teammates passed the ball from left to right. The striker was out wide near the left touchline when the right back launched a sixty yard pass behind the American defense. Arnie Mausser ran to intercept it at the corner of the penalty area, but the ball took a funny bounce just as he was about to scoop it up.

Vandenbergh saw that the keeper was going to get to this one first and, especially this early in the game, planned to avoid making any contact. He curled his run to be nearby in case Mausser fumbled the ball, but was caught by surprise when the American unexpectedly dove into his path. He tried to leap over him, but the striker caught the keeper in the head with his left knee. Both players ended up on the turf, but all the attention was paid to Mausser, who was not moving.

The ball was still in the American goalkeeper's grasp as he laid face-down, unconscious, on the grass. Medical technicians were immediately called onto the pitch and Johnny Jackson began to get ready, even before Schneider requested it.

"I hate going in this way," Jackson said to Maxwell, who was helping him warm up. "You think Arnie's gonna be OK?"

230

"He'll be fine," Jimmy replied, "until you steal his spot for good."

Before Johnny could react to that statement, his friend said, "You've got to be the best keeper you can be, and let Willy make the hard decisions."

"I know, but..." he still felt bad. Inside the fierce competitor was actually a really nice guy.

"But nothin', you don't want to spend the rest of the World Cup on the bench with me, do you?"

"Good point," Jackson said with a smile, "you aren't very good company."

"Exactly," Maxwell agreed, and his friend checked in with the officials.

Three minutes into their second match, Willy was replacing his starting goalkeeper with a twenty-five year old who had all of *four* international appearances under his belt. He knew the Belgian attackers would try to test his young keeper quickly. He thought (and hoped) Johnny Jackson was up to the challenge.

It took only five minutes for the first test, and Johnny lived up to Willy's expectations. A corner kick whipped into the goal box forced the keeper to take quick and decisive action, punching the ball away amid a crowd of red jerseys. He handled the pressure, and dished out a little punishment for good measure. Two Belgian players were left on the ground, assuming they had crashed into each other. They hadn't.

231

The first half-hour of the match was ugly. Neither team was able to establish much of a rhythm, nor maintain possession. Ten minutes before halftime, though, Belgium would take advantage of a rare mistake.

Brandon Rafferty routinely came back into the defensive third of the field to receive the ball from Arnie Mausser, but Johnny Jackson wasn't as comfortable playing him the ball in the middle of the field. Jackson motioned for Raff to go wide for the ball, but the captain insisted on staying central. *No problem*, the keeper thought, *Espi's out wide.*

Johnny had picked up an ambitious through-ball and, after allowing his teammates to recover, looked for an outlet pass. First choice was downfield, but no one was open so he tossed a side-arm pitch to Espinoza out near the right touchline. Rafferty had come back into the center of the defense and wanted the ball, but Juan saw some space in front of him and chewed it up, as usual, while Raff moved into the area behind him for support.

The right back was looking for Grey, but couldn't find a path to get the ball to him, so he turned his back to the approaching pressure. Rafferty was thirty yards away, between him and their goal, and Espinoza made the simple pass to him in order to keep possession and restart the attack. Neither of them saw the Belgian forward lurking ten yards away, but it wouldn't have mattered if Rafferty's first touch hadn't let him down.

When the ball arrived at his feet, Rafferty was mugged by an opponent who had timed his run perfectly. He stole the ball and left Raff in a heap, wondering what had just hit him. Two seconds later,

232

Franky Vercauteren was one-on-one with the backup American keeper, and he placed his right-footed shot just inside the far post. The twenty-five year old Belgian was having quite a tournament – he had the assist in their win over Argentina, and now he had a goal of his own.

35th minute: Belgium 1, United States 0.

This was not what Willy had hoped for, but he had confidence in his players and he knew they could work it out. Steve Newton, on the other hand, was not as calm.

"What was Rafferty thinking?" he asked to no one in particular. "You've got to pull him, Willy." Schneider wasn't paying attention to his assistant's rants. He had a bigger problem to deal with. His *fresh* center back was on his knees at midfield, throwing up.

David Knott looked terrible. The recovery from his concussion was just assumed, as they always were, to take a week. He had been fine in training and Willy had kept a close eye on him, just to be sure. Maybe the combination of the added pressure of the match and the oppressive heat had caused an adverse reaction, but none of that mattered right now. "Smitty, you're in." Willy wouldn't wait to see if Knott was going to shake it off, not that it looked likely.

Bobby Smith was ready to go in a few seconds and entered the match with less than ten minutes remaining in the first half. He and Doc had worked the backline together enough to know how each other moved. Both men just tried to stay central and direct

233

those in front of them until they could get in for halftime. *No mistakes*, Smith said to himself, *no mistakes*. They made it with little effort.

The priorities were almost always the same for a halftime break: Hydrate, discuss weaknesses, hydrate, discuss opponent's weaknesses, hydrate, rest, and hydrate some more. With today's heat, everyone was grateful for the cases of chilled Gatorade provided by their sponsor. The liquid refreshment claimed to be a major factor in the US squad's superior fitness late in games, and had paid several players to endorse their cause. Billy Ford had been the first to sign on.

Ford's first nationwide ad campaign, *Mama made me fast, but Gatorade keeps me runnin'*, paid him $75,000. He reportedly offered to claim that Gatorade *also* made him fast – for another twenty-five thousand.

Willy Schneider pulled Brandon Rafferty aside after his captain grabbed a drink. "What's going on, Raff?" he asked, knowing he didn't need to elaborate.

"I'm OK, Willy," he replied. "Just had a bad couple of minutes."

Schneider was not convinced. He was an expert at reading people – and Raff wasn't a very good liar. He put his hand on Brandon's shoulder and said, "You'll let me know if you're having any problems, right?"

"Sure, coach," he said as he turned away. Brandon Rafferty had never felt like he did right now. As he approached his thirty-third birthday, he was suddenly starting to feel old. His play with the Patriots was still solid, but he knew it was largely due to the influx of new, younger, players around him. He had been going forward less and less, taking up a position deeper in the midfield and using his vision and leadership to direct traffic. He had become a field general, but Willy needed him to be a warrior. He wasn't sure if he could still do it, but he had to try.

The team doctor informed Willy that David Knott was being transported to the local hospital for evaluation, making him a little uneasy about having started him in the first place. "His parents are in the stands," he informed the physician, "make sure they know." They would reluctantly leave the game and escort their son to the nearby medical center. Arnie Mausser was already stitched up, showered, and dressed in his training gear. He was feeling better, and held an icepack on the inch-long gash in his head to keep the swelling to a minimum. He knew the drill.

"You doin' alright?" Johnny Jackson asked Mausser, as soon as he could get to him. Everyone wanted to check on the veteran keeper as soon as they entered the locker room.

"I'll be fine," Arnie said. Then he smiled at the young man who would be claiming his position. "It's on you now," he said quietly, "make the most of it."

"Thanks," Johnny replied, somewhat relieved, "I will."

Being down a goal at the half wasn't such a big deal to these guys – they had been around enough to know that they had the ability to come back against any team in the world, especially a mid-level European squad that hadn't exactly overwhelmed them in the first forty-five minutes. *Just stick to the plan and the goals will come*, Willy reassured them.

235

Both teams started the second half as they had ended the first, personnel-wise. The big difference was how the Americans applied pressure. Willy had asked his forwards to back off the Belgian defenders for the first period, retreating to their own half of the field each time their opponents regained possession. They would start the second half like banshees, jumping all over the backs that had become complacent. It paid immediate results.

For the first forty-five minutes, Leslie King and Barrett Grey would quickly drop back to their half when the ball was lost, allowing the defenders to look around for a target with no pressure. Six minutes into the second half, Billy Ford played a through-ball to Grey, but led him by a yard too much. The Belgian sweeper picked up the loose ball and paused to look for a teammate to pass to. He wasn't aware that the American striker had continued his run and, before he knew it, he was on his face and Grey was racing into his penalty area with the ball.

As Barrett Grey approached the opposing goal, he expected the keeper to come out and cut down his angle. The striker's plan, as usual, was simple: Let the goalie come out, cut the ball to the side, shoot into the empty net. Jean-Marie Pfaff had a different idea.

He planned to commit early, and charged out at Grey. His objective was clear when he dropped to the turf two yards inside the eighteen-yard line just as the American was entering the penalty area.

Barrett Grey saw the keeper slide before he had decided which way to go, so he just chipped the ball over him and continued his run. Pfaff did what he had to do - he reached up and grabbed Grey's boot as he was

236

stepping over the keeper's outstretched arms. As the ball rolled harmlessly toward the goal, the referee blew his whistle and pointed to the penalty spot. When Grey picked himself up, he noticed that the ball had stopped about a foot from the goal line.

Brandon Rafferty was calm as he placed the ball on the spot, twelve yards from the Belgian goal. If there was one person on Earth who would not be shaken by this situation, it was *Captain America*. Raff had been the go-to guy for penalties since he took over Team USA's playmaking duties nearly eight years before. His record of fifty-six national team goals was somewhat tainted by the fact that forty-two were scored from the penalty spot, but his teammates were glad they had a guy who could be counted on to finish a PK when it really mattered. The players knew it wasn't as easy as it looked, and Brandon Rafferty made burying a penalty kick look very easy.

"Make Jackie proud!" Leslie King shouted to his buddy as both teams prepared for the shot.

Jack Rafferty's dad smiled at the inside joke. Two days earlier, while kicking a ball around on the beach near the hotel, Jack had proudly announced to his father his intention to become a striker – instead of a midfielder.

"Ugh! Why would you want to do *that?*" Brandon asked, with feigned disgust.

"I want to score goals," the youngster replied, "lots of goals."

"*I'm* a midfielder, and *I* score lots of goals!"

"*Real* goals, Dad," the boy was serious, "not penalty kicks." Brandon was sure Uncle Les had put him up to this – at least, he hoped so.

Raff closed his eyes for a few seconds, like he always did, and visualized the scene playing out in front of him. He knew this keeper always dove to his left when facing a right-footed shooter, so he would place his shot in the other side of the net - with enough venom, of course, to beat him in case he suddenly changed his habit. It happened just like the American captain imagined it and, for the forty-third time in his long career, Brandon Rafferty converted a penalty for his country. *Now is the time*, he thought. When he could catch Willy's attention, he gave him a subtle signal. "Maxwell," Schneider called down the bench, "get warm!"

53rd minute: Belgium 1, United States 1.

Schneider wasn't sure what was wrong with Rafferty, but he knew that his captain wouldn't give him the universal signal for a substitution unless he needed to come out. He had appeared fine before the penalty. *Maybe he injured something on the kick*, Willy thought. He was considering how to use his last sub anyway, and this swap was tops on the list.

Maxwell jumped right in and began probing the Belgian defense with his usual pinpoint passes to the feet of his forwards. Noting how the backs played their marks and where they would allow space would enable him to take advantage of them later. He covered the field from side-to-side twice before an opportunity presented itself. It was just a matter of time. Six minutes, to be exact.

238

Leslie King was covered by Luc Millecamps, the backbone of the Belgian defense. He wasn't as big as King, but he was strong and determined. The center back had been applying high pressure to King's back for nearly an hour, and Les was getting tired of it. Jimmy Maxwell saw a way to make him pay.

The first step would be to get Grey out of the way. Then he would use the defender's pressure against him. All three Americans were inside thirty yards of the Belgian goal, with five defenders in the vicinity. Billy Ford and Brad Mishigawa were staying wide as Maxwell had requested during his trips across the pitch. Stoyan Petrov was back near the midfield stripe, just in case.

King was pushing his mark as far back as he could, and the Belgian was trying to hold his ground. Maxwell made eye contact with him and quickly turned away, ball at his foot, and headed toward Barrett Grey. Grey was outside the penalty area on the right side when he saw Maxwell start his run. He did what came naturally – he cleared out. As Grey moved wide, he opened up space and Maxwell turned into it. King's defender was holding on tight, keeping the American from backing him down. Perfect.

Jimmy Maxwell knew just what to do. A simple change-of-pace move froze his mark and he blew past him with the next step. Twenty-five yards out, he was driving straight at King, who was still holding his ground, just inside the eighteen. Two defenders converged as Maxwell slipped a little pass into the space to the right of the striker. King stepped forward as the ball rolled to his left, feeling the pressure from the Belgian on his back. Then he spun and struck the ball with his right foot - directly at Pfaff, who made a brilliant "self-defense" save.

After playing the perfectly weighted pass, Maxwell made a beeline for the left post – preparing for the pass if King decided not to shoot. His run was well-timed and aggressive, which was usual for the Real Madrid playmaker. He would score his first-ever World Cup goal, and the game-winner, because of it. He would also be a little embarrassed.

Leslie King could crush a soccer ball, and with the added power from his spin move, this shot was nearly lethal. The Belgian goalkeeper was lucky to get his hands up in time to keep the ball from hitting him square in the mouth. His deflection would have sent the shot well outside the penalty area - if it hadn't hit Jimmy Maxwell in the face and caromed into his goal. Bad luck for Belgium.

60th minute: Belgium 1, United States 2.

"Beautiful shot," King was the first to con-gratulate him, but Maxwell wasn't quite sure why. After a few seconds, the crowd noise gave it away.

"Did that go in?" Jimmy's face had taken the full brunt of the deflection. He was still seeing stars and wasn't quite sure what had happened. Brad Mishigawa grabbed him around the waist and lifted him in the air as the rest of Team USA celebrated what would be the winning goal of their second game of this tournament. None of them would have bet that Jimmy Maxwell would score his first World Cup goal with his nose. He shook it off and got back into his groove.

240

The next half-hour showcased the playmaking abilities of the young American, as he picked apart the tired Belgian defense. Barrett Grey's first-time shot in the 74th minute ricocheted off the post, and he and King were unlucky not to score until the match was almost over. With less than two minutes remaining, Leslie King took a pass from Maxwell, faked the return part of the give-and-go, and turned on his man. Since they were twenty-five yards from goal, the defender backed off, allowing King to unleash a rocket that caught Pfaff by surprise. In his defense, the Belgian keeper didn't have a chance to keep the shot out. It was well-placed in the upper corner and blew past him before he had time to react. *A Leslie King Special*, according to the reporter from the New York Times, who had seen several.

89th minute: Belgium 1, United States 3.

The referee's whistle announced full-time a few minutes later. The American players shook hands with their opponents, who were somewhat shell-shocked. They had beaten Argentina less than a week before and had taken Team USA too lightly. Now they were in trouble – Argentina had demolished Hungary the day before and was now tied with them for second place. Belgium would have to make the most of their next game against Hungary.

Once they entered the locker room, the high fives started flying. It was a good result, worth maximum points, and Willy was pleased that his boys had overcome some adversity along the way. Brandon Rafferty was on the trainer's table when Billy Ford found him.

"Hey bro," he said, quietly, "you alright?" He knew Raff too well to accept a cursory answer to the affirmative. He would want the truth, and his friend knew it.

"My calf just stopped working," he pointed to his right leg, which was partially obscured by a clear plastic bag of ice. "They think it may be torn."

"But ..." Billy wasn't satisfied with the answer.

"But we'll know more in a few days," Raff cut him off, and offered a strained smile to his old friend.

This would be the hardest part of his plan.

Chapter 21

ARGENTINA

Chang was the one Jimmy had worried about the most, probably because of the mysterious nature of his culture. He was born on a rice farm near a poor village in China and sent to the government soccer school when he was barely ten years old. The Communists had invested a great deal of time and money in his development, forcing him to make the most of his natural talents, which had been discovered by an astute physical education teacher. The combination of speed, strength, and agility would normally have qualified the boy for the state-run gymnastics academy, but his size made him better suited for soccer. He had no choice but to be a great player and a billion countrymen were depending on him.

There was also *Uche,* who would use his soccer skills to escape the mean streets of Lagos, Nigeria, where he grew up homeless and orphaned, and *Josmer* from Haiti, whose parents had sold him to a scout when he was nine - for three chickens and a hambone. But there had never been a *Diego* .

Chang, Uche, and Josmer - like many others - were fictional characters who actually lived in the imagination of Bobby Maxwell. He would tell his boys stories to motivate them, always ending with the same line:

"When you meet up with this kid," he would say, "are you going to be ready?" He would look them directly in the eye, forcing them to think about their answers. "He practices every day to make himself a better life, to escape poverty, and he WILL be ready."

While Bob and Dale listened and surely understood, their little brother took every word to heart. Jimmy Maxwell was determined to be ready. The thought of a kid his age having to work for a living wasn't hard to do, since growing up on a farm was similar to indentured servitude, but he realized the difference in the approach to their chosen profession. While he frequently played for the pure enjoyment or the satisfaction of mastering a skill, he knew his competitors were forced at an early age to train like professionals. He worried about these imaginary opponents every day but now, for the first time, he would face one in person. On Wednesday, June 23rd, 1982, the United States would take on Argentina, and their newest star – Diego Armando Maradona.

It had been fifty-two years since the Americans played Argentina in a World Cup. No one on the field today was even born then – Willy Schneider excluded. Under normal sports reporting guidelines, the story would have focused on the match in Uruguay at the first World Cup in 1930, where the Americans were dealt a 6-1 defeat in the semi-finals - but this wasn't a normal matchup.

There were two main stories leading up to this match, with each getting considerable coverage in the Spanish media. First, many experts were surprised at the success, thus far, of the Americans. Most noted that a much-needed win by Argentina was not a foregone conclusion, as this US team seemed to be getting better as the tournament progressed – and that this wasn't the same Argentina from four years ago, when they won the World Cup. Second, they were busy comparing the two new stars of Spanish football. Jimmy Maxwell was just coming into his own with the US National Team, but he was already well-known in Spain. In contrast, Diego Maradona was known throughout the soccer world as a great young talent, but was especially interesting to the local press following his recent transfer to FC Barcelona.

Madrid's *El Pais* featured a pullout section entitled *"Un Duelo de Numero Diez"* that looked like a boxing magazine's "tale of the tape". They listed each player's vital statistics, including height, weight, appearances, goals, etc. The number that stood out most was the Argentine's transfer fee – Barcelona had reportedly paid $7 million!

While this was an obvious attempt to generate interest in two of the game's rising stars, the press could not overestimate the fan frenzy involved in this match. Real Madrid's star playmaker was leading his country against an Argentina squad which boasted Barcelona's newest signing. The *Madridistas* hated Maradona already, just as the *Barca* fans were preparing to hurl their usual insults at Maxwell. With their own national team assured a spot in the second round, Spanish fans now had a new game to care about.

Nearly thirty thousand fans filled the Estadio Jose Rico Perez for the final match of Group III, with those pulling for Argentina outnumbering the American supporters by a 2-to-1 margin. The Sam's Army contingent covered most of the South stands in red,

245

while large swaths of the crowd donned the light blue of Argentina. The red-and-blue FC Barcelona colors outnumbered them both, and many of the remaining fans were wearing the traditional white of Real Madrid. All had one thing in common – their hope that both teams had come to play.

The seaside city of Alicante was nearly the same distance from Spain's two largest cities, but had its own distinct style. Five days earlier, they had hosted the Argentina-Hungary match where the South Americans had bounced back from their first-game defeat in style. The locals had embraced Maradona and his teammates during their stay, evidenced by all the photographs in the tabloids. Using a bustling resort city as your base during a major tournament could have its distractions and, for those looking for excuses, could contribute to a team's demise.

Due to the result of the Belgium-Hungary match a day earlier, both squads knew what they needed to do to move on to the second round. Argentina had ridden the emotional roller coaster during that game, but the 1-1 score meant that they needed a win or a draw in order to avoid an early exit. Team USA was assured at least second place, even with a defeat. The Spanish fans were enthused when they saw Willy Schneider's starting lineup.

Team USA fielded the same group that had finished the Belgium match four days earlier, with two changes. Leslie King was replaced by Rick Davis, and Pooky Bauer was in Petrov's usual spot, at defensive mid. Barrett Grey was the other forward; Ford, Maxwell, and Mishigawa filled out the midfield; Mayer, DeSantis, Smith, and Espinoza were in front of Johnny Jackson. This was definitely not a second-string lineup.

246

Bauer was given a special assignment: Mark Maradona out of the game. Willy told him to do whatever it took to contain the Argentine playmaker - within the rules, of course. Pooky's athleticism would prove a difficult challenge for his opponent, and Schneider was curious to see how Maradona would react to being hounded by a defender who was bigger, stronger, and at least as fast. Stoyan Petrov had picked up a slight ankle sprain in training and, though available, could use the rest. *Not a bad backup*, Willy thought.

The first twenty minutes resembled a heavyweight boxing match, with both sides poking and prodding, looking for a crack in the other's defenses. With few exceptions, the ball was knocked around the middle third of the field while providing little in the way of an attacking threat. Then Argentina's new Number Ten saw an opening.

Maradona was used to being closely marked - standard fare since the Under-17 World Cup a few years earlier when he led Argentina to the trophy. He was already well-known for his ability to take advantage of the slightest opportunity, using his dazzling skill and agility to make the most of his limited chances. At the twenty-five minute mark, he saw his first chance of this match and put his team up.

While Pooky Bauer was doing a fantastic job of keeping the ball from reaching Maradona, the crafty Argentine playmaker knew he could take advantage of the high pressure – if the right situation arose. Mario Kempes, star of the 1978 Cup, saw what his young teammate wanted and faked a pass to Maradona's feet. As Bauer stepped up to intercept, his man turned and headed for goal.

247

Kempes slotted a diagonal pass between Pooky and Bobby Smith, toward the left corner flag. Johnny Jackson shifted over to cut down the angle, and noticed two Argentine attackers charging into the penalty box – looking for the crossing pass that didn't come. Maradona's left foot hit the ball with his first touch and he blasted a shot between Jackson and the left post.

The American had violated the Goalkeeper's Golden Rule – *Never Get Beat Near Post*. He was leaning to his left, also looking for the cross, when the ball was struck and couldn't shift his weight back in time. He felt awful, but was comforted by Bauer while Argentina celebrated.

"That was my fault," Pooky said, "won't happen again."

"I should've had the post covered," Jackson replied, head down, hands on his hips.

"I know," Bauer got in his face. "That's why Arnie told me not to let him shoot. My bad." They both managed little smiles. "C'mon, back to work!"

25th minute: Argentina 1, United States 0.

Bauer stepped up his pressure on Maradona, and by half-time the referee had whistled him for three fouls that left the Argentine playmaker writhing on the ground in excruciating, game-delaying, agony. Pooky's job had gotten more difficult since the goal, due to his opponent's desire to waste time after every perceived infraction. Fortunately, the Bolivian official was growing tired of the simulated injuries that had suddenly afflicted the South Americans. While leaving the pitch for half-time he told both captains that he would not stand for it any more.

Argentina's strategy for the second half was decidedly different, and they appeared to be content to pack it in and hold on to their one-goal margin. The Americans were not going to go down without a fight. The night air was cooling as the play was heating up.

With most of their team playing defense, Argentina's goal was going to be difficult to penetrate. Willy's boys knew how to level the playing field against this type of tactic. They would play for set-pieces, especially corner kicks.

Even when a team pulled most of their players back to defend in numbers, most of them would revert back to the standard set-piece defense that they spent weeks practicing. Argentina was recently criticized for their poor form on set-play defending, and the Americans felt they could capitalize on their weak zonal marking. Since attacking down the middle wasn't working anyway, Team USA would try to use the flanks more often, increasing their chances of a corner kick.

The Argentine defense had done a terrific job of stifling Grey and Davis - and had been lucky a few times, as well, when Maxwell bounced a free-kick off the post and Billy Ford missed an easy shot from eight yards out. The second half was proving to be frustrating for both team's attackers, especially for Maradona. He was consistently stripped of the ball by Bauer, or prevented from receiving it altogether. This half, though, his cries to the referee were ignored. It was about to get worse.

Twenty minutes into the second period, the Americans were awarded their fifth corner kick after a spectacular save pushed Barrett Grey's header over the crossbar. Previous attempts had been disappointing, but the odds were in their favor as the number of free kicks grew.

Jimmy Maxwell placed the ball in the left corner for the third time tonight, and looked for possible targets. This time, his strike was precise and Marco DeSantis met the in-swinging kick at the top of his leap and buried the ball in the back of the net. Grey's attempt was still fresh in their minds, so two defenders had decided to concentrate on *him* - which left Doc one-on-one. At this level, a mistake that small often made all the difference.

66th minute: Argentina 1, United States 1.

For the next fifteen minutes, Argentina seemed to have a renewed sense of purpose and pounded the American defense. If not for several acrobatic saves, the score line surely would have tilted back in their favor. The attack stopped when Diego Maradona momentarily lost his mind.

With just under ten minutes left to play, Argentina's number ten was dispossessed by Bauer - again - a few yards outside the US penalty area. The tackle was fair, but Maradona was dumped to the turf - again. This time, instead of rolling several times and holding his shin, he reached out and kicked Bobby Smith square in the knee, dropping him instantly. He had had enough.

Unfortunately, for Argentina, the Bolivian referee was only four yards away and looking directly at the carnage on his field. He had witnessed the whole scene and was momentarily stunned. After two or three seconds, which seemed longer, he blew his whistle and reached in his pocket. Diego Maradona was shown the red card and ejected.

Petrov came in for Smith, and Pooky Bauer dropped back to the defense. At this point, both teams were content to let the clock run out. The match ended 1-1, sending the United States and Argentina to the second round.

While Doc was being interviewed following the game, he overheard the conversation between Diego Maradona and a horde of reporters:

"It is so unfair that I was sent off," Maradona charged, looking like he was about to cry.

"The ref was right there," a reporter pointed out the obvious, "he SAW you kick their defender!"

"But I meant to kick *Bauer*, not Smith," he explained. "I was ejected for something I didn't *mean* to do!" The room filled with laughter, but Maradona was serious. "That's not fair!"

As Group III winners, the United States was placed in Group C with Italy and Brazil. The South American champions were certainly a force to be reckoned with, but Italy had advanced without winning a single game! Three draws, and one more goal than Cameroon, had put them through. Surprising no one, Brazil had won all three of their games.

Argentina would be playing Poland and the Soviet Union, two teams that were unimpressive in the first round, in Group A. The defending World Cup champions were favored to move on to the semi-finals, but would have to play Poland without their suspended star.

The next two days saw all the first round matches completed. England, the only other unbeaten team, was placed in Group B with West Germany and Spain. Austria, France, and Northern Ireland would make up Group D.

Chapter 22

ITALY

For the Americans, the second round would begin on Tuesday, June 29ᵗʰ, following a weekend off for the twelve teams still involved. Willy Schneider gave his charges two days of rest after the Argentina match, and most spent the extra time lounging around the hotel in Lloret de Mar. Two of the players made a little road trip.

Alexi Mayer had been looking forward to visiting Madrid since he had first heard Jimmy Maxwell's tales of the night life in the Spanish capital. As a member of the New York Cosmos, Mayer had plenty of opportunities to enjoy big-city entertainment, but his new friend had painted such a vivid picture he had to check it out for himself. Perhaps, as a native of the Big Apple, Alexi was immune to some of the more exciting aspects of his hometown. Or maybe it was all the talk of Brazilian supermodels.

The two had Willy's permission to take the train to Madrid and return in Maxwell's car. *One day there, get a good night's sleep, then drive back – very carefully!* Schneider was initially concerned about the drive, but he reminded himself that Maxwell actually lived here and had been navigating the Spanish roadways for the last three years. His real concern was what the two of them might be doing with their *spare* time, but he trusted them enough to know they would be OK.

The train ride was long – nearly four hundred miles – and boring. Maxwell slept most of the way, but Alexi Mayer was too excited to sleep. Jimmy had set him up, telling him about the girls who lived in the apartment next door and their friends who loved to drop in for friendly visits.

"I called Carmen before we left," Jimmy confessed, "so she could pick up some groceries." She lived next door, and loved cooking for the young American.

"She *cooks* for you?" Alexi asked, with a great deal of interest.

"Sure. Cleans my place, too," he added. Alexi imagined what she must look like – and smiled. "We should arrive just about dinner time. Perfect."

As expected, their train pulled into the Atocha Railway Station just after six o'clock. Maxwell's apartment was only a ten-minute cab ride from there, and taxis were plentiful this time of day on a Thursday – especially if you were a celebrity. When they piled in, the driver said something to them in Spanish, and Maxwell answered with a laugh. Alexi didn't understand a word of it.

"What was that all about?" he asked.

"He was just giving us a hard time for not beating Argentina." The cabbie was a die-hard Real Madrid fan, which meant two things: He certainly knew the young man who just got into his taxi, and he hated Barcelona – and by extension, Diego Maradona. "He'll try to refuse my money," he added, "so *you* pay, and act like you don't understand."

A few minutes later, they pulled up in front of a stylish apartment building in a newer section of Madrid, just northwest of downtown. Two universities were within walking distance, and the neighborhood was bustling with activity. Alexi was hungry, and hoped Jimmy's girlfriend was a good cook. They took the stairs up to the third floor, where they were greeted in the hallway by two middle-aged women.

"Jimmy!" both screamed with Spanish accents. They immediately rushed to the tired Americans. Maxwell was showered with hugs and kisses, which sort of spilled over to Alexi, due to his close proximity. Neither complained.

"Come in," the dark-haired woman said, motioning to Jimmy's apartment a few doors away. "I am Carmen," she introduced herself. "And this is my friend, Elsa. You must be Alexi."

"Yes, Ma'am," he replied, with a laugh. "It's good to meet you both."

Carmen and Elsa led the way, and Jimmy grabbed the overnight bags. Alexi turned back and said, "Not what I expected, Jimbo."

"Trust me," he said in a reassuring tone. "Supermodels can't cook."

It's good to be home, he thought. They would stay in tonight and enjoy a home-cooked meal, then hit the road early the next day. Maxwell was itching to get behind the wheel of his new car, and there would be plenty of time to party *after* the World Cup.

Breakfast consisted of an assortment of fresh pastries, compliments of the girls next door, while Maxwell made coffee, espresso-style, for all three. Carmen gave Alexi fair warning.

"It's a bit stronger than you're used to," she said. "Not like that awful stuff in New York." Carmen had traveled to the United States several times and always complained about the lack of good coffee. "This is much better, but *be careful.*"

"Whoa!" Alexi agreed, reaching for the sugar and milk. "You aren't kidding."

"I'm going to open a chain of coffee shops back in the states when I retire," Maxwell said. "This stuff will sell like crazy." He had actually given it some serious thought.

"You're nuts!" Alexi replied. "Americans will never buy this – it's too... *European.*" They all laughed, especially Carmen.

After breakfast, and brief good-byes, Jimmy and Alexi crossed the street to the garage where Maxwell's new car was kept. Alexi had no idea what was under the tan canvas cover, but he had high expectations. He had asked several times, only to be told *wait and see.* It was time to finally see what all the fuss was about.

"Let me introduce you," Jimmy Maxwell said, with just the right amount of reverence, "to Rhonda." He removed the cover to expose his newest, and most-expensive, toy.

"She...is...gorgeous!" Alexi said quietly, almost to himself.

Maxwell's pride and joy was delivered just two days before the team started camp and they hadn't had much time together. The garage owner had offered to keep it for him since they had been hired to perform a complete inspection - and Jimmy paid well. He knew the mechanics would drive her a little but, of course, who could blame them.

"Nineteen-sixty-nine Chevy Camaro Zee-twenty-eight," Carlos the mechanic began, in passable English. "Two hundred ninety horsepower, 302 cubic inch, V-8," he was pretending to be a model at a car show, "Hurst shifter, twin Holley carburetors, cowl-induction, and she will do zero-to-one hundred in just over seven seconds!" He knew his stuff.

"He means kilometers," Jimmy added, for his teammate's benefit. "And she can do a quarter-mile in fifteen seconds." So did he.

"Let's hit the road!" Alexi was ready to go, excited about the mode of transportation. Both were anxious to get back to the team. The stakes were much higher now.

Italy had advanced to the second round out of Group I by tying all three of their games, and scoring one more goal than Cameroon. They were well-known as a national team that started slowly, but had the firepower to play with anyone in the world. It was assumed that they would be ready for the next match.

Paolo Rossi had been surprisingly quiet, which had the press wondering if he would be included in the lineup against the Americans. The twenty-five-year-old

257

striker starred for Juventus, who had just won their 20th league title in Italy's top division. Five of his club teammates were also a part of this squad.

Coach Enzo Bearzot was determined to win this group and move on to the semi-finals. He saw Brazil as the only team in the way, which made sense – the last time the United States played Italy, they were blown out. Bearzot did not know that a few things had changed in American soccer since 1975. Team USA would seek to take advantage of this oversight.

The second round had started a day earlier, on Monday, June 28th, with Poland surprising Argentina. Despite fielding ten players from the cup-winning squad of four years ago, Argentina was outplayed by the Poles and lost 3-0. Maradona's suspension may have hindered their attack, but the champions' defense was tired and Poland's Zbigniew Boniek made them pay, scoring all three goals himself. Not surprisingly, France beat Austria 1-0 in the other Monday match.

The Estadi de Sarria was the home field for RCD Espanyol, Barcelona's *other* club. Though Espanyol could claim to be their country's first club actually formed by Spaniards (instead of expatriates from other countries), they couldn't compete for trophies with the big boys. Their loyal fans didn't seem to mind, though, and routinely filled every one of the 44,000 seats for home games. All three Group C matches would be played here.

Based on the mood in the locker room, Willy Schneider could tell his guys were ready. Team USA was coming together nicely and the players were comfortable in their roles. Several expected to start every game, and an equal number didn't expect to play at all. Those left over knew they would get in when Willy needed them, and they trusted his decisions. The injury list hadn't grown since the Argentina match – but it hadn't shrunk either.

Rafferty was still unable to play, having been diagnosed with a severe calf strain. He had taken to mentoring Maxwell and the other midfielders, and was actually enjoying coaching more than he thought he would. Knott was out indefinitely and had accepted his fate. Still only twenty-five, he could easily be back for the next cup campaign. Arnie Mausser and Bobby Smith, on the other hand, worried they were spending their last World Cup on the bench.

The United States would start with Johnny Jackson in goal; Alexi Mayer, Marco DeSantis, Pooky Bauer, and Juan Espinoza in back; Billy Ford, Stoyan Petrov, Jimmy Maxwell, and Brad Mishigawa in the midfield; Leslie King and Barrett Grey at forward. This was their strongest lineup so far.

Italy came out, as usual, with Dino Zoff in the net. The forty-year-old goalkeeper was as fit and strong as ever – and was the oldest player *ever* to appear in the World Cup finals. He was a formidable opponent, having once gone over eleven hundred consecutive minutes without giving up a goal! His Juventus teammates, Claudio Gentile, Antonio Cabrini, and Gaetano Scirea, formed a wall in front of him that only gave up two goals in the first round. They were joined in the back by Fulvio Collovati of AC Milan. Paolo Rossi got the start, after all, and would look to prove his detractors wrong. He was paired up top with Fiorentina striker, Francesco Graziani. Giancarlo Antognoni, Gabriele Oriali, Marco Tardelli, and Bruno Conti made up the Azzuri midfield.

The Italians were the home side and wore their traditional blue jerseys, white shorts, and blue socks. Team USA donned white (again). Steve Newton was excited about the next match when they could finally wear the red jerseys. Kickoff was set for five-fifteen local time, and the weather was perfect.

Italy chose to start the match with an unusually *offensive* mindset. They had limited knowledge of this American team, but they did know that they were missing their starting goalkeeper and one of their center backs. Graziani and Rossi were pushed up as high as possible and tried to get behind their marks at every chance. Even with the additional pressure, the US defense had little difficulty with the Italian attackers. Team USA weathered the first twenty minutes with no trouble, then implemented Willy's *Phase Two*.

Schneider knew this Italian squad would come out one of two ways: Either their normal *catenaccio* style (with everyone behind the ball), or they would attack with abandon expecting to score early and often. He hoped for the first option, but made a game plan to work either way.

For the first twenty minutes, the American squad would mirror the typical Italian style – with all players behind the ball, all the time. If the Italians came out in a similar defensive posture, the US' style might encourage them to attack more, which, in turn, might open up some counter-attacking possibilities. If they came out in full attack mode, Team USA would be able to withstand the pressure with little effort. That was Willy's *Phase One*.

After sufficient time had passed, Willy hoped the Italians would become frustrated. It wasn't the first time they had seen this type of strategy – Peru and Cameroon had done the same thing in the first round and Italy hadn't responded soon enough, resulting in two draws. Schneider thought the Italian coach would misread the situation and assume that the Americans were bunkered in because they were afraid to push numbers forward against a superior opponent. Enzo Bearzot swore he would not be caught off guard again.

When the Italian midfield began pushing forward, Willy Schneider knew his plan would work. In their previous matches, the Azzuri had kept their midfield players fairly deep, only allowing one at a time to venture into the attack. This defensive strategy was useful against a team of equal or greater strength, but had been a waste against weaker teams. Willy knew his boys could take advantage of the Italian defenders in a fair fight, and after twenty minutes they would get their chance. The Italians' arrogance would be their undoing.

Italy was preparing for their third corner kick when the clock passed the appropriate mark. All the American players noticed and, without a word, made sure they were in position for *Phase Two*. The first two corner kicks had resulted in weak headers that Johnny Jackson grabbed with little effort. Each time he held onto the ball like it was solid gold, allowing several seconds to pass before punting it far downfield – to the waiting Italian defenders. That was part of *Phase One* and, as expected, the Italians had gotten used to it.

This time, instead of dropping all the way back to defend, Billy Ford crept out wide and Jimmy Maxwell stayed about ten yards outside the US penalty box. Ford would be the primary outlet option, Maxwell would be secondary. Leslie King was the best header on the team, offensive or defensive, and could not be sacrificed for this attack, but Barrett Grey would release when the ball was played – as long as it wasn't coming toward his mark. *A counter-attack of epic proportions* is what Willy had called for in the locker room before the game. His players were glad to oblige.

Graziani played the corner in from the left side, toward Marco Tardelli who was marked by Grey at the edge of the penalty area. The American striker leaped high and headed the ball to Maxwell, twelve yards downfield and to his right. Maxwell cushioned the pass with his chest, dropping the ball to his left side, and turned. He was fifteen yards from the touchline when he launched a seventy-yard pass to the feet of Billy Ford on the far side of the pitch, near the center stripe. Grey had started running after his clearance, and was crossing midfield when Billy took his second touch.

Willy Schneider used the term *helicopter view* in practice - often. He wanted his players to visualize how a team moved by imagining they were hovering above the field - where you could see team shape most clearly. He wished he was hovering above when both Italian central defenders shifted toward Billy as he played the ball on the diagonal behind them, into the path of Barrett Grey. Grey took one touch to control the ball at the edge of the penalty area and blasted a shot into the Italian goal. He had started the play inside his own eighteen yard box and had finished it with the biggest goal of his career.

22nd minute: United States 1, Italy 0

While the Italian coaches didn't seem too concerned about the goal, their players were visibly stunned. They hadn't seen this level of attacking skill from their previous opponents, and had assumed that the Americans would be just as overwhelmed as Peru and Cameroon. Doc did his best to make them feel even worse.

"Nice finish for a backup forward," he said to Rossi, in perfect Italian. "Number twenty-one, Maxwell, he's a backup, too."

Rossi just shook his head and jogged back to the center circle. Like most of his teammates, he hadn't heard of Grey or Maxwell either. He began to wonder if they had underestimated the Americans. It seemed like they had been set up.

Steve Newton was consumed with fear that Italy was going to unleash some awesome force on them after the goal. "Here it comes, Willy." He sounded sick.

"Here *what* comes?" Schneider asked. He looked sideways at his assistant coach, and smiled. "In case you didn't notice, they were hitting us with all they've got for the first twenty minutes. Bearzot made a crucial mistake, though."

"What's that?"

"My grandmother used to say it like this, 'it's only OK to mess with a dog's tail *if* you've got a plan to deal with his teeth'"

"He had no plan," Newton agreed with his boss.

"Worse," Willy added, "he didn't think this dog *had* teeth!"

The rest of the first half was horribly boring for the fans. Italy was now reluctant to send too many players forward, fearful of another American counter-attack. Team USA was content to keep possession and watch the clock wind down, only pushing the action when the situation was close to perfect. After forty-five minutes the teams left the field for the locker rooms, the score still 1-0.

As the players passed the benches, a group of Italian fans were chanting in unison, trying to get under the skin of one of the American players.

"JIM-MY CAR-TER!" They yelled at the top of their lungs.

"JIM-MY CAR-TER!" Over and over.

"Is that for you?" Brad Mishigawa asked Maxwell. He was trying to understand the significance.

"Yep," Maxwell replied, "the Barca fans started it last year after I scored a hat-trick against them. I suppose they think I should be offended."

"That's pretty funny," Mish laughed, and then stopped. "Wait a minute. You scored three goals against Barcelona!"

"Actually, this one was a *maestro* – left-foot, right-foot, and header."

"Dude," Mish asked, incredulously, "you name your *hat-tricks*?"

"Sure," Maxwell said, matter-of-factly, "makes it easier to keep track."

Both squads began the second half as they had finished the first. Lineup-wise, anyway. Coach Bearzot implored his players to get forward and grab the tying goal, but they could not penetrate the American defense while always looking over their shoulder for another US counter-attack. Willy had messed with their heads in a major way and he had his confirmation when the clock reached the sixty-minute mark.

Italy's substitutes were all in by the time the United States made their first one. Willy knew that swapping forwards for forwards wouldn't make a difference against his backline, especially since their subs weren't nearly as dangerous as their starters. His only concern was that Bearzot might bring on attacking players to replace defensive ones, but that didn't happen. Italian sub number three came in with a half-hour left in the match and Team USA knew it was over. All they had to do was manage the clock.

The basketball team at the University of North Carolina had their "four corners" offense, where the players would spread the floor and pass the ball around in order to kill off a game. Any soccer team with Jimmy Maxwell had a similar weapon at their disposal.

With Billy Ford and Brad Mishigawa spread wide, Leslie King and Barrett Grey as high as they could be, Stoyan Petrov deep in the center of midfield, and Maxwell roaming all over the field, the US National Team could implement their own stalling offense. The problem the Italians had was that Maxwell was nearly impossible to dispossess and, if they committed too many players to him, he always found an open man to pass to. Time expired with no doubts about which team had won.

"Barrett?" the reporter asked. "Your lone goal held up. How do you feel?" Since this was their first match in Barcelona, he hadn't interviewed any of the Americans yet.

"I'm just happy we got the win," Grey began his normal speech. "You know, we gave it 110%, and I think we got the result we deserved. It was a total team effort. The Italians deserve a lot of respect, they never quit. But, I think, at the end of the day, we just wanted it more." Then he smiled and walked away.

The reporter watched Grey enter the tunnel and exchange high-fives with a dozen laughing teammates, unsure if they were congratulating him on his goal or that awful interview. *These Americans are strange*, he thought.

Team USA would have to face Brazil in three days. Starting with a win put them in an excellent situation, but now the perennial favorites would certainly not take them lightly. Many prominent sportswriters had picked this Brazil team to win it all, and they would be rested and ready for the Americans.

Chapter 23

BRAZIL

The first FIFA World Cup was played in 1930. As the reigning Olympic champions, Uruguay was granted host duties and twelve other countries joined them to play in the inaugural tournament.

Argentina and Uruguay won their semi-final matches by identical 6-1 scores and met in the final on July 30th in Montevideo. The hosts had beaten Argentina in the 1928 Olympic final in Amsterdam and were determined to win the first World Cup on their home soil. 93,000 fans filled the Estadio Centenario for the match and saw the home side take the cup with a dramatic 4-2 victory.

Uruguay and Italy would each win two of the first four World Cups and West Germany would lift the cup in 1954 but, since then, one country has dominated world football. Brazil.

No other national team had ever won a World Cup outside their own continent, and Brazil has done it *twice*. Sweden 1958 saw the emergence of, arguably, the greatest player ever when 17-year old Pelé scored two goals against the hosts en route to a 5-2 victory in the final match. The Brazilians defended their crown in Chile in 1962 despite injuries to several of their stars, including Pelé.

267

Mexico 1970 saw the return of Brazil, with Pelé back in form amid a team of superstars. This squad is considered by many to be the best national team ever as their dismantling of Italy in the final proved.

Willy Schneider certainly knew all this, and more, about his next opponent but the interviewer felt the need to remind him. He really hated these pre-game press conferences.

"So," he smugly asked, "what do think of your chances?" Then the reporter shoved his microphone in Willy's face. His expression showed a great deal of artificial sympathy.

"I'd say our chances are very good," Schneider replied with his usual level of confidence. "Have you seen us play?" He turned the tables. Willy didn't accept the argument that his boys were inferior to anyone.

"Surely you know how impressive the Brazilians were in the first round," the reporter persisted, "Scoring ten goals while only allowing two!" He couldn't believe the American coach would disagree with him on this.

"Have you *seen* us play?" Willy asked again. "My guys have played Italy and Argentina our last two games. Brazil has played Scotland and New Zealand. My guess is that *we* are going to be ready." He was nearly out of patience.

"But, coach," he wouldn't let it go, "you must admit that Brazil's pool of players is *vastly* deeper than yours, right?" Perhaps, he thought, he had finally made his point.

"OK, I'll admit that."

The reporter was surprised by Schneider's response. Word around the press box was that the American coach was something of a curmudgeon. As the smile started to appear on his face, Willy added his final statement.

"Maybe their top hundred players are better than our top hundred," he sounded like the professor that he was, "but this game is played eleven versus eleven." He started to turn and walk away, but pointed at the Spanish reporter and added, "Please think about that."

The reporter actually did think about it - and wondered if it was too late to put a few hundred pesetas on Team USA.

The teams entered the Estadi de Sarria through the tunnel from the locker rooms looking like their respective countries' flags. Steve Newton's eyes filled with tears when he saw the American players walk onto the field wearing the red, white, and blue uniforms he had designed. The Brazilians wore their traditional yellow jerseys with blue shorts and white socks.

Forty-four thousand exuberant fans filled the stadium, many of them new supporters of the United States. The Spaniards had started partying before the game and planned to continue right up to, during, and (hopefully) after the Spain-West Germany match later that evening. Sam's Army was always raucous, and the Brazilians weren't called the *samba kings* for nothing. Barcelona was ready for a party and these two teams were prepared to be the main event.

Brazil had enjoyed eight days off since their last game, when they handily defeated New Zealand in Seville. Training had been loose and unfocused - until Team USA beat Italy three days earlier. Like the Italians, Brazil was ready to overlook their first foe and concentrate on the big matchup later in the round, but the upset forced them to pay attention to the Americans.

Head Coach Tele Santana made sure his players understood the gravity of this situation, constantly reminding them that this game against the United States would likely decide the group winner. *Italy*, he would say, *has self-destructed. We will win this group on July 2nd by defeating the Americans.*

Santana was also concerned that his team had had too much time off, and hadn't yet been adequately tested. Even against relative minnows like Scotland and New Zealand, they had struggled to control the matches, not to mention the early goals given up against both the Scots and the USSR. His style of full-blown attacking soccer was entertaining and difficult to contain, but the *jogo bonito* hadn't yet produced any significant results. He would start the same team that he had started against the Kiwis, nine days earlier.

For the first time as National Team coach, Willy Schneider would use the same starting lineup two games in a row. Due to the limitations placed on him by injuries, and the level of comfort he had with this squad, Willy left the lineup alone. After the Italy result, no one questioned his decisions.

The attacking prowess of the Brazilians was legendary, and this team was on par with any of their predecessors. Six different players had scored in the first round, totaling ten goals. Brazil's number ten,

270

Zico, led the way with three. Midfielders Èder and Falcão had two each, and even defender Oscar had one. Sócrates and Toninho Cerezo filled out the midfield and Junior, Luizinho, and Leandro were the other defenders. Serginho was listed as the lone forward, but veteran goalkeeper Valdir Peres was the only member of this team who didn't get involved in the attack.

Kickoff was set for five-fifteen local time - same as the Italy match. Marco DeSantis and Sócrates met at the center circle for the coin toss, which was won by the American. Doc chose to kickoff; both captains shook hands; and the referees prepared to start the game. It was time for Leslie King to satisfy one of his sponsors.

Just before the opening whistle, King motioned to the Mexican official to "hold on". His left shoe was untied and, as he knelt down to tie it, he flashed a little smile to Barrett Grey. Leslie King was fully aware of the close-up attention his new white boots would be getting from the massive international television audience. PUMA had delivered his new "Kings" a week earlier, but Les wanted to wait for the proper stage to debut them. He could not have planned it better.

When Pelé performed the same stunt in Mexico at the 1970 World Cup, soccer's version of *product placement* was born. PUMA became an overnight sensation and, since then, several World Cup stars have worn their boots on the game's highest stage - most recently Johann Cruyff in '74 and Mario Kempes in '78. The shoe company had hedged their bets in this tournament, ensuring Diego Maradona and several Brazilians were also wearing their cleats, but only Leslie King had the newest style.

271

His all-white "Kings" wouldn't even hit the stores for three more days, adding to the demand generated by a media campaign over the July 4th weekend in the United States. A lot was riding on Leslie King's performance, and he rarely disappointed when the stakes were high.

"I can't believe you are *actually* wearing those," Grey was embarrassed for his strike partner. The bright white boots looked almost radiant against his blue socks and the dark green turf.

"You're just jealous," King laughed and nodded to the ref. He was ready.

Willy Schneider assumed the Brazilians would come at them with everything early, hoping to set the tone and force the Americans to pack it in and defend with numbers. This time, though, Willy got it wrong.

In their previous matches, against lesser opponents, Brazil had looked almost lethargic in the early stages, giving up a goal twice in the opening minutes. Team USA had planned to pressure them early and try to force a mistake. Instead, their opponents had decided to play through the first part of this game by keeping possession and allowing their defenders to get comfortable with the American forwards before going on the attack. It back-fired on them in the tenth minute.

Despite answering Steve Newton's standard *Are you ready?* with his usual *Yep,* Jimmy Maxwell didn't feel quite right during warm-ups. His touch seemed off, *like my cleats are on the wrong feet,* he thought.

272

Granted, his *bad* touch was still better than most players' *best*, but it made him a little less confident in his playmaking abilities. Fortunately, this had happened to him before and he knew how to respond. He remembered Coach Franklin's speech from eight years ago like it was yesterday.

During a playoff game against Little Rock, Maxwell became frustrated with his touch. It seemed like every pass was just a little off and it was even difficult for him to maintain possession. His best friend, Chester Alquist, was on his case about it and the two were jawing at each other pretty viciously at halftime.

"Jimmy," Ken Franklin called him out, "two-touch only, and pick up your defense." He knew Maxwell was trying to do too much, and had a simple remedy. He also knew what his young playmaker would hear of that order.

"My DE-fense?" His voice cracked, which made everyone laugh and Franklin quickly replied, "I know your touch is off, but we can't help that. It happens. But you can always play hard defense." Simple as that. Then he added, "You too, Chet," just to be fair. Concentrating on their defensive duties and being forced to play quickly allowed the boys to simply *play* when they had the ball, which solved the touch problem. It also caused considerable difficulties for the opposing midfield, resulting in four unanswered second-half goals for the Mules - and an early exit from the playoffs for Little Rock.

Like a heavyweight title fight, the first minutes of this match were safe, calculated – and boring. Brazil's fans quickly tired of their team's frequent back-passes to keeper Peres when they felt any pressure.

273

The Americans tried to force the issue a few times, but neither team mounted a decent attack in the opening ten minutes. Then Zico thought he saw an opening.

Èder and Falcão had been patrolling the midfield looking for potential holes in the US defense. Zico was the playmaker on this squad and his teammates looked for him to create chances for them, even when they saw none. He thought he saw an opportunity to spring Falcão with a long ball over Juan Espinoza, but first he needed to pull the American backs far from their own goal. He had also grown tired of Petrov's high pressure in the center of the midfield and desperately wanted to get out of his range. The next time a ball was played back to the Brazilian defenders, Zico would make his move.

He simply pointed to his feet and Luizinho knew what he wanted. A quick check over his left shoulder confirmed that Petrov was not following him as he approached his defensive third of the field, and prepared to receive the fifteen-yard pass from his teammate. Zico should have checked over *both* shoulders.

Jimmy Maxwell waited for the ball to leave the Brazilian defender's foot, then bolted toward his opponent. Junior yelled "Man on!", but it didn't matter – Maxwell got there first and picked up the ball on a full sprint. Two touches later, his cross was headed into the back of the net by Billy Ford, who was possibly the only person on the planet fast enough to get to the pin-point pass. The Brazilians were behind again, but they had been here before.

11th minute: United States 1, Brazil 0.

"Nice steal," Petey high-fived his midfield partner. The two had become a force to be reckoned with, and were enjoying it.

"Thanks for loosening him up for me," Maxwell replied. He had never told Petrov about his tryout with St. Louis Busch – hadn't actually thought about it until now. The possibility of playing club soccer together was interesting. *I'll have to mention it later,* he thought.

Brazil was not a team to sulk when scored upon. Quite the contrary, they seemed to focus intently on their primary mission in life – scoring goals. While some of his critics complained about the lack of attention paid to the defense, Coach Santana felt that his squad could simply outscore anyone. He had yet to be proven wrong.

For a few minutes after Ford's goal, the Americans seemed to be playing short-handed. Brazil's precision passing suddenly found gaps in the defense, forcing Johnny Jackson to make three saves in a span of two minutes. Doc finally settled his backs down and Team USA was able to withstand the worst of the onslaught.

Pooky Bauer had started man-marking Serginho, which allowed Doc to play as a sweeper behind his three defenders. It wasn't their normal zonal style, but it worked for two reasons: Bauer was an incredible individual defender, and Doc was able to direct play on *both* sides of the field – which he did as well as any central defender in the world. The new system was working well in the back and the midfield was starting to hold their own against the Brazilians. The American forwards were finally generating some shots.

Leslie King had a chance to double Team USA's lead in the thirty-third minute, but sent his twelve-yard strike into the stands behind the goal. Two minutes later, Falcão sent a left-footed blast right at Jackson, who parried it over the crossbar. Both sides had several chances, but neither scored until Stoyan Petrov made an uncharacteristic mistake just before halftime.

Playing the lone striker role meant that Serginho often had to be like a low-post player in basketball, keeping his back to goal and holding possession while his teammates tried to get open. His strength and vision made him a star with São Paulo, and had cemented his spot on his national team. He was a true number nine, who could finish as well as set up other players.

Wearing the number ten meant certain things. Typically, it signified a team's playmaker that coordinated the offense and was their prime mover in the attacking end of the field. *Wearing the number ten for Brazil* was another thing entirely. Legends had worn that jersey and the whole world knew it. Rivelino had inherited it after Pelé retired and Zico was wearing it for the first time in a World Cup. Both of his predecessors had lifted the cup and the pressure was immense, but Zico was more than capable of filling his country's ten shirt.

As a boy in Rio de Janeiro, Arthur Antunes Coimbra was small and not particularly athletic. Nicknamed Zico, he would become a gifted midfielder who could score with either foot or set up a teammate for a goal. Hard work, determination, and a disciplined training regimen helped him become one of Brazil's greatest players and a star for his club, Flamengo. Chief among his talents was his ability to bend a free kick around a wall of defenders, earning him another nickname - the "White Pelé".

Pooky Bauer knew all about Brazil's number nine and had been stuck to him like glue. The striker was getting annoyed with the pressure and tried everything he could think of to create some space for himself, but the American stayed within a few yards wherever he went. That's why it made no sense for Petey to commit the foul just outside the penalty box.

Serginho posted himself up and Pooky took his position just behind him, always keeping the ball in sight. If a pass was delivered to him, the only option would be to drop it right back to a teammate since Bauer was too big and quick for him to turn on. Éder played a simple pass to the striker's feet and made a run to the right, while Petrov dropped to help cover.

When Serginho received the ball, he took a little touch away from Bauer to try and relieve some of the pressure. His move took him into Petey's path and the American plowed through him like he wasn't even there. The referee blew his whistle and pointed to a spot three yards outside the US penalty area, lined up with the right goal post. This was Zico territory.

"Petey, what are you doing?" DeSantis was livid. All the American players, and most of the rest of the world, knew how dangerous the little Brazilian was from this range. Worse, there had been no reason to foul Serginho at all.

"I didn't *see* him," Petrov tried to explain. He wasn't used to being yelled at.

"You can't.....not....." then the captain was interrupted.

"WALL!" As everyone looked at Johnny Jackson, they realized it was Pooky Bauer calling for their defense to get set up. JJ quickly assessed the situation, called for a five-man wall, and lined them up with the post on his left. The human wall would cover half of the goal and Johnny would be responsible for the rest. Zico, as expected, stepped up to take the free kick.

While Willy Schneider certainly understood the physics behind making a soccer ball bend, most players who could perform this feat knew only how and where to strike the ball to achieve the desired result. Zico's fans claimed his foot was blessed with a certain type of magic only available to those wearing the ten shirt for Brazil. Jimmy Maxwell would disagree, of course, but he would not get a chance to prove it this game.

The tallest American field players formed a human shield between the ball and the right half of the goal. It would be nearly impossible for anyone to put a shot over the heads of King, Grey, Bauer, Petrov, & DeSantis and make it dip under the crossbar from this range. Zico understood this – so he went around the wall.

Johnny Jackson didn't even see the ball until it entered his net.

43rd minute: United States 1, Brazil 1.

The half ended soon after and both teams entered their locker rooms feeling like they could win this game. Willy thought he might need to pick them up

278

after Brazil's late goal, but it wasn't necessary. They would soon be past it.

"Sorry, guys," Petrov apologized for his transgression, to no one in particular.

"No sweat, Pete," Brad Mishigawa replied for the group, "but I must say, that goal was gnarly!" He had the optimum angle to view Zico's shot. Heads were nodding all over the room – these guys appreciated greatness when they saw it.

"Still," Petrov needed to make sure they knew he was sorry, "I know I shouldn't have fouled there. It won't happen again."

Brandon Rafferty stepped into the middle of the room and pretended to puff on a cigar. With his free hand he pointed right at Petey, only two feet away, and said, "And now you know, and knowing is half the battle." Rafferty laughed. Alone.

"What is that?" Leslie King thought he should know if Raff was doing a movie or television character, but he didn't recognize this at all. Only Dennis Hutton knew who he was trying to emulate. His son was about the same age as Jack.

"G.I. Joe," the backup keeper shouted out, "from the cartoon!"

"Thanks, D," Raff felt a little better. Everyone else laughed at their former captain and got back into their halftime routine. *Mission accomplished*, Rafferty thought.

279

The second half started with the same players on the field for both teams. Brazil seemed to be a little more comfortable on the ball and was able to maintain possession for long stretches. Team USA held firm and let their opponents knock the ball around in the back or the midfield, but quickly shut them down when they tried to advance into the American defensive third. The game was starting to resemble a chess match, and both coaches felt they had the edge.

Tele Santana made one slight change to his team during the halftime break. Despite multiple attempts to drive through the middle of the American defense, the Brazilian attack was shut down with relative ease every time. Santana simply instructed Zico to look for his wide midfielders more often when they approached the American penalty area. Twenty minutes into the half, it would pay off.

While most of the defensive focus was on the lone Brazilian striker, Zico played a through-ball to Falcão who was blazing down the right side. His first-touch crossing pass was perfectly placed and Serginho's powerful header beat Johnny Jackson to the left side of the goal. Brazil had scored on their first chance of the half. Chessmaster Tele Santana thought of one word – *Check*.

66th minute: United States 1, Brazil 2.

Like their South American opposition, Team USA was not inclined to lie down and give up in this situation. As difficult as it would certainly be, they knew they had to dig in and do everything possible to get the job done. Even though the scoreboard showed them to be behind, the Americans had been in the driver's seat for much of the match. Possession was nice, but scoring chances mattered more - and Willy's boys had been creating chances at a consistent clip. The problem had been the finishing – or the lack of it.

Barrett Grey had missed wide twice and Leslie King actually whiffed at a pass that Mish had laid back for him. Not to be outdone, Jimmy Maxwell committed the ultimate offense on a twenty-five yard shot, mis-hitting the ball so badly that it went out for a Brazil throw-in. *No problem*, Willy kept saying, *just keep doing what you're doing.* Sooner or later, he knew something would go in. Meanwhile, Brazil was preparing to put the game on ice.

As the match entered the last ten minutes, Santana ordered two of his subs to warm up. Edevaldo and Batista were defenders and their insertion into this game would be the signal that Brazil was closing the door on the Americans. Entering for Zico and Leandro, the change reconfigured their lineup into a defensive shell that would be difficult to penetrate. When Willy Schneider saw which two Brazilians were entering the match, he made a subtle change to his formation.

"Doc!" he called out to his center back, "Move Pooky into the midfield." The American captain made the switch, taking over Bauer's marking responsibilities. They had discussed the new 3-5-2 setup, with Bauer and Petrov behind Maxwell, but had never used it. Time was running out.

Now with one more midfielder than Brazil, Team USA suddenly had much more time and space to operate. They would need to throw everything they had at the Brazilian defenders, and they had to hurry. Rather than play long balls into the penalty area, Maxwell and Company began utilizing the flanks to

281

send in driven crosses which were much less likely to be scooped up by the goalkeeper.

With time expiring, Juan Espinoza overlapped Mish on the right side and Petrov played him a long pass toward the corner flag. Espi hustled to get to the ball before it went out but overplayed his cross, which was easily headed out by Oscar. The big defender had time to plant his feet firmly and sent his clearance a good fifteen yards outside of the penalty area, where it landed on Leslie King's chest.

King had dropped back to help defend a few minutes earlier and, while making his way back to his forward position, he slowed down to watch Espinoza chase Petey's ambitious pass. He was surprised when Espi actually got his cross off, but stayed in the midfield to watch Oscar's clearance. He was more surprised when the defender sent the ball right at him.

A small window of opportunity presented itself as King received the ball on his chest, thirty-two yards from goal, while running forward at half speed. Defenders were closing in on both sides as he was approaching a third directly ahead. Leslie King had, in his mind, only one option.

As the ball bounced softly off his chest the striker accelerated a little and lowered his gaze, looking intently at a spot two yards ahead where his size twelve PUMA King (the all-white version) would meet the Adidas Tango España soccer ball. Time slowed for King as he approached the strike point. He strode into the shot with his right foot, meeting the ball with the laces of his cleat just before it reached the turf.

The ball left his foot on a trajectory that should have landed it in the eighth row of the second level of seats behind the Brazilian goal. While the initial track wasn't of any concern, the velocity and the topspin on the ball caused it to dip rapidly and Valdir Peres couldn't react fast enough to keep it from crossing the goal line just under his crossbar.

89th minute: United States 2, Brazil 2.

As he laid face-down on the grass, listening to the cheers of the American fans, the Brazilian goalkeeper couldn't believe what had just happened. He wasn't alone.

Over the next two weeks, slow-motion replays of Leslie King's shot would circle the globe. The one from an angle directly behind him famously showed three fans in the second level starting to lean to their left to avoid being hit by his errant shot - which would ultimately miss them by nearly ten yards. Physics professors would make guest appearances on sports shows to try to explain how much force a person would have to generate in order to create the shot. Several would proclaim it to be impossible – after seeing it with their own eyes.

The game ended in a draw and both teams felt beaten. In reality, the statistics showed a very close match that could have been won by either team, and sharing the points was probably the fairest result.

Three days later, Brazil and Italy faced each other in an epic match. These two powers of international football had last met four years earlier in the third place game of the 1978 World Cup, where Brazil defeated the Azzuri 2-0. Even though Italy knew they could not advance out of the group to the semi-finals, no one considered lying down for their bitter rivals. They saw this as a chance to avenge the loss in Argentina and make amends for their poor showing against the USA. Brazil needed to win in order to stay in the tournament.

Paolo Rossi, the Italian star who had not yet scored, put his team on the board only five minutes into the match. Brazil, once again, had given up an early goal. The *samba kings* controlled the midfield as the Italians dropped back to defend their lead and Socrates tied it up seven minutes later. Brazil continued to press, forcing Dino Zoff to make several saves. In the 25th minute, Rossi would strike again on a counter-attack, putting his squad up going into halftime.

For the first twenty minutes of the second half, Brazil pounded the Italian defense until Falcão unleashed a long-range blast that tied the game again. Since a draw would still send them home, the South Americans had to push for a third goal. Paolo Rossi would make them pay with a third of his own in the 74th minute.

The Brazilians tried everything they could, but the Italian defense held on. Rossi had finally earned his star status - one game too late.

Thanks to the Italians, and Paolo Rossi, the United States would face Poland in the semi-finals three days later. West Germany and France would play in the other.

Chapter 24

SEMI-FINALS

Of the four remaining teams, two were expected to be there and two were not. The second semi-final featuring West Germany and France was already being called the "real final". The early departure of giants Brazil, Italy, and Argentina left a power void, at least as far as the press was concerned.

The only country left who had ever won a World Cup was West Germany, so they became the instant favorite. Even though Poland and France had made it to a semi-final in previous cups, the two teams were seen as heading in opposite directions. The Poles were carrying nine players from the 1978 squad that did not advance out of their group, and top-scorer Zbigniew Boniek was suspended due to a second yellow card in the last round.

France, on the other hand, was filled with young stars playing attractive, attacking soccer. The French midfield was skilled, fast, and stylish, drawing comparisons to Brazil's *jogo bonito,* or beautiful game. The analysts expected this French squad to give the Germans a game. They were right about that.

The United States National Team was starting to attract some attention, which was seen as both good *and* bad. Largely unknown to the European media prior to this tournament, Team USA had displayed a level of proficiency that surprised many of the reporters covering them – which was expected, though, since the US squads of the recent past had been less than impressive. The press was already calling this the finest American team ever, and hoped they could continue to perform at this high level. It was always nice to read positive articles about your team. That was the good part of the additional attention.

The not-so-good part was that it brought more requests for interviews and the guys could no longer throw out a few clichés and duck into the locker room. While most of the reporters didn't mind waiting in line to speak with the likes of a Leslie King or Billy Ford, a few ventured out to find new subjects. One had actually done some research.

"Alfred," she began, "I've noticed that you are playing center back instead of your normal position. You play center-midfield for your team in St. Louis, right?"

"That's right," Bauer answered her question, unsure if he should elaborate. He was impressed by her already and didn't want to blow it. He was still uncomfortable around beautiful women.

"Yet you are still listed on the roster as a midfielder," she continued to probe. "Did you know you were going to be asked to play in the back?"

"Coach Schneider talked to me about it during the qualifiers," he was trying to concentrate on his answers, and her Spanish accent wasn't helping. "I knew it was a possibility."

"What did you *think* about that?" There it was, the dreaded question no one wanted to get. Fortunately, Pooky Bauer *had* thought about it and had an answer.

"Well, I figured I had two options," he held his large hands out in front of him, palms up. "One, I could tell Willy I demand to play in the midfield, which would have made it easy for him to leave me home. Or two, I could do whatever my coach wanted me to do – and try to help the team." He was pleased with himself for getting it all out, and was feeling much better about this interview. "I chose option two."

"And are you happy with your decision?"

"Next Sunday, I'll be lifting the World Cup instead of watching someone else do it on television." He didn't really think about that one – it just slipped out. "What do *you* think?" Bauer asked with a big smile.

"I think you seem very sure of yourself, Alfred," she returned the smile.

"Please," he said, offering her his right hand, "call me Pooky."

Another five-fifteen kickoff in Barcelona, just like the Italy match, but with one major difference. While Group C was based in the Catalan capital, all games so far had been played at the Estadi de Sarria – home of Espanyol, the "other" club in town. The Poland-USA semi-final was to be contested in the considerably larger

287

Nou Camp, home of FC Barcelona - and one American's favorite stadium.

The level of animosity between Real Madrid and FC Barcelona is unlike anything in American sports. When a Red Sox fan says he hates the Yankees, or a Cosmos supporter claims to despise the Aztecs, they are more like a six-year-old boy who *hates* taking a bath. Sure, they have an allegiance to their team – but "hate" is a bit strong. The giants of Spanish football *really* hated each other – and had some good reasons.

Imagine if the United States had had professional soccer, or any pro sport, during the Civil War. Now try to picture how the Atlanta supporters would welcome a visiting team from Philadelphia. How about Richmond visiting Washington DC? Real Madrid and Barcelona experienced a similar history during much of the twentieth century, and the rivalry was passed from generation to generation. Players for both teams would be remembered for how they performed against their biggest adversary, and Jimmy Maxwell was proud to be a villain in the Nou Camp.

The catcalls started as soon as the American Number Twenty-One emerged from the tunnel, and continued through the pre-game warm-ups.

"Lots of fans here, I see," Steve Newton said to Maxwell, while making his normal rounds. As the designated worrier, he needed to make sure every detail was discussed at length. "Are you *sure* you can handle this?"

"Yep." The standard answer, of course. With a big smile this time.

"Ninety-five thousand people in here and it sounds like half of them are booing *you*." Newton wasn't buying it. No one could perform in this cauldron – he could barely hear himself think.

"You should be here for a club match, Steve," Maxwell leaned in close so he wouldn't have to yell. "I get all 95,000 of 'em."

Willy made one change to the lineup from the Brazil game, replacing Barrett Grey with Rick Davis. Since Grey was nursing a twisted ankle and Davis had been sharp in training, the decision was an easy one. So was the decision to keep the rest of the starters intact. "Not broke, so don't fix it," was Newton's response when Schneider handed him the lineup. "And we get paid for this," Willy joked.

Poland had advanced to the semi-finals on the strength of their defense. Three of their five matches had been scoreless draws, but they *had* beaten Argentina (without Maradona, of course) and Peru - convincingly. Willy assumed they would play in their usual defensive shell and try for counter-attack goals. He was right but, without Boniek, the Polish attack was lifeless. Poor Grzegorz Lato was all alone up top and, at thirty-two, he was nowhere near the striker he used to be.

The Americans were in white-blue-white and Poland wore red-white-red. Like his counterpart, Coach Antoni Piechniczek was dealing with injuries to some key players. Unlike Willy Schneider, he wasn't able to field a team nearly as strong as he would have liked. Both coaches were aware of the role luck played in a World Cup and, while the Pole was cursing his, Willy was hoping his wouldn't expire anytime soon. He knew he had dodged a few bullets while in Spain.

Besides having to replace his top goal-scorer, Piechniczek was also missing one of his best defenders. Jan Jalocha, considered the best right back Poland had ever produced, was still out after an injury suffered against Peru and Marek Dziuba would replace him. Billy Ford and Alexi Mayer would make Dziuba wish he was still on the bench.

On paper, the Poles played the same 4-5-1 formation as Brazil. On the field, however, the differences were monumental. While the South Americans liked to throw everyone into the attack (sometimes to their detriment), Poland was reluctant to commit more than two or three players to the cause. Their coach was a big fan of "safety first" soccer, and he would rely on his team's defense-by-numbers style to hold the American forwards in check. His plan would work in one regard: Rick Davis and Leslie King would be almost invisible, at least for the first half. Too bad he didn't have a plan for a certain US defender.

By the thirtieth minute, Maxwell and Mishigawa had each taken three shots, and Ford had two. King and Davis were content to play the decoy role, keeping the Polish defenders occupied while the American midfielders charged ahead. Since the Poles were reluctant to send their own midfielders forward, Maxwell and his mates were free to attack at will. Seven minutes before halftime, an unlikely player would register his first World Cup goal.

The Polish defense was held up by its sheer strength of numbers for most of the first half, even while the American midfielders peppered their goal with long-range shots. None had scored yet, but a few caused goalkeeper Mlynarczyk to have to make some acrobatic saves. In the thirty-seventh minute, he parried one of Brad Mishigawa's shots over the crossbar, giving the Americans their second corner kick.

Billy Ford crossed the field to the right-hand corner flag and prepared to take the kick. His left-footed in-swinger would normally be aimed at the edge of the goal box, hoping to find the head of one of his strikers – or a tall central defender. Marco DeSantis was Ford's favorite target, but he had stayed back at midfield to discuss some tactical matters with his outside backs. He sent a substitute instead.

"Pook!" DeSantis shouted to his partner, fifteen yards away, "I'm staying here – take my spot." Bauer usually stayed with his mark, no matter what, but Doc waved him forward and said "Hurry up!"

Billy Ford was just about to launch his corner kick when he saw Pooky Bauer running forward to get in the mix. All the Polish players were already in the box, so Bauer was unmarked as he raced ahead. Billy quickly changed his plan and played a hard pass into Pooky's path, twenty-five yards from the goal.

Most of the time when a defender gets an opportunity to strike a long-range shot in a big game, the results remind us of one reason why the player is in the back in the first place, but the *If a defender could shoot straight, he'd be a forward* theory didn't apply here. Pooky Bauer was no ordinary defender.

Running full-speed to meet Ford's pass, Bauer unleashed a powerful blast that beat the Polish keeper to the far side of his goal. Pooky then dropped to his knees, right where he landed after striking the ball, five yards outside the edge of the penalty area, and held out his hands - palms up. He hoped the pretty Spanish reporter noticed before he was mobbed by his teammates.

38th minute: United States 1, Poland 0.

The half ended with Team USA content to keep possession and the Poles happy to pack their defensive end of the field. Going into the locker room down a goal to the Americans was bad enough, but knowing that they hadn't been able to generate anything resembling a decent attack in the first forty-five minutes was intolerable. Piechniczek now knew how the Argentine coach must have felt when they had played ten days earlier. It was imperative that he make a change to improve his attack, but his top goal-scorer was unavailable.

Lato could see the writing on the wall, so he immediately let his coach know that he was "good to go" for the second half. The only switch actually made at the break was Andrzej Palasz for Wlodzimierz Ciolek. It was a forward-for-forward swap, but it signaled to the Polish players that their coach was fed up with the way they were playing. Everyone would have to take responsibility for the lack of goal-scoring chances – or face the consequences.

Willy Schneider made no changes to his lineup at halftime, and said very little to the team while they were in the locker room. *Just keep doing what you're doing.* He knew that, barring a miracle from Poland, his

292

boys were going to be playing in the World Cup Final in three days. Usually the least-superstitious person in the locker room, Willy noticed he was afraid to even *think* about the final. *Stupid*, he thought – but he didn't mention it to anyone, just to be safe. Seven minutes into the second half, Leslie King would make it OK to think about.

Alexi Mayer and Billy Ford were taking turns racing down the left flank again, just like they had done for most of the first half. Marek Dziuba, the backup right back, was exhausted and in need of help when Mayer made another overlapping run toward him. Billy played a little pass inside to Jimmy Maxwell, who simply turned and passed the ball into the space ahead of Alexi.

Mayer reached the ball ten yards from the end line and made a crossing pass to the far edge of the goal box. King had drifted outside the penalty area, trying to elude his markers, and began his sprint to goal when Alexi struck the ball. He leapt high, towering over two Polish defenders, and headed the ball past the keeper who felt it glance off his right ear on its way to the back of his net. While accepting the congratulations from his teammates, Les made his way to the end line behind Poland's goal and pointed to a friend in the stands.

52nd minute: United States 2, Poland 0.

"Was that Bill Murray?" Maxwell asked, as they jogged back to their half. He thought he recognized the fan pointing back at King with his hand over his heart.

"Yeah - it was." He and the comic/actor had met when King hosted SNL five years earlier. A mutual friend died a few months before and Les had made a

293

promise to dedicate a goal to him. Of course, no one else knew about it.

"That's cool," the youngster was impressed.

"Thanks," he knew Maxwell wouldn't probe him for more information – and appreciated it. "Nice pass to 'Lexi.'"

"Goal was OK, too," with an accompanying high-five.

A two-goal lead is the worst lead to have. All the players, and both coaches, had heard that old axiom many times. Willy Schneider laughed every time his assistant coach would mention it, usually asking Newton if he thought they should give up a goal to help their cause. Sure, some teams might become complacent after going two goals up, but he wasn't worried about these guys.

With more than a half-hour remaining, the Americans knew they couldn't let up – not yet. Keeping possession in the midfield had become a little more difficult since Poland had moved one of their defenders up, so Team USA just continued to mount a consistent, if half-hearted, attack. The only excitement in the last thirty minutes came when Pawel Janas became frustrated with a cocky young American.

The harassment from the Nou Camp faithful had diminished some since Team USA doubled their lead but every time Maxwell touched the ball (which was often) the whistles came alive. Now that the outcome looked certain, Sam's Army's shouts of "Olé" each time an American received the ball were beginning to drown out the boo's. Willy's new playmaker was enjoying this immensely, which was obvious by the smile on his face. Not everyone on the field was as pleased.

With five minutes left on the clock, Jimmy Maxwell was dribbling across the field midway between the center stripe and Poland's penalty area, just killing time. Janas quickly approached him from the left, hoping to catch him off guard, but Maxwell simply turned and put the ball through the defender's legs. *Ball or man, not both* was ingrained in the Pole's subconscious and, fueled by no small amount of repressed rage, he decked the American with a forearm to the jaw.

It took Stoyan Petrov less than one second to retaliate. Petey's shove to Janas's chest caused both sides to respond similarly – by trying to get between the two aggressors. Maxwell was the first to grab one of them from behind, dragging his midfield partner to the ground nearly five yards from the altercation.

What could have turned into a street fight quickly turned into a hilarious situation · with a surprised American on his back and Jimmy Maxwell sitting on his chest, using his knees to pin Petrov's arms to the turf. Growing up with two older brothers caused one to become proficient in a number of things and, though many were socially unacceptable, wrestling was certainly one of them.

"Get off me!" Petrov wasn't used to being bullied. His teammates were as surprised as he was, but their shock quickly turned to laughter and several Polish players joined in.

"Not until you calm down," Maxwell was trying to be serious. "C'mon, man, we can't afford to lose you for the final." Then it sunk in.

Both players climbed to their feet just as the Uruguayan referee prepared to show Petrov his card. Neither knew which color to expect – red was certainly justified – and held their breath for a second. The eleven Americans on the field were joined by several million back home in breathing a sigh of relief when the yellow one was held up. *Thank you, sir.* Willy's luck was holding up.

As the players prepared to finish the match, Petey thanked Maxwell for intervening. "And I heard what you said to the ref," he continued, "pretty funny."

"You speak Spanish?"

"Yeah, but it's a good thing he didn't know I'm not married!"

Both laughed and finished the last two minutes of the game with a renewed sense of purpose. *We're going to the World Cup Final!*

• • •

As soon as the semi-final matchups were decided, the media spotlight shifted to Seville. The Estadio Ramón Sánchez Pizjuán was about to become the site of a World Cup Classic that would exceed even the highest expectations.

The second match of the evening of July 8th began at nine o'clock local time, with 70,000 enthusiastic fans in the stands. Both teams knew who had won the other semi, and could have been forgiven for thinking about the chance to play in the final against a relatively unknown US team, but neither did.

France and West Germany were approaching this match like it really was the final. Both squads understood the obvious importance of winning this game but, with a perceived *minnow* waiting for them, the stakes were even higher. Neither would hold anything back, and it would take over two hours of soccer to determine a winner.

The first half saw each team score once: Littbarski in the 17th minute and Platini nine minutes later. The play was intense, leading to a controversial decision with a half-hour remaining in regulation time when French substitute Patrick Battiston, who had been on the field less than ten minutes, was savagely taken out by the German goalkeeper. The Dutch referee apparently missed the collision in the penalty area entirely – awarding no penalty kick, no ejection, not even a yellow card! Battiston was carried off on a stretcher and would not return.

Despite spirited play by both sides, the second half ended with the game still tied 1-1. Thirty minutes of overtime to play (two 15-minute halves with no sudden-death) and, if still tied – penalty kicks.

France came out with all their guns blazing and thought they had finished the Germans off when Alain Giresse scored their *second* overtime goal. Down 3-1 less than ten minutes into the extra period, West Germany needed a miracle – and they got one. Karl-

Heinz Rummenigge, the German star who had not started due to an injury, entered the match in the ninety-seventh minute and scored five minutes later. The French were reeling when Klaus Fischer tied the match midway through the second half of the overtime, and this game was going into the history books. For the first time ever, a World Cup match would be decided in a penalty-kick shootout.

After the first five kicks the match was still tied 4-4. A place in the final was now to be decided one shot at a time. The next player to take his penalty kick was Maxime Bossis. The Frenchman tried to beat the German keeper to the post but was denied. The man who should have been sent off for his flagrant foul in the sixtieth minute was about to become a national hero.

After the save, all Horst Hrubesch had to do was score his penalty and his team was in the final. With the pressure off (since he could miss and they still had a chance) the German number nine calmly put his country in the World Cup final for the fourth time.

Chapter 25

THE FINAL

Friday's headlines said it all: "US Tops Poland – Face West German Machine In Final" – *New York Times*, "West Germany In Fourth World Cup Final - Favorites Against Upstart Americans" – *Bild*, "USA, Maxwell To Battle Mighty Germans" – *El País,* and "West Germany Versus Who?" – *London Times.* Underdogs. Again.

"I hear the odds are three-to-one against us," Steve Newton had already read the *Times* and *El País*. His boss was trying to enjoy his breakfast, preferring to spend his morning reading time in the comics section.

"What were the odds against us beating Italy?" he asked, without looking up from his paper. "Or Poland, for that matter?"

"I, uh, ... OK, point taken," Newton understood what Schneider was saying, but he worried that the players might be affected by the predictions. He was right.

"Hey coach," Billy Ford said, as he and Brandon Rafferty passed by on the way out of the hotel dining room. "We're going to find a bookie. Can't beat 3 to 1 odds!" Willy knew he was kidding, and laughed at the joke - and at his assistant's worried look.

"Lighten up, Steve," he said, rising from his seat. "These guys know how good they are."

Twenty-eight thousand fans saw Poland and France meet on Saturday in Alicante. While the French had the edge in skill and speed, Poland held on to win the match 3-2. Largely due to the toll taken by the marathon game they had played only two days before, France simply ran out of gas.

All the American players knew that the Germans would be weary but, unlike France with their free-flowing attack, West Germany would be content to play an organized, defensive-minded game and wait for the United States to make a mistake. And they would not take their opponents lightly.

Head Coach Jupp Derwall made sure his team knew who they were up against, reading them the scorelines from each of the US games.

"They defeated Belgium and Hungary," he hesitated to let that sink in, "then drew with Argentina.

"Next round, they beat Italy and tied Brazil, and" he continued, "you saw how they dismantled Poland Thursday night.

"Gentlemen, we cannot expect anything less than excellent football from the Americans," he finished, not realizing how right he would be.

West Germany started the final with their normal lineup, now that Karl-Heinz Rummenigge was back. The striker was still not at full strength, but

Derwall hoped that having him on the field was worth the gamble. His inspirational performance against France had buoyed his teammates and the coach felt they might need another miracle. Besides, he wasn't going to leave his leading scorer on the bench for a World Cup Final.

After their poor performance in the tournament opener, where they lost to tiny Algeria, the West Germans had rebounded to win Group II. Their second round opponents weren't as strong as advertised and, with a scoreless draw against England and a 2-1 win over Spain, they advanced to their historic semi-final with France.

Klaus Fischer was the other forward and, even at thirty-two, he was still an easy choice. His spectacular bicycle-kick goal late in the overtime period had forced the penalty kick shootout against France. His two goals tied him with playmaker Pierre Littbarski, ten years his junior, for second on the team. They played together at FC Köln with goalkeeper Harald "Tony" Schumacher.

Rummenigge's Bayern Munich teammates Wolfgang Dremmler and Paul Breitner played wide midfield. Brothers Karl-Heinz and Bernd Förster joined Hans-Peter Briegel and Manfred Kaltz in the defense. As a unit, they were big, strong and disciplined. All the West German players were employed in their home country, except one.

While the majority of the players in this final considered the Estadio Santiago Bernabeu in Madrid a neutral site, two of them felt right at home. Jimmy Maxwell and his Real Madrid teammate, Uli Stielike, who was the defensive midfielder for the Germans. The twenty-seven-year-old was a fan favorite, having just been voted "Best Foreign Player" in the Spanish league for the fourth year in a row. He would often tell the press his job was to "clean up Maxwell's messes", but he knew he was lucky to be playing behind him. *I'm not even the best foreign player on my team*, he thought.

Willy knew how the Germans would play, having spent much of his childhood watching matches with his father and uncles. The elder Schneider liked to say "The Germans don't *play* soccer, they *work* soccer!" which *he* meant as a compliment. His son disagreed.

To Willy Schneider, there was a limit to how far hard work alone could take you as a player. At the highest levels, which was where he coached, hard work was a *given* – you certainly wouldn't last on his Cosmos or the US National Team without busting your butt every day. Athleticism was also a basic requirement, since you couldn't get to the TPL without being an exceptional athlete. Willy wanted his teams to have something else, something more. Most importantly, they had to make him happy.

There was something special about watching a really good soccer team put all the pieces together. To Willy Schneider, it was like creating a unique dish, where several disparate ingredients are mixed with one another, heat is applied, and the resulting flavor is magical. He always marveled at creative players like Puskas and Di Stefano, only to be told that they weren't "real" soccer players. Then again, his father never understood his love of cooking, either.

Willy knew how the West Germans would play because they always played the same way. While all national team programs went through highs and lows, the Germans were among the most consistent in the world because they always played to *not lose*. But, without the creative talents of a Franz Beckenbauer or a Gerd Mueller, this squad would have to hope for a scoreless draw, or a lucky goal, in order to beat this American team. The bookmakers had this one wrong.

The United States fielded the same team that had started against Brazil and Italy. Barrett Grey was back in form and he joined Leslie King at forward. Jimmy Maxwell, Stoyan Petrov, Billy Ford and Brad Mishigawa made up the midfield with the normal back four behind them. Marco DeSantis, Pooky Bauer, Alexi Mayer and Juan Espinoza took the field in front of Johnny Jackson.

Since West Germany's traditional national team jersey was white, it didn't really matter that the US was the designated home team. As expected, Steve Newton looked like a proud papa when he saw the team come out of the tunnel in their red-white-and-blue uniforms. He was surprised to see Willy Schneider wiping his eyes and wanted to say something, but didn't know what. Willy caught his glance and immediately approached his long-time assistant.

"We wouldn't be here without you," Schneider said as he offered his right hand. Newton knew this was a lie - but appreciated the sentiment.

"Thanks, Boss," he said as they shook hands.

"So, what should we be worried about this time?" Schneider asked.

"Nothing," Newton replied, appearing as calm as Willy had ever seen him. "I think we'll be OK."

"We finally agree!" Willy said. "C'mon, I found us some great seats."

Ninety-thousand fans filled the Estadio Bernabeu on Sunday, July 11th, 1982, for the final match of the twelfth FIFA World Cup. The West German contingent outnumbered Sam's Army by a two-to-one margin, due mainly to geography. About half of the remaining seats were purchased by locals, who had no allegiance to either country's team, especially since Real Madrid was represented by both sides. These fans would wait to see who would earn their praise.

The first half began as expected, with most of the Germans planted comfortably in their own half and Team USA knocking the ball around in the midfield – looking for openings, but finding none.

Thirty minutes in, with the crowd growing restless, West Germany was still content to play in their defensive shell and look for the occasional counter-attack. The United States continued to probe – playing passes to the feet of Grey and King, who promptly gave the ball back to their teammates in the midfield. The Germans were too disciplined to commit rash fouls, so this chess game would need to be decided by some individual brilliance.

Paul Breitner was playing left midfield and had ventured forward a few times. Mish and Espi were aware of his abilities – he had a powerful shot and was not shy about using it – but felt they had him covered.

The Bayern Munich star had recently been honored as German Footballer of the Year. Oddly, he lost in the final balloting for *European* Footballer to his teammate, Karl-Heinz Rummenigge.

The thirty-year-old midfielder made another run down the left flank, only to be ignored by his teammate, forcing him to hustle back on defense. Juan Espinoza took note of the run and devised a plan. He noticed that when he drifted into the center of the field, leaving the German lots of space to run into, Breitner tried to exploit the space. *Every time.* After a few more tests, Espi was sure his plan would work.

The first half ended with no score, but it was obvious which team was in charge. The West German defenders and midfielders were exhausted and their forwards were frustrated. The Americans left the field knowing that all they had to do was keep up the pressure – and avoid any mistakes.

Forty-five minutes of chasing the ball would tire any team and, after their extra-long match against France three days earlier, the West German players were starting to feel the effects. Juan Espinoza had a plan to take advantage of them and Willy couldn't have been prouder of his right back.

"All we have to do is wear Breitner out," Espi told the group inside the locker room. "He keeps making these runs down the flank, and he's almost done." Then he made the point that caused his coach to smile. "And the guy behind him - number four, Förster - is hobbling a little bit. Hamstring, I think." The younger brother, Karl-Heinz, had indeed strained his hamstring and had opted to try to tough it out.

305

One of the more radical ideas that Willy Schneider proposed to his players, club and national team, was that if a coach put a weak athlete on the field, it was *necessary* to attack that player. *How else would their coach learn?* Willy would ask. A team had to be punished for their mistakes, or those of their coach, or no one learned anything. And, in Willy Schneider's mind, that would be a shame. If Derwall kept Förster in the game, he would be the first target.

When the teams took the field to start the second half, all the Americans noticed that number four was again taking his spot in the West German defense. The plan was to attack down the right side every time Breitner made one of his speculative runs down the flank. Juan Espinoza would set the trap, luring the German midfielder out, then Team USA would pounce on the exposed defender. The first two times proved too difficult, but the third time Leslie King made it count.

Each time Espinoza moved inside, Breitner tried to race into the space out wide while looking for a long pass from his backs. The few times the ball was actually played his way he was shut down by the quicker, stronger, American defender. While Espi could do this all day, his counterpart was getting tired. Twelve minutes into the second half, it was time.

Barrett Grey and King liked to change sides of the field frequently, but almost never ventured more than twenty yards apart. Constantly moving, they would drift in and out of the penalty area, dragging defenders with them just to see who would come – and who would stay. When Paul Breitner made his sprint into Espi's trap, they were half-way between the center stripe and the German eighteen yard line, surrounded by Hans-Peter Briegel and the Förster brothers.

Right back Manfred Kaltz tried to make the long pass through the midfield to Breitner, but the ball was intercepted by Stoyan Petrov before it got to him. Petey quickly gave the ball to Jimmy Maxwell, who was racing across the field five yards ahead. Maxwell was headed diagonally toward the right corner flag while Brad Mishigawa sprinted, unmarked, down the right touchline. Uli Stielike knew as well as anyone what his Real Madrid teammate could do and stepped up to pressure him – half a second too late.

The instant their eyes met, Uli knew it was bad. As soon as the ball left Maxwell's foot toward the space in front of the streaking Mishigawa, the West German turned to see if his left back was going to cover for him. Since Breitner was still thirty yards up the field, and in no shape to help, he had hoped to see Karl-Heinz Förster sprinting out to track the American down. Instead, he saw a look in his teammate's eyes that simply said, "Help". Stielike put his head down and tried to catch up to Mishigawa, but it wouldn't matter.

The pass Maxwell played into the space was perfectly weighted so that all Mish had to do was serve it with his first touch. Without breaking stride, the midfielder struck the ball with the inside of his right boot and sent a crossing pass to the far side of the West German penalty area, ten yards from the endline. Grey and King watched the ball soar over their heads – and saw Billy Ford running to get to it. Both immediately prepared for another opportunity.

Billy headed the ball back across the goal mouth to the edge of the six-yard box near the right post where Karl-Heinz Förster was waiting to clear it out. As the five-foot-ten-inch defender tensed his neck muscles in preparation for the contact between the ball and his forehead, he was mauled by a six-foot-four-inch American striker he never saw coming. Leslie King was already on his way back to midfield before Förster knew what hit him.

52nd minute: United States 1, West Germany 0.

When Mishigawa's cross sailed over his strikers' heads, all eyes followed the ball toward the opposite side of the penalty area. Defenders shifted to stay goal-side of their marks, and Leslie King saw an opening. Instead of joining the others who were jockeying for position in front of the German goal, he took four steps back – away from the mix. He was trying to get to a spot where the defenders couldn't see both him and the ball at the same time. It worked perfectly.

Two German backs picked up Barrett Grey at the near post when Billy sent his pass back into the box. Karl-Heinz Förster was all alone, or so he thought, at the other end of the goal. He didn't know that King was lurking three yards away, behind him, waiting to attack. The theme from "Jaws" would have made an appropriate soundtrack for the slow-motion replay, as the defender waited for the ball to arrive only to have his world turned upside down by a monster in a red jersey.

Les buried his header, as usual, with power and precision – and total disregard for the poor defender between him and the ball. Even at one-hundred percent, Förster could not have stopped him.

"Number five," Marco DeSantis pointed out while administering a bear hug. King's goal tied him with Rummenigge for the tournament lead, and Team USA's captain wanted *his* striker to have that honor – alone.

"OK," King said.   He didn't care about the personal accolades. "So, let's get a few more."

The all-business attitude of the West Germans suddenly turned ugly.   Shumacher was yelling at Förster,   Kaltz   was   yelling   at   Shumacher,   and Rummenigge was yelling at all of them. While they had been down before in this tournament, the situation they found themselves in this time was very different.

Being behind against Algeria in the opener, twice, didn't seem to faze the stoic West German players. *No problem*, they thought, *of course we'll come back.* Two quick goals from the French in extra time of the semi-final match were more of a shock – but then there was no time to bicker. They simply dug in and, inspired by their captain, fought back to tie the score. The circumstances in the final were unlike any this team had faced in a long time and they were starting to realize they might actually lose.

The next few moments would be crucial for the United States, and everyone knew it. He didn't need to, but Jupp Derwall encouraged his players to attack with everything they had, hoping to take advantage of an American letdown. The minutes immediately following a goal were well-known to be an opportune time to catch a team off guard, but Willy's boys were experienced – and unwilling to concede anything to the Germans.

Maxwell's idea to *jump all over them* was accepted this time – seems his stature had grown a bit since the Haiti match in qualifying – and the Americans decided to intensify their attack, hoping to force their opponents to forego their plans of grabbing a quick tying goal.   It was also obvious that the Germans were starting   to   wear   out   physically   so   the   appropriate action, according to any decent predator, was to finish them off quickly.

"Let's put 'em away," the playmaker said to the contingent of Americans congratulating King after his goal. "Second goal now and this one's over."

"Don't look at me," Marco DeSantis said, "that's *your* job!"

"Thanks, Doc," Maxwell replied, "I'm on it." And he meant it.

Whether it was the renewed confidence of his captain, the deafening pro-American cheers from the previously unaffiliated fans, or just a sense of the historic place he now found himself in, Jimmy Maxwell suddenly felt different. He hadn't thought about it before, but *he* was now the Number Ten for the United States National Team. The twenty-one on his back was just a formality - and was certainly temporary now — and, for the next half-hour, the game seemed to move in slow-motion to him. Maxwell was in his zone.

In the 59th minute, his left-footed shot was parried over the crossbar by Schumacher. Two minutes later, Alexi Mayer whipped in a cross that Maxwell met with a full-volley at the top of the penalty area, only to be headed away by Kaltz. The clearance sent the ball out to the left corner of the box where Wolfgang Dremmler and Stoyan Petrov collided.

Petey was trying to send the ball back into the mix and Dremmler was just holding his ground, hoping to help clear it out of his end of the field. Both men were going for the ball and neither saw the other before it was too late. Their skulls met, Petrov's left temple and the bridge of the German's nose, as the ball bounced off Dremmler's head and fell to Billy Ford's feet, just outside the West German penalty area. It was Billy's opportunity to show that his class was as remarkable as his speed and skill.

Ordinarily, having a clear path to goal with only a keeper to beat would be considered a good situation, especially in a World Cup Final. Billy Ford knew instantly what had to be done when he collected the ball and his decision surprised everyone – except his team-mates, his coaches, and his wife.

Seeing the only German defender between him and the goal on the ground clutching his bloody face, Ford immediately turned to his left and kicked the ball out for a West German throw-in. Medical staffers were called in to tend to the wounded and players from both teams showed their appreciation with pats on the back or thumbs-up gestures. Many wondered if they would have done the same thing, and several weren't sure. One player didn't even have to consider it.

"Are we even now?" Billy asked, flashing his big smile.

"You need to get over it," Grey replied. A year earlier, in a club match against Billy's Detroit Chrysler team, the striker had stolen the headlines with a similar act. Even though Detroit had beaten Dallas 2-0, the *Detroit Free Press* story raved about Grey's integrity and honor. To make it worse, Billy's two goals were hardly mentioned.

Barrett Grey had been battling with a Detroit defender all night, as usual, and the two got tangled up on a corner kick. Grey was pulling on the other guy's

311

jersey and, as they were going for the ball, both toppled over in a heap. The referee blew his whistle, which was expected, and pointed to the penalty spot – which was not. The Dallas striker actually joined the Detroit defender to argue the call, but the official stood firm. *Simple fix*, Grey thought as he placed the ball on the spot.

His first thought was to shoot wide, but he couldn't convince himself to miss on purpose. Besides, he was trying to point out to the ref that he had made the wrong call. He simply passed the ball on the ground to the Detroit goalkeeper, who scooped it up and nodded his approval. Barrett Grey wasn't trying to become a hero, but Billy had never let him forget it. "OK," he said, "we're even."

Dremmler left the match for good as West Germany made the first substitution of the game. Horst Hrubesch came on and took his usual spot out wide on the right. He was being called upon to jump-start the offense, but his primary duty - trying to stop Ford and Mayer from running roughshod over their defense – would prevent him from making any serious attacking runs.

Maxwell continued to have his way with the West German defense, despite Stielike's attempts to stop him. Uli knew he couldn't allow his teammate a free kick opportunity inside thirty yards, so he made sure to trip him up - or, at least, try - before he could get in range. He and Hans-Peter Briegel were growing tired of the brash young American with his constant smile. Briegel had voiced his discontent after Maxwell's earlier attempt on goal, chastising Stielike for letting him shoot with his left foot. After he struck the full-volley with his *other* foot, Briegel offered to help with a double-team. It didn't matter. Jimmy Maxwell would take them both for a ride in the 69th minute.

Leslie King was posted up with a defender on his back two yards outside the eighteen-yard box. Maxwell played him a hard pass from fifteen yards away and made a run to the left, toward the corner of the box. King simply deflected the ball back into the midfielder's path, where he picked it up in stride and headed into the area with the ball on his left foot. Two Germans, Stielike and Briegel, tracked him into their penalty area to cut off his direct shot.

Maxwell quickly stepped over the ball and cut it back with his right boot, reversing course and heading for the eighteen yard line. Two steps later, as the defenders were catching up, he turned to his left and made a dash toward the center of the field, just outside the penalty area. All the West German defenders knew he was going to attempt to get off a shot with his preferred right foot, and two of them joined Stielike and Briegel to take that option away.

As Jimmy Maxwell dribbled across the top of the box with four West Germans blocking his right-footed shot, he made his move without a second thought. Near the middle of the goal, Maxwell put on the brakes and cut the ball behind his left leg – straight at Shumacher. His opponents tried to stop, but the American playmaker was now staring directly at their keeper from fifteen yards away. He took one touch to the left and ran past the ball, opening his body so that he was facing the right side of the goal. Schumacher tried to cut off the angle and protect his near post, but Maxwell went the other way, curling his right-footed shot into the netting just inside the far post. The Germans didn't yell at each other this time.

69th minute: United States 2, West Germany 0.

The players made their way back to midfield for the kickoff and Karl-Heinz Rummenigge did two things he had never done before. He shook Jimmy Maxwell's hand, and told his coach he needed to come out of the match. Hansi Mueller came off the bench for the West German captain, who received a standing ovation for his service.

"Why didn't you just pass that one in with your left," King asked his young teammate. He was known as an efficient scoring machine, and wondered why Maxwell had decided to make this one more difficult than necessary.

"Four guys trying to stop my *right*," he said, "that's why." Both laughed, and Leslie King shook his head. *Glad I've got a few more years left*, he thought.

Four minutes later, Maxwell's petulance got him in trouble. He had chased a ball into the corner, and Uli Stielike had followed him – alone. With no real options, and a two-goal lead, the American just decided to hold the ball in the corner and see what happened. Uli put immediate, hard pressure on Maxwell's back and they both knew where this was going.

The two were intense rivals on the Real Madrid practice field and often had to be pulled apart to prevent serious injuries. With a head coach who liked their competitiveness, most of their battles were allowed to get much more heated than a real referee would have consented to.

The Brazilian official had been watching these two for a while and, when Maxwell reached back and grabbed the German's shirt, he put his whistle in his mouth. Before he could blow it, Uli swept his teammate's feet out from under him, missing the ball completely and leaving the American falling onto his back. He still had a handful of West German jersey and pulled Stielike down with him.

Both were laughing as the ball rolled across the endline for a German goal kick, but Mr. Coelho was not amused. The referee promptly showed his yellow card to both the West German number fifteen and the American number twenty-one.

West Germany had enough left in the tank for one more flurry of offense, but were denied twice by Johnny Jackson in a two-minute span. In the seventy-fifth minute, Littbarski forced a corner kick with a long-range blast that JJ had to push wide. Klaus Fischer nearly scored on the corner with a strong header over Juan Espinoza, but Jackson, again, came up with a big save.

That's it, Willy thought. He had expected West Germany to get another chance after the second US goal, and had told Steve Newton that if they could weather that storm, it was "game over". He didn't say it out loud though, since his assistant would have reminded him that there were still a lot of time left.

With ten minutes left in the World Cup final, the West Germans made a mistake that would cost their captain his share of the Golden Boot. Maxwell found his way, again, into the German penalty area and slipped a pass across the top of the goal box. Barrett Grey was preparing to put Team USA up 3-0 when he was tripped from behind by Bernd Förster. Penalty.

As the players took up their positions outside the penalty box, all the Americans were looking at Leslie King while King was waiting for someone else to take the penalty kick. He had forgotten that Rafferty was on the bench.

"Les!" Doc yelled, over the crowd noise. "You've got this."

"I don't *do* penalties," the striker replied, shaking his head. Raff always took them for the National Team and Joe Manfredi took them for the Dodgers. Besides, they just weren't fair. *And what would Jack think?*

"Got to be you," DeSantis pointed to his captain's armband, then the penalty spot, asserting his authority. "Go get number six."

Leslie King reluctantly stepped up to the penalty spot, twelve yards from Tony Schumacher's goal, placed the ball on the grass and took three steps back. He looked up into the sky and said something to his father, then blasted a shot past the West German goalkeeper, who was fortunate the ball missed him.

81st minute: United States 3, West Germany 0.

"What did you say before the shot?" Maxwell had finally gotten up the nerve to ask.

"Don't look," King said as they exchanged high-fives.

316

Two minutes later, more World Cup history was made when Paul Breitner scored. The United States was finally content to lay back and let the game clock expire when Hans-Peter Briegel made a powerful run down the left flank and Espi fouled him just outside the US penalty area.

Hansi Mueller took the free kick and placed it perfectly for Klaus Fischer, who was six yards from the goal. The German striker misplayed the ball, as did Pooky Bauer, and it fell to Breitner, who put his right-footed shot just inside the left post. Paul Breitner just became the third person to score in two different World Cup final matches, having netted a goal in the 1974 final against the Netherlands, but it was no consolation for the thirty-year-old.

83rd minute: United States 3, West Germany 1.

Johnny Jackson was furious with the poor clearance and immediately let Bauer know it. Pooky hung his head and waited for JJ to get closer, then looked up and stopped him in his tracks. When the American keeper saw the smile on his old friend's face, he planted a two-hand shove firmly in Bauer's chest.

"Sorry about your shutout," Bauer said sincerely, "but lighten up, we're about to win the World Cup." The two had been fierce competitors for ten years and it was hard to turn it off – even when they were on the same team.

"Not if you keep playing like that!" JJ said, returning the smile.

The final ended ten minutes later, after three agonizingly long minutes of extra time. Breitner's goal had invigorated his team, but the renewed enthusiasm lasted only a few moments. They all knew they did not have enough time, or energy, to come back against this American team that had outplayed them in every way. When Arnaldo Coelho blew his whistle signaling full-time, the match was over and the celebrations began.

Nearly all the American players had some family or friends in attendance, and their contingent was promptly escorted to the field to join in. Jimmy Maxwell's favorite groundskeeper – the one who kept the lights on for his extra practice sessions – was put in charge of "family detail" and his crew made sure to get everyone to the staging area behind the benches. As soon as the players had finished shaking hands and swapping jerseys with the West Germans, the family members and friends were allowed to take the field for sweaty hugs and kisses.

Ten minutes later, the runner-up medals were awarded to the West German players who were obviously spent, both physically and mentally. It was the second time their country had made it to a final and failed to win, having lost to hosts England in 1966. They could be proud of the fact that they had won two World Cups, in 1954 and 1974, but that didn't matter now. This team had been beaten, and everyone knew it.

After Rummenigge and his team had some pictures taken and made their way off the podium, Team USA responded to the roar of the crowd and headed for the stage. The players were awarded their individual medals by João Havelange, FIFA president, and congregated in the center of the large podium to receive the team trophy. All but one.

318

"Where's Maxwell?" Steve Newton was counting off the players in his head, voluntarily making it his job to keep things moving and his number twenty-one was missing. *Who would miss this?*

"Here he comes," Mish spotted him running toward midfield. He had been in front of the goal behind the stage and no one there could see him demonstrating a move to the little boy in the red Number 10 jersey.

Jimmy Maxwell jumped onto the stage to receive his champion's medal and joined the rest of his teammates. Havelange first announced that Leslie King was being honored as the winner of both the Golden Boot, for most goals, and the Golden Ball, for best player, of the tournament. For only the second time in World Cup history, the high scorer was on the winning side and, for the first time in his life, Leslie King was speechless.

The World Cup trophy was handed to Marco DeSantis, captain of the United States National Team. Amid the resulting explosion of cheers, fireworks, and stadium speakers blaring *We Are The Champions,* Brandon Rafferty asked his young replacement a question.

"What were you doing back there?"

"Sorry," Maxwell answered with his usual smile, "I was showing Jack how to score *real* goals."

EPILOGUE

He pulled the bright red jersey off the press, careful not to let the hot letters touch. The name and number were centered perfectly, of course – he had performed this operation thousands of times. A few minutes to cool, then he would hang it in the main window, just in time for opening. The day after winning the World Cup was a big day for American sports, especially if you owned a soccer shop in South St. Louis.

"Hey, Mr. Bayless," Kevin Jenkins and his friends were the first customers this Monday morning. Neighborhood kids who mainly came here to hang out and listen to the elderly man's tales of the *good old days*, they did keep his replica jersey sales brisk, and he appreciated their passion for the game he loved.

"You know that jersey is wrong, don't you?" Kevin asked, surprised that the shop owner had made a mistake of this magnitude. Hanging in the large window at the front of the store were three red US National Team jerseys. Leslie King's Number Nine, Marco DeSantis' Number Four, and a Maxwell jersey with a *10* on the back. "Jimmy Maxwell doesn't wear ten for the national team."

Bayless winked at the boy and said, "Not yet."

APOLOGIES

I started writing this story with the end in mind, and worked backwards. Obviously, to make my ending work, I had to change or delete some events that actually happened. For instance, it is easy to see that if the United States was *in* the 1982 World Cup, someone else from CONCACAF *wasn't*. Sorry, El Salvador. No offense meant.

Along the way, a few real people's actions were embellished – some positively, some not. It's all part of the story and it isn't personal. Most of the accounts involving real people were based on actual events, but not always. Offended? Sorry.

Italy deserves praise for winning their third World Cup in 1982 and Paolo Rossi certainly deserved his awards. *Scusami, mi dispiace.*

Rick Davis, Bobby Smith, and Arnie Mausser are real people who surely would have been in the squad if the United States had qualified for the 1982 World Cup. Of course, I had to replace them with my fictional players to make it work. Sorry.

- MM

.

6383624R0

Made in the USA
Charleston, SC
18 October 2010